# Thrash Track

## Detective Mahoney Series
## Julie Hiner

Killers and Demons

First Printing in 2024

Publisher: Julie Hiner

KillersAndDemons.com

Editing by: Taija Morgan

Cover Design (front): 100 Covers

Cover design (back): Killers and Demons

ISBN: 978-1-7389176-2-4

First Edition

# Dedication

To the visionary fusion of thrash metal and rap: Body Count, The Children of KoRn.
To the grittiest of the grunge: Nirvana.
To the kings of thrash metal: Hazzerd, Slayer.
To the rulers of the hair, the heavy, and the wild: Lÿnx, Black Label Society, Rob Zombie, Skid Row, Queensrÿche.
To the gods of classic rock: Led Zeppelin.
To those whose skin wrapped the lamps, bowls, and legs of The Butcher of Plainfield.

KILLERS AND DEMONS
THRASH TRACK
- the soundtrack
PARENTAL ADVISORY
EXPLICIT CONTENT

Thrash Track has a *custom* 2 track soundtrack.

Lyrics by Killers and Demons

Music by Hazzerd

Track 1: Stella's Scream

Track 2: Skin Peeler

Digital album comes with album booklet including album artwork, lyrics, and more.

GET YOURS:

https://killersanddemons.bandcamp.com/

# Contents


1993 MTV ... 1

1. The Cecil ... 3

2. The Hunt ... 7

3. Vintage Track ... 11

4. Recording Studio ... 14

5. Rock Candy ... 17

6. Imperfect Performance ... 22

7. OK Hotel ... 25

Body Count ... 27

8. Killer Case ... 29

9. Leopard-Print Vomit ... 33

10. Missy Chrissy Sissy ... 40

11. Back-Alley Scan ... 44

12. Familiar Eyes ... 46

13. Music Fusion ... 49

14. Skin ... 52

15. High-Tech 90s ... 58

16. Time Warp ... 63

17. Dark Instincts ... 66

18.  Night Cap     69

Children of the KoRn     73

19.  Jakey     75

20.  Follow the ID     77

21.  Children of the Korn     81

22.  Banditos     84

23.  Skin     89

24.  Land Lady     93

25.  Poetry Slam     97

26.  The Mint     99

27.  Bourbon Numb     103

28.  Rockstar     106

29.  Back Alley     108

30.  Night Recap     110

31.  Criminal Profiling     112

Oxytocin Suffocation     121

32.  Hot Dog     123

33.  Closing in on Electric     125

34.  Put the Rum in the Coconut     131

35.  Metal and Chemicals     136

36.  Follow the Drugs     139

37.  Investigative Triangle     143

38.  Drug Connection     144

39.  Fix My Brain     147

Disco Biscuit Bourbon High     149

| | |
|---|---|
| 40. Murder Wall | 151 |
| 41. Bea | 156 |
| 42. Open Your Heart | 160 |
| 43. Close It Up Again | 162 |
| 44. Chilly Case | 168 |
| 45. Anticipation | 171 |
| 46. Ice Air | 174 |
| 47. Pure Love | 177 |
| 48. Vintage | 181 |
| 49. Killer Concert | 184 |
| 50. Strawberry-Whiskey Groupie | 187 |
| 51. Riding the Pure-Love Wave | 190 |
| 52. Endless Pure-Love Wave | 194 |
| 53. Sneaky Treat Retreat | 197 |
| Thrash Metal Murder | 199 |
| 54. The Performance | 201 |
| 55. What the Fuck? | 204 |
| 56. Thrilling Commute | 206 |
| 57. Solo Investigation | 208 |
| 58. Walkman | 212 |
| 59. Late-Night Trace | 215 |
| 60. Fresh Start | 217 |
| 61. Stopped Dead | 219 |
| 62. Broken Detective | 222 |
| 63. Fucked-Up Murder Scene | 226 |

64. In Over Her Head                    228

Saliva Bath                             231

65. Damning Statement                   233

66. DNA Profile                         236

67. Hunt                                238

68. Wild Energy                         242

69. Vinyl Uncut                         244

70. Olive Skin                          247

71. Worlds Collide                      250

72. Earth and Spice                     252

73. Killer Sex                          257

74. Getaway                             259

Wear Your Skin                          261

75. Back on the Case                    263

76. Saliva                              265

77. Muse                                268

78. Reunited                            271

79. The Afterparty                      274

80. Off-Kilter                          276

81. Recording Studio                    278

82. Stella's Skills                     281

83. Elevator of Doom                    284

84. Whiskey-Infused Skin                286

85. Skin Peeler Eyes                    287

86. Open Up                             292

87. MTV 1993      295

Skin Peeler      299

88. Criminal Profile: Skin Peeler      301

About Author      307

Acknowledgments      309

Also By      311

1993 MTV

# Chapter 1

# The Cecil

*O*ctober 9, 1999

Darkness cloaked the damp alley. A persistent drip rippled through the silence. Stella exhaled. A puff of hot breath simmered through the crisp air.

She'd come this far. And she needed this.

She pumped her legs, amping up her pace before she changed her mind. The heels of her boots clicked along the pavement. The unsettling blue-purple of the neon sign pulsed ahead. *The Cecil.* Her hunting grounds. Or so it used to be. She hadn't frequented the joint in a while. She'd been coming a lot less since her prime target no longer existed.

At the height of the Poison Sisters case, she'd been pulled into a torturous vortex by the weird chanting of The Devil's Track. Her boss, Detective Sutton, had found her in a hypnotized state, hunting knife in one hand, glass of bourbon in the other, hiding in the darkness of her apartment, staring at the target she'd been preparing for: Sargeant Tomlinson. The polished, politics-playing, money-hungry lead of the murder case that swallowed her father. She'd been practising her stalking skills for him.

Sutton had extracted her from her devilish state. She'd realized that killing Tomlinson wouldn't inject life into her father. The only outcome would be the loss of her badge. She'd stewed night after night in her apartment with no purpose.

She'd stopped thinking about hunting Tomlinson down and sliding her knife into his gut.

The Poison Sisters case ended months ago. The scar across her upper arm was the only reminder of what went down in the woods behind the house where humans were burned alive. A string of one-off murders, boring cases, landed her right where she started. She wanted more. More purpose.

The neon pulse snapped her from her thoughts. She halted in front of the rickety door tilted on its hinges. She slid her hand under her long, leather coat, to the back of her belt, and down the hunting knife. She'd let her plan to hunt Tomlinson fade away. But she couldn't bring herself to get rid of her prized weapon.

She took a deep breath and whipped the door open.

The moist heat of sweat and booze drowned her. She walked straight to the bar without hesitation, looking like she was just another patron needing a dose of alcoholic relief to drown out reality for a few hours. She slid into her favourite spot, halfway up the bar. The perfect position to view the exit to the alleyway and the entrance from the hotel lobby. *The Cecil* had been fancy once. The now tarnished brass fixings, faded chandeliers, and dull marble counters were screaming for an overhaul. This place wouldn't be redone. It was lucky if it didn't get bulldozed. It used to be a stop for high-class businessmen. Now it was the nightly spot for drunks and murder.

"Usual?" her favourite bartender, Todd, asked her from across the counter. His dark hair feathered over his muscular shoulders. He wore his typical black tank top.

"Yeah." Stella smiled.

Todd left to tend to her drink. She'd met him the first time she'd come in here, when she was sixteen. Her mother had brought her *home* to visit all her friends from another time. A time when they lived here, when her father was still alive. Before they left him. Her teeth ground together as she thought about how her mother had whisked her away. She knew now that she couldn't have prevented her father's death. But she would always wish she'd had more time with him. She'd wished she'd been there during those brief moments when he wasn't hunting a human monster. All she'd had was his voice over the phone.

Todd slid a healthy glass of bourbon over the counter. "On the house."

"What? No. You have to make a living." Stella took a sip.

"Whatever. I only do it for you." He winked, then walked to the other end of the bar to tend to a restless patron.

Stella took a lengthier sip of the bourbon and relished in the sweet burn at the back of her tongue. She put the glass on the dull marble counter with a click, then slid her hand into the inner pocket of her coat.

She took a peek at the photo, wrapping her palm around it in case of prying eyes.

Dirty Joe licked his crusty lips. What a creep. He deserved to die.

The case had gone cold. He'd been the prime suspect at one time, but the investigation was dead now, lying at the bottom of a box in a basement. Nothing but a stack of files that no one would ever read again. Except her. This was her purpose.

She'd cleared her apartment wall of the photos of the grisly cases that had pulled her father down a dark path. She'd taken a fresh approach: heat up the cold cases, give these human monsters a taste of what they'd fed their victims. Problem was, it was taking too long to get formal clearance to re-open cases. Stella couldn't sit on the sidelines waiting for these killers to leave another body dumped in a ditch.

This one had left at least half-a-dozen young women tossed into ditches on the side of the highway. All the locations had been within thirty kilometres of the city limits, in different directions. She'd re-examined those who'd been interviewed. Then she'd dug into those lingering outside of the inner circle of the victims. There was a recurring theme. His real name was Joseph. She'd followed him for weeks, until one night, she'd caught him stalking a girl with a similar profile to those of the victims from five years ago.

Todd had confirmed seeing him in here. Always the same night. The same time. Shouldn't be long now until he made an appearance.

Stella polished off the bourbon and made eye contact with Todd, pleading for another.

The door to the hotel lobby opened. Sweet giggles rippled through into the lounge. Stella snuck a quick glance. There he was. Six foot. Doughy around the middle, but muscular. Probably from lifting bodies. Rough skin, but chiselled features. Could be nice looking. If he wasn't a murderer. Heavy boots, dark jeans, and a plaid shirt. A young woman hung off his arm. A replica of the women tossed aside, bruised and bloody. Long brown hair. Her demeanour and her skin suggested she was in her early twenties. Her eyes said otherwise. A shiny coat over years of a rough life. The others had similar pasts. They'd been on their own far too young. No one to watch over them. Or to notice if they didn't come home one night.

*Not tonight.* Not on Stella's watch.

# Chapter 2
# The Hunt

Dirty Joe led the young woman toward the door to the alley. He'd fed her four stiff cocktails. She wobbled as she clung to his arm.

Stella slid the empty glass of her second bourbon over the bar. She'd nursed it for the last couple of hours. She glanced at Todd. He was occupied. She placed a bill under the glass, pulled her coat tight around her, and slipped off the stool. Looking at the ground, she took her time getting to the door. Staying under the radar was crucial.

The cold air bit at her face as she left the lounge. The door creaked behind her. The heat of the stuffy joint dissolved in an instant as the chill fall night took her in.

It was a quiet night. Unusual for *The Cecil*. The day of the week wasn't a deterrent for a night out for those living day to day.

A muffled cry came from the direction of the alley leading toward the river. Stella approached the entrance to the alley as she wrapped her fingers around the handle of her hunting knife. She rounded the corner and looked into the darkness. As her eyes adjusted, the hefty silhouette of Dirty Joe came into view. He hovered over a smaller figure cowering against a brick wall. The young woman. Alone in this world. A dose of desperation-induced naivety taking her down the wrong path for the evening.

*Not tonight.* Not on Stella's watch.

Stella unsheathed the knife, the weight of the handle comforting against her cold palm.

She walked straight up to Dirty Joe, keeping the click of her boots to a minimum. He was too engrossed in his prized catch to notice. Joe wrapped his monstrous hands around the girl's neck.

The girl spat in his face, shooting alcohol-doused words at him. "Let me go. Fucker."

"No. You're gonna calm down now." He squeezed her throat.

She choked, clawing at him. Her nails scraped the rough skin cratering down his cheek. Blood trickled.

"Bitch." He squeezed hard.

"Stop." Stella pressed the tip of the blade into the back of Dirty Joe's neck.

Dirty Joe released the girl. She crumpled to the ground, choking and cursing.

Joe rotated to face Stella. She kept the blade pressed against his neck. His eyes narrowed as he glanced down her body. "Well, well...what do we have here?" He licked his thick upper lip.

Stella's stomach lurched. Who the fuck did this guy think he was?

Before he had a chance to react, she sliced his cheek clean open with the knife.

He stumbled backwards, slapping his palm against the fresh cut. He pulled his hand away and looked at the blood staining his hand. "What the fuck?" He glared.

"Joseph Rolen. This is the end. No more girls. No more murder."

"What?" Dirty Joe sneered.

"The girls. Jolene, Sheeba, Mya, Lindsy, Emily, Kylie. All long, brown hair. All early twenties. No family. Living alone. Until you came along."

Joe's expression cooled. He lowered his hand. Blood trickled down his face.

"All of them, left in a ditch on the side of the highway. One thing in common. They all knew you. In fact, you were the last one to see any of them, weren't you?"

The rough contours in his face deepened as his brow furrowed. "Police don't know that."

"I *am* the police." She swallowed down any hint of weakness in her voice.

"Case went cold. Saw it on the news." He narrowed his eyes again, summoning a fresh smirk.

"I'm re-opening it. Now." She needed to get his confession, before he had time to make a rash move. She gripped the knife hard, wanting to gut him like the animal he was, but knowing she could only use it to pressure him. A cold wave erupted from the pit of her gut as she waited for him to speak.

The silence clung to the air as their breath formed white wisps.

"You just admitted you were last to see each of those girls." She pumped aggression into her voice, like she was in control.

"Yeah. So what?"

"So. That's a confession." She held her knife steady, slipped her badge from her pocket and flashed it. "I *am* the police. Case just cracked wide open."

His eyes darted. His arm came round fast. She tried to block it. His fist connected hard with her upper arm, right where her scar was. Her knife clattered across the pavement. Her badge clanked to the ground as she instinctively clasped her arm. Bone crunched as Joe's fist hit her cheek.

Stella cringed then threw a right hook, jabbing him in the side of the head. Dirty Joe stumbled. He recovered with a kick, his right boot connecting with her left shin. Her jaw clenched. She thrust her right leg straight out, connecting the heel of her boot with Dirty Joe's knee. A sickening crunch echoed through the silent alley. He clutched his leg as he crumpled to the pavement. Stella took a couple steps backwards.

In her periphery, Stella could see Dirty Joe's victim crawling across the slick pavement.

"Joseph. This can end now. A full confession can shorten your time in a cell." She bit her lip on the lie.

Dirty Joe's eyes met Stella's. Her shoulders relaxed. She waited, not releasing his gaze.

Suddenly, he thrust from the ground straight at Stella. Sharp pain sliced her abdomen. She gasped, glancing down at her torso. A slice opened her shirt, below her ribcage. Blood seeped through the material. *Fuck.* She looked up. Dirty Joe stood, clutching a small knife in his hand.

Out of nowhere, the young woman lunged at Joe. She plunged Stella's recovered knife straight at Joe's gut. The blade slid in. His own blade clanked over the ground. He crumpled to his knees, landing hard.

Dirty Joe hunched over, grabbing his gut. Blood bubbled from the corner of his mouth. "You...bitch..." he sputtered.

He fell on his side.

Stella stood, grimacing against the pain slicing her side. She pushed her boot into Joe's arm, rolling him over. His head hit the pavement with a wet thud. She leaned over, pulling her knife from his severed flesh. Crouching beside him, she wiped the blade clean with his plaid shirt, stood, then re-sheathed it in her belt.

The girl walked up to Joe. She spat in his face.

She faced Stella, her lips trembling. "I thought he was going to kill you."

Stella nodded. "He probably was."

Stella scanned both ends of the alley. They were alone. "Get out of here."

The woman froze, eyes wide. "I thought you were the police."

"I am. But they'll treat you like every other tightly clothed lady who clings to The Cecil." The words that Todd had spoken to her in this exact alley years ago slipped from her lips. "You know the truth. Live it." She waved her hand, gesturing for the young woman to scurry along.

Without a word, the woman walked away from the next-murder-victim path she'd nearly ventured.

Stella witnessed Joe draw in his final breath.

She'd come here for a confession, intending to take a killer and throw him in a jail cell. Intending to show her boss he must re-open the unsolved cases she wanted to pursue. She'd gotten what she really wanted, deep down. To see Dirty Joe gutted. She *should* be satisfied.

The cold trickle in her gut was anything but a sign of satisfaction.

She watched the woman disappear into the black night. She wanted to believe she'd done the right thing, but she'd never know. She picked up her badge and walked into the darkness.

# Chapter 3
# Vintage Track

Orange flames licked the top of the brick fireplace, casting a glow over the living room and reaching fingers up the bay window facing the street. A television sat on an antique table, the round volume knob cranked to max. A large '*M*' with a smaller '*TV*' scribed beside it flashed onto the screen. A lyricist, his tousled too-blond hair flying through the air, lunged at the screen. Intense emotion dripped from his voice. The sleeves of his silver shirt shimmered as his green eyes pierced her soul.

Lolita pulled her legs into her chest and rested against the plush velour of the sofa. Her long, dark dreadlocks tinged with chocolate streaks fell over her knees. She rocked back and forth as her face twitched.

Words appeared in the lower left corner of the screen.

*Nirvana "Heart-Shaped Box" In Utero DGC Records*

A performance from another time.

The first bars of the song always soothed her. She had to watch the video every day. Sometimes multiple times, if her switch had clicked on. It was an internal switch, something inside of her, moving her into a state of anxiety and thrusting her into memories that were so vivid she could swear she was reliving them.

By the time the singer reached the chorus, her being always settled, and her switch usually returned to *off*.

Usually.

She drank in the voice emanating from the television, gripping her heart. It was a song of love, grief, and devotion. A love poem. His voice, filled with sorrow and etched with angst, had a powerful hold on her.

They didn't play the video on MTV very often anymore. She didn't watch any of the TV stations anyways. The only reason she possessed the lone outdated television was to play a constant stream of videos. When one tape ended, she'd slip the next one in the player. Her house existed within a bubble of a year that had come and gone.

1993. The year had been the most significant of her life. Sometimes, she slipped so deeply into the memories of those few months that had a grasp on her heart that she'd forget what year it actually was.

The singer's angelic voice became harsh and jagged at the end of each line. She narrowed her dark eyes and focused on his lips. They glided with precise and exaggerated motion. It reminded her of how Orson's mouth had moved when he used to rhyme.

The thought of him increased her rocking motion. Her shoulders twitched. She scrunched her lips into a contorted frown, the drooping left side of her mouth refusing to comply. The droop itched. She rubbed at it with her sleeve. As she focused on the face of the singer on the scratchy screen, it morphed and shimmered, revealing Orson's smooth skin and striking emerald eyes. The colour of tourmaline.

Her rocking eased. Her shoulders relaxed. She stared into those eyes. It *was* Orson. He was alive, on the screen, right where he belonged. His own MTV video.

She knew he'd be big. She'd told him over and over. She'd put *everything* into his success. Night after night, showering him with support, announcing to anyone she encountered how he was the newest big thing and they *had* to catch his show.

The tape reached the end of the track. The video came to an end. The next track played.

Lolita snapped from her reverie and blinked several times.

The video trance had taken her. Her energy had responded, following its regular path of anxiousness transforming to calm *rootedness*. It was the only way she could describe it. When she was here, in this zone, she felt as if her feet were roots reaching into the earth, down to its core. She could think. She could breathe. A warmth surged through her. The fire flickered. The flames reached for her. She let their heat wrap around her.

She took a deep breath, rested her head against the sofa, and exhaled as she closed her eyes.

Riding the *rootedness* for as long as it would last, her being settled. For now.

# Chapter 4
# Recording Studio

The cool air permeated from the basement below. Lolita flicked a switch on the wall. Light glimmered below, casting a yellow glow up the wooden stairs. Citrus wafted from the mug in her hand. She gripped it tightly, not wanting to spill any of her special tea, then settled her other hand on the railing. As she reached the bottom of the stairs, she scanned the room.

She felt most at home down here.

It wasn't an ordinary basement. The house was old. She'd lived in it for a long time. She'd found it years ago when Orson was still around. They'd moved in together, full of excitement at the potential offered by the unique structure of the house. It was already old when they stumbled upon it. The door dangled askew on the hinges. The frame of the house seemed slightly off-kilter. The shape of the basement offered an interesting layout. The composition of the walls—the plaster not used anymore in the construction of homes—provided a sound-dampening barrier, inside and out.

The perfect basement for a home studio. A private place to record their music.

To top it all off, the house was located blocks from the buzzing lights of Electric Avenue. Far enough off to be sheltered from the noise, close enough to allow them to submerge themselves in the flourishing music scene.

She hadn't been sure about the move to Calgary. Growing up in the prairies, she'd been shielded from the madness of city life. When she'd met Orson, he'd instantly filled her head with wild ideas of what the city life could offer. If they could get to the biggest city within their reach and make it there, then the next stop could be Seattle, or even L.A.

They would go far. That's what he'd said.

Her skepticism quickly faded and blossomed into full-on excitement. Complete *belief* in their dream.

*Their dream.*

She bit down on her lower lip, wrapped both hands around the warm mug, and breathed in the fresh citrus scent of her lemon balm tea. She closed her eyes, took a deep breath, and let the powers of the perennial herb reach healing fingers through her brain. The citrus had a beneficial effect on the limbic centre, helping her to control her emotions. An improved alternative to popping too many pills from her ample collection. Barbiturates, benzodiazepines, GHB...she'd dabbled in a slew of anti-depressants, tranquilizers, and party drugs, both over the counter and from the street, hoping to ease her overactive, damaged brain. Under the guidance of her mother's doctors, Lolita's amygdala had been both stimulated with corticotropin-releasing hormones and stifled with oxytocin, despite the potential damage to her young uterus. A mother would do anything to ease her o wn guilt.

She couldn't allow her mind to weave down the path from the past. Not right now.

Last night, as she curled under her covers and closed her eyes, she'd promised herself a full day of practising. She refused to let go of her dream. The *perfect performance.*

When she was in her state of *rootedness,* her heart told her *the performance* was within reach. It never fabricated quite right. she had to persist in trying. It was her sole purpose now.

She shuffled across the basement floor, hands wrapped around her mug, and settled into a chair in front of the control panel. She inspected the recording equipment. Orson had bought the best. She'd kept all of it. Even the ADAT—Alesis Digital Audio Tape. One of the first, and rather eccentric, eight-track-recording devices that had tipped the music power from major labels to smaller studios. Leaning against the plush fur wrapped around the chair, she took a long sip of tea and stared through the noise-reduction glass separating the control room from the recording space.

As she drew a long breath, a glimmer crossed her dark eyes. A shine from the star-struck feeling that swelled within her, refusing to release. She pictured herself in front of the microphone, stroking the silk scarf she used to tie around the top of the microphone stand, when she used to perform for live audiences. The side of her mouth twitched. The side that now drooped, her lip responding to the condition simmering in her temporal lobe.

She shook her head. *No.* This wasn't the time to drown her rootedness in an anxious aura infused with sad memories of the past.

This was here. This was now. This was her time.

Today, she'd nail the performance. No matter how long it took.

The microphone sat, waiting. Her own olive-skinned face shimmered in front of her. Her lips hovered over the silver bulb as she executed the rhyme. One that had birthed from her creative vibes. One that came from within her warm core.

She watched her own perfectly formed lips move over the microphone. She heard her sweet voice. The rhyme seized control.

Whirling the chair around, she set the mug on a wooden table, away from the controls. Opening a drawer, she retrieved a book. Her book. The one that she captured her personal rhymes within whenever they surfaced. She picked a 2B pencil from the collection in the drawer. She preferred something with a soft edge, reminding her the lyrics were only a rough draft, easing her anxiety about getting them right the first time.

Curling her legs into herself and resting her feet on the chair, she flipped to the opening blank page. It was becoming quite crowded. She'd had a lot of inspiration lately. Resting it on her knees, she pressed the pencil to the page and let her fingers move freely. The words came. Her fingers scrolled. The page filled.

The creativity swelled within her, surfacing as lyrics. Rhymes. Spoken word to be transformed into music. A specific type of music.

Sinking into the inviting hands of inspiration, the time ticked away as she continued to write.

As the words slowed, her hand halted. She flipped through the book. Pages had been filled. As she read over her work, excitement trickled through her. It was excellent.

And she was her harshest critic.

Today would be the day. She'd record the ultimate performance. The pain of the past would disintegrate. It would be just like it was. In 1993.

# Chapter 5
# Rock Candy



*October 11, 1999*

*Rock Candy, Seattle*

Stella slithered her way through the tightly packed pit of the basement joint. *RKCANDY* was splashed across the wall behind the stage in bold white, giving the place the title it deserved. *Rock Candy* was an epic place in the live-music scene in Seattle. Any metal band who was worth talking about had played here at some point. Likely before they became famous, if they became famous at all. Fame didn't matter to the metal heads who swarmed down the stairs to the black pit to drink in the devil's music like heroine.

She'd been here before.

After watching Dirty Joe's next victim slide a knife into his gut at *The Cecil* two nights ago, Stella needed to get away. It was exactly as she'd predicted. A tiny article hidden at the end of the paper declared another night and another murder at the rundown hotel. A drug deal gone bad, the paper speculated. Assigned to another department. Nothing was happening in her homicide unit. Ever since the Poison Sisters murders, she'd been straining to stay *in line.* She'd gotten along with Sutton *and* Parker, her new partner. The feeling of impending self-implosion swelled within her with increasing intensity each passing day.

She'd said her goodbyes to her father as she set his ashes free over the ocean. If she learned anything from the Poison Sisters case, it was that she was not responsible for his death. There was nothing she could have done to stop him from going into the basement of Saul the Slayer to prevent him from slaughtering another member of his horror-doll cult. Her father had made his decision to do what he needed to do. The same way she had made the decision to go into the basement of the little house on the edge of the forest, hunting a witch to halt the burning of another young victim.

She thought she had it together. All she had to do was get along with her boss and her partner and solve murder cases. The cases had been a bore. Nothing had happened in months. After ripping down the collage of horrors plastered over her apartment wall, depicting the human monsters that her father had hunted, the wall had remained clean for a few weeks. As the days passed, the hours ticked by, she'd stared at the wall hours on end, feeling its vacant glare. The wall wanted to be used. She'd given in. She'd perused cold case files from the evidence room, focusing on those from the early 90s. Long enough ago to be forgotten. But still recent enough to be solvable. Soon, her nightly routine became a late happy hour of sipping bourbon as she sharpened her hunting knife and pasted photos of the cold case she'd dug into at the office that day.

Two nights ago, behind *The Cecil,* Dirty Joe had caught her off guard. If his next victim hadn't slid Stella's hunting knife into his gut, Stella might have been seriously wounded while Joe got away.

She'd wanted to prove to Sutton that the unsolved cases she'd begged him to let her pursue were worth his time.

With a crushed cheekbone, bruised black and purple, and a stab wound that wasn't deep enough to do serious damage, she'd called Sutton the next morning and asked for a couple days off. He'd been ecstatic. He didn't like her habit of never using her vacation time.

A thrill rushed through as she'd browsed a series of concert postings and discovered that Type O Negative was playing at Rock Candy the next night. She'd hopped on the first plane to Seattle. After a night at Radiator Whiskey, swimming in high-end bourbon, and a day in a hotel bed watching bad TV, she'd sunk far enough into a bubble shielding her from facing reality that she was ready to burn off some bad energy.

One good thing that came from the case that took her father was that she'd discovered Type O Negative. Kings of gothic metal. Ahead of their time. Saul the Ripper might have been a human monster feasting on the blood of young girls, but he had a discerning taste in music. The moment she'd pressed play on October

Rust, she'd been transported to another world. Somehow, it brought her closer to the father she'd barely known.

The brick in her belly and the sadness in her heart seemed to have subsided significantly since she had boarded that plane.

A rumbling erupted through the claustrophobic pit of the basement dive. A wiry young man in tattered jeans, long hair concealing his face, strummed a shiny black bass onstage. If you could call it a stage. It was nothing but a rectangle of wood wedged in the corner, a mere few inches off the ground. Sound check. The show would start soon. It was time to find that sweet buzz.

Stella strolled over to the shifty counter plastered in band decals and stickers posing as a bar.

"What's your poison?" the bartender greeted her before she had a chance to blink.

"Bourbon. Double. Straight up." She wondered if she'd blended the thick layer of foundation over her cheek well enough.

He raised his pierced eyebrow. "Nice." His dark eyes settled on her for a moment.

Tingles erupted up her insides. Maybe tonight would be double-treat night. Maybe. It depended on Ian, the mysterious front man who would be making his appearance any moment now.

The bartender went to work on her drink. She leaned over the bar and watched his moves, biting her lip against the burst of pain across her abdomen. Nothing a few bourbons couldn't numb. He was thin, yet muscular. His hair was styled with a wild but controlled flair. His t-shirt was crisp and clean, despite the angry letters in neon-yellow plastered over a skull.

He returned, his eyes finding hers again, and settled the drink on the bar. "New Riff. Last bit. We don't often carry that."

Impressive. Places like this didn't usually stock anything but the cheapest poison. "How much?" Stella stretched her scarlet lips into a sly smile.

"On the house." He winked.

"Really..." Her eyebrow lifted.

"Just the first one. Keep you wanting more." He smiled, revealing a dimple.

"Thanks." She tilted the glass toward him, then took a sip.

He left to tend to the growing crowd pushing against the bar. Stella sipped the free bourbon while she watched the sound check. It wasn't long before the bourbon was gone and the lights had dimmed.

Mid-turn to order another, the bartender appeared, drink in hand.

"It's like you can read my thoughts." She winked.

"Just good at my job."

The way he was looking at her said otherwise. She slapped a bill on the bar and grabbed the drink. "Keep the change." She swept her gaze up and down his muscular frame, then walked away. He was tempting, but she had to acquire a prime spot before the show started. She had a gothic metal god to devour.

Purple, blue, and red pot lights blurred into a cosmic glow. Bass rumbled. A drum beat thrummed, steady and slow. An electric guitar riff ripped through the pit of the basement, vibrating the walls.

Stella stood front row and centre. Fellow leather-and-spike-clad metal lovers crowded around her. It was tight, but comfortable. Most of the front-row seekers were women. They were all there for the same reason.

Stella sipped her drink, the sweet bourbon sliding over the back of her tongue, weaving numbing fingers down her throat.

The voice—rich, luxurious, and hypnotizing—crept from the corner. It reached for Stella, clutching her in its mesmerizing grasp. She surrendered. She closed her eyes. There was nothing but the voice. It heightened. He was approaching. She could sense his presence. She could detect his scent.

As the opening lines of *Everyone I Love is Dead* wove through the hot air, his voice captured every soul in the room.

The lyrics were haunting. They came in gradual, dramatic waves. Her heart seized as he sung of kisses of death and grief.

Stella opened her eyes. He was right there, a few arm lengths away, lost in the vocals, performing his hypnotic dance with the silver microphone. She dared to drink him in from bottom to top. Black boots rose up his legs. Tight pants stretched over his muscular thighs. His ample manhood bulged. Flowing sleeves fluttered as his arms swung to the song. Luscious locks of hair moved as if there was a breeze.

His eyes. Dark. Deep. Knowing. She gazed into them, imagining he was staring right at her despite the lineup of leather and glittered gems hovering at his feet.

The guitarist approached the lip of the stage, dark hair flowing over his shoulders, tight pants hugging his contours, black leather jacket revealing his sweat-coated chest. He thrust his guitar into the air as the riff suddenly erupted. The powerful electric chords seized Stella.

The mysterious front man stepped forward as his vocals erupted alongside the guitar. His eyes found hers. Electric tingles wove through her. She didn't back away. For a moment, he sang to her. Her expert-level positioning may have been the reason, but she allowed herself the luxury of thinking it was more than that.

He moved on, seeking others, feeding the crowd. An expert lead man, he knew what he was doing. He gave each one of them what they came for.

The song unfolded. He sung to her of tears and laughter, flames, smoke, and shame. His voice—dark, melancholic, mysterious, hypnotizing—entranced her. His hair flowed around his shoulders and fluttered over his face as he made deliberate movements. She lost herself in the words she'd heard many times. Words that accused her pain of rendering her weak and being nothing more than a painting over the dirt inside of her.

The guitarist eased his gut-gripping riff, moving into a softer strum. The voice retreated to a sorrowful plea, expressing to her that she can't win at the game of life and that the truth is in the mirrors.

As the track concluded, Stella relished in the last morsels. Something serendipitous had aligned this show on this night at this venue, with the band choosing to open with her favourite song. She succumbed to the overdrive her senses were in and let the night take her away.

# Chapter 6

# Imperfect Performance

Lolita pulled at her dreadlocks with both hands. Her shoulders twitched. She loomed close to the control panel. The rocking started. She couldn't control it.

She could *sense* her internal switch click. The feeling of serenity, of being grounded to the earth, slipped through the imaginary fingers she could perceive, trying to grasp it, trying to hold on. Tendrils of anxiety crawled up through her from her gut to her brain.

Shut in her basement recording studio all day, she'd performed the freshly written lyrics over and over. A million times. At least.

Why wasn't this working? Where had that star-struck feeling of hope gone?

She grabbed her open notebook and scanned the page again with wild eyes. Tossing it aside, she didn't need it. She'd memorized the lines hours ago. They flashed through her mind now like bright signs. Refusing to dim. The words wouldn't let go of her until she got it right. The performance.

She snatched the mug from the table behind her and swallowed a swig of chilled tea. Her mouth, dry from hours of practice, screamed for a break. She couldn't stop. Not now.

She placed the mug down with a clack and walked confidently to the door of the recording space. Hovering over the controls, she found the button and clicked the recording feed to live. Flinging the door open, she made her way to the microphone. She grabbed a set of studio earphones from a stand and slid them underneath her thick dreadlocks, over her ears.

She took a deep breath. An attempt at calm washed over the anxiety gripping her insides.

As she wrapped her hands around the silver stand, her lips hovered near the bulb.

She concentrated and half-sang, half-spoke the words that had come from her creative core. The lyrics trickled from her mouth. Her voice weaved through the microphone, over the recording waves, onto the tape, and into her ears through the headphones.

At the end of each line, a raw edge coated her sugar voice.

The angst-tinged sweetness of the sound pulled her into a trance. Her mouth moved. The words came. The rhymes laid themselves down onto the tape.

The roots of her calm began to ascend up her body.

The performance unfolded, just how she'd imagined it.

As her body relaxed, her shoulders unclenched and she sank into the creativity oozing from her core.

Then her lip caught. The droop that pulled the left side of her lip into a downward contortion distorted a critical word. She slurred it. Then the next. And the next.

Her shoulders clenched. The tranquil roots retreated into the earth beneath the house. Her lips snapped shut. The words stopped. The rhyming was ruined.

Her brain buzzed. Hot tears trickled down her cheeks. A tear caught in the droop pulling her lip downward.

She flung the microphone aside and threw the headphones to the ground. She stomped to the door. Wrenching it open, she burst into the control space and slammed her hand against a button, ending the live feed.

Another one to be thrown away.

Her exhausted mind heaved a heavy sigh.

She pulled at the thick weaves of her hair. Her gaze landed on the eight-track recorder. The one that had been spinning only moments ago. The one that held the dozens of garbage recordings from the day. She stomped over to it, yanked open the plastic door, and pulled the cassette from within. Clutching it in her trembling hand, she pulled the tape out in long strands. Lengths of shiny black polyester flew through the air, whirling in streams and settling in crumpled bunches on the studio floor.

Every moment of angel voice tinged with a distinctive edge fluttered through the room, clinging to the destroyed tape.

No one would ever hear it.

Any ounce of stardom acquired on the recording disintegrated in a matter of minutes.

The last inch of tape fell to the ground.

Still clutching the cassette in her hand so hard that it started to crack, Lolita stood, breathing heavily.

Panic clawed at her mind, her limbs, her internals, as she whirled around, absorbing the damage that she had created. Without the perfect performance, she had nothing.

Salty tears clung to her face. She licked the side of her mouth, her tongue catching on the contorted skin of her drooping lip. She sank into the chair facing the control panel. Her shoulders slumped. Defeat prevailed. It would only be a matter of seconds before her body commenced rocking herself back and forth.

This space between the switch being in off and on modes, the one that controlled every part of her, left her empty and weightless. Like she was floating between two worlds.

She had no control.

# Chapter 7
# OK Hotel

A *buzz* followed by a *clatter* jolted Stella awake.

She moaned, rolled over, and pulled the scratchy comforter over her face. The buzz persisted. The clatter followed.

*Dammit.* She opened one eye, lowered the hot-pink comforter plastered in bright-blue flowers, and glared at the nightstand. Her murder phone bounced across the chipped wood.

She reached from beneath the covers, grabbed the phone, and flipped it open. "Mahoney." She didn't even try to sound alert.

"Stella. I need you home. Now," Sutton's voice blared into her ear.

She sat up. Her head thrummed as the cheap seventies décor whirled around her in a booze-infested collage.

She closed her eyes and swallowed. "I'm on vacation. You approved it."

"I know. I'm sorry to have to call you." He paused. "I need you here, Detective."

She still wasn't used to him calling her that, even though she'd begged for it for almost a year. "Can't Parker take it?"

"Sure. But I need you with him. Just get here. You'll see."

He was serious. This wasn't another humdrum case. "On my way."

She flipped the phone shut, tossed it on the nightstand, then sat up on the edge of the bed.

The night returned to her in a series of cosmic purple-and-blue flashes. The way-too-many bourbons served by the way-too-cute bartender. The dark-haired metal god. During the show. And after. Slipping into the cheap hotel in the belly of the seedy side of downtown. The *OK Hotel.* Drifting into a booze coma as she watched the sky shift to pink as the sun reached golden fingers over the horizon.

She'd planned to stay another day, walk her way to the quaint back alley corridors of the famous fish market, settling her angry stomach with a dose of greasy breakfast at *Biscuit Bitch* and cleansing her system with fresh air.

Sutton's voice rang through her mind. *I need you here, Detective.*

He didn't say things he didn't mean.

Stella shook her head and slipped from the bed. She always packed light. It wouldn't take her long to hop on a plane and return home. By sundown, she'd be inspecting a murder scene.

As she shoved her pleather and fake fur into her backpack, she wondered what kind of killer she was up against.

BODY COUNT

# Chapter 8
# Killer Case

The tires on her Sunfire squealed as Stella executed a hard right. She was minutes away from the murder scene.

They'd have been processing the scene for hours by now. Part of her advised her it was a bad thing that it was taking all day. Only the most chilling murder scenes necessitated that amount of time. The other part informed her it was good. She hadn't missed out. She'd get to see it for herself.

That it would be the work of the kind of killer she wanted to deal with.

Despite the body count it would bring.

A rock voice blasted through her Sunfire as she pulled up behind Sutton's shiny blue Chevy. She absorbed the best part of the chorus. *Primal Scream* had to be her favourite Mötley Crüe track. With a guitar riff that ripped through her gut, she couldn't resist. She usually preferred heavier metal, but something about the animalistic vibe coated in a layer of glam piqued her interest. As the pretty blond singer screeched about letting out the primal scream scraping to the surface, she closed her eyes and imagined doing just that.

She killed the engine, slid out of the car, and walked briskly across the street. The body had been dumped in an alley behind a line of shops. She pulled her leather jacket closer around her. October was a bitch. Warm one minute, cold the next. She suspected the first snow wasn't far away.

She strolled down the line of shops, around to the alley. The heels on her boots clicked against the pavement. Sutton saw her and promptly met her halfway from the entrance to the alley and the taped-off scene.

"Great hustle." He cringed when he got close enough to see her. To smell her.

"You said hurry. I didn't have time to go home first." The last thing she needed was another scolding about her appearance. *He* called *her,* for fuck's sake.

"What's with your cheek?" He twisted his mouth into a frown.

"It's nothing." She clenched her jaw and stared him down.

"Fine." He raised his hands. "We don't have time for this now. I *need* your detective skills. I'd warn you, but I know you don't require it. Not after the burned bodies from the Poison Sisters murders." He motioned for her to follow and headed back to the scene. "I need you to focus. Really dig deep. Examine the evidence, slowly, cautiously. Listen to your gut."

The familiar green rabbit foot rested against his jeans, hanging from his belt, partially concealed by his jacket. She'd gotten used to his gnarly good luck charm. The whole team had. She slipped her hand into her pocket and touched her matching version in deep purple. The one he'd given her after she'd chased down the Poison Sisters.

"Techies processed the body and surrounding area. Parker's working with them down the alley."

Stella glanced down the alley, locating her clean-cut partner. She didn't hate him anymore. Now she was working on liking him. It was easier than she wanted it to be.

"Blackwood?" she asked, not seeing the medical examiner.

"Did an initial scan of the body. Went to greet the body haulers and fill them in. She had specific instructions for them."

They reached the scene. Stella halted and took her time dissecting the display.

A young man—likely in his twenties, his body less than fresh—was sprawled out on the pavement, nestled against the wall. His hair, so blond it must have been bleached, was ragged and tangled. His eyes were wide open, a striking emerald, glassy and lifeless.

Stella caught her breath. His hand. The skin was gone. The fleshless fingers clutched a book. Stella approached, fixated.

"The hand," she whispered.

"Skin is gone," Sutton said. "Seems to be the only area. We'll know after the clothes are removed."

She crouched, wincing at the pain across her abdomen. She peered at the book, hoping Sutton hadn't noticed. "No title. Some kind of notebook, maybe." She narrowed her eyes. "Strange binding."

"Odd place to stow a body," Sutton said.

"Yeah." Or was it? This was barely over the line of where Electric Avenue started, the party street. An entire downtown avenue of nightclubs and bars. She hadn't been here in a while.

"Take your time. I'm gonna check in with Parker. Work with Blackwood when she returns. Get as much as you can before they move the body." Sutton walked away.

"Got it, boss," Stella responded.

She crouched lower and leaned toward the dead man. The skin on the body had a green-blue tinge. Black areas had started eating in on the flesh. The body was moving quickly from bloat to active decay. Likely the insides were infested with eggs, soon to hatch, spewing a non-stop supply of flies. Either he'd been here a while—unlikely, with the amount of traffic in this area—or someone had moved him here days after he'd seen his end.

His clothes seemed far too...*fresh*. Not wrinkled. No blood. No dirt. The jeans were tattered, but clean. A long-sleeved, shimmering-silver shirt covered his arms, the buttons open and exposing his bare chest. His face seemed...*polished*. Either there had been some sort of post-mortem cleanup, or the struggle was kept to a minimum.

Stella fixated on the skinless hand clutching the book. She pulled a pair of latex gloves from the inside pocket of her coat and snapped one over each hand. Gingerly pulling the sleeve of the shirt up the arm, the flesh remained intact above the wrist. It appeared to be peeled away in symmetric strips. A flawless circle wound around the wrist. The flesh above was intact and in full decay.

She released the sleeve with the utmost caution.

Why the skin? Why the hand?

The cover of the book was blank. It was open, about halfway, perched as if the dead man was reading.

Stella sidled up against the wall next to the body and peered at the open page.

Writing. In scarlet letters. Perfect penmanship.

*I've been trapped*

*Deep inside the walls*

*Of your love morphed box*

*I've been entranced*

*By your pull*

*Trapped by your dream*

*I'd die to swallow*

*The poison running through your veins*

*To warm your ice-cold body*

*To bring you home again*

A message. From the killer. To the victim?

Stella reached her hand inside her pocket and stroked the purple fur of her rabbit claw. Instinctively, her other hand slid over the scar she'd earned from the Poison Sisters case.

Whatever it meant, it was from the killer. And he was the real deal. She could feel it in her gut. This time, she wouldn't hold back.

# Chapter 9
# Leopard-Print Vomit

Wisps of cotton clouds stretched over the black-tinged denim sky. It was getting late fast. With the night came the chill. Stella pulled her coat tighter around herself. The techies were making a final scan of the alley. Medical Examiner Blackwood directed her team around the corner at the end of the alley as they meticulously removed the body. Sutton, a few feet away, was engaged in a summary with the lead tech. He'd been the only one to say anything about Stella's black and blue cheek, but she'd gotten plenty of shocked glances. She wished she had time to return to her car and cover it up.

Stella perused the pages of notes she had collected during her detailed examination of the body, the surrounding area, and the entire alley.

"I can't shake off the skin," Detective Parker said as he approached from behind. His Versace Blue Jeans scent clouded the air. He was attractive, but he wore the same cologne as her father had, and he was way too boring for her to risk mixing her separate lives of lust and murder. "I mean, it was clearly peeled off his hand. Who does something like that?"

"Someone with a fetish for hands," Stella said.

"A killer with a fetish."

He still sounded like a goddamn parrot. She'd have to get used to that. "Paraphilia." The words from the criminal profiling book she'd been devouring sprung from her mouth as if she had written them.

"What?"

"It's a fixation. Sexual. We all have them."

He twisted his mouth and narrowed his eyes.

"For most of us, it's mild. For serial killers, it's consuming. In fact, they tend to have four to five paraphilias. Stacked. It drives their kills." She snapped her notebook shut.

"So, what? Our killer, he's aroused by skin? Peeled flesh?" Parker followed her gaze along the back door.

"Could be either. Or a combination."

Parker shuddered. "Geez. Where do you get this stuff from?"

She thought of the stack of books she'd inherited from her father. "Books. About serial killers. Behavioural profiling." She nodded at the door to the joint the body had been dumped behind. "I want to know what's inside."

"Cheetahs. Strip Club. Closed when we arrived. An officer was stationed at the door."

"What else is on this block?"

"Not much. Fast-food place. Liquor store. Mac's. Only thing open when we got here was the Mac's. Clerk was interviewed. Nothing." Parker crossed his arms.

"Hey! Detectives," an officer called from the end of the alley. "Owner's here."

"Cheetahs?" Parker yelled.

The officer nodded.

Stella jogged across the pavement, Parker in tow.

"Says he needs to open up. Told him he had to wait. He's not too happy," the officer blurted, trying to keep up with Stella.

As she rounded the corner, she saw him. Slicked-back hair. Thin moustache. Silk shirt. Polished shoes. He could easily pass for a star in a low-budget eighties porno. Why did she always get the sleazeballs? He tapped the toe of his dress shoe on the pavement.

"What's the hold up?" He glared.

She flashed her badge as she closed the distance. "Detective Mahoney."

"Hey, what's the problem, *Detective?* I got a business to run here." Sleazeball put up his hands and shot her a suave smile.

Her stomach roiled. "Found a body behind your joint. We need to talk."

"Hey, I don't know nothing about a body. I just got here. Opening time's in an hour. I got shit to do." He continued to tap his foot, his hands on his hips.

He was ridiculous.

"You can't open until we talk." She snapped her badge shut and shoved it into the pocket of her coat. Her face a few inches from his, she stared him straight in the eye.

"Okay, okay. Don't get riled up. We can talk, inside." He held up a ring of keys and jingled them. "What the fuck's with your cheek? You beat people up when they don't do what you want?"

"I'll ask the questions." Stella motioned for him to open the door.

"This your partner?" Sleazeball rolled his eyes at Parker.

Parker hovered behind Stella.

"Yes. Detective Parker." Parker flashed his badge.

"Well, *Detectives*. After you. I insist." Sleazeball opened the door and waved his hand, motioning them to step inside.

Stella walked through the door. The smell of sweat and sex invaded her senses. A red glow dimly lit the joint. Dark silhouettes of tables and chairs dotted the main space. A bar ran along the left wall.

Sleazeball stepped in behind them, closed the door, and flicked a switch on the wall. A buzzing vibrated through the space. Purple, pink, and red lights brought it to life. It was like a cheetah had vomited over the entire dive. Golden animal-print drapes covered the back wall across a stage mounted a few feet from the floor. The same pattern clothed chairs and pillows lining the shiny dance floor adorned with silver poles. Oh yeah, this guy had a real business to run. Stella choked back a comment and pivoted to face Sleazeball.

"You the owner?" She had no time, or desire, for small talk.

"Yeah. Jean." He extended his hand.

Stella looked him up and down, ignoring his hand, and proceeded to the front of the room.

Parker followed. He shot her a gaze that said, *Is this guy for real?*

She fought the urge to laugh.

"How long you owned this place, Jean?" Stella scanned the performance area. Along with the plush leopard-print drapes, matching chairs, and pillows, the checkered tiles of the dance floor had a yellow tinge to them. It was excessively adorned with leopard print. Or cheetah. Whatever the fuck it was supposed to be. It was making her eyes blur.

"Just over two years." Jean settled against the stage, leaning on his elbow and eyeballing her up and down.

Stella twirled around, taking in the dance floor, the bar, and a sequence of tinier rooms off the wall to the side. "Say, Jean, you run a proper business here?" She nodded toward the suspicious rooms.

"Yeah, of course." Jean shifted on his feet, digging his hands into his pockets.

Parker stood back, letting Stella take the lead.

"How long you owned this place?" Stella leaned against the stage, making it appear as if she was relaxed. She wanted him to know she had the upper hand. But she didn't want him to stop talking.

Jean's shoulders slumped slightly. "Just over two years. My cousin Jimmy used to run it."

"Oh yeah? Did Jimmy run the same business?" Stella rolled her shoulders and relaxed her jaw.

"Oh no. He was a big shot. From L.A. Lots of connections. He opened The Westward here. Big live-music place. Until it went under."

"When was that?"

"A few months shy of the tenth anniversary. Just over two years ago. Jimmy was crushed. Had some big shows here."

Stella flipped open her notebook casually. "Oh yeah? Who?"

"Chili Peppers. The Hip. Even Nirvana. In '91. It was big time. Jimmy was going all the way with this thing. When Electric Avenue was alive." Jean shrugged. "But it simmered. After the violence got bad. A lot of places shut down. Fewer people. Fewer shows."

She remembered. When she'd returned with her mother four years after her father died, she'd got a glimpse of it. Mobs of people streaming down the several-block cluster of nightclubs. Now, only the vintage joints remained.

"Yeah. The avenue shrank down to one block," Stella stated.

"You got it." Jean nodded. "It was wild in those days. At least four blocks. A mini-Vegas right here. Nightclubs. Bars. Lights. People. Lots of people." Jean's eyes lit up.

"You help Jimmy run his place?"

Jean nodded again. The memory seemed to bring him alive. "Yeah. Well, he ran the business. I helped out wherever I could. Westward was one of the few live-music places. Electric Ave was mostly bars. Place to get drunk. Party it up. Some clubs had DJs. But most of them didn't spring for live music. Too much overhead. Wasn't worth it. Unless you could bring in the big names. Party crowd wouldn't splurge for cover. Didn't want to waste their drinking money." Jean motioned over to the bar. "Say, you want a drink?"

Of course she did. But it wouldn't go over well with Parker. And she didn't want to make Jean think she liked him.

"We're on duty," Parker said.

Right on cue.

"Okay. I got it." Jean put his hands up. "You remember it? Electric Ave?"

"I'm new in town," Parker said.

"But *you* do." Jean glanced at Stella. His lips stretched into a slick smile.

"Not totally." She wasn't here during the height of the electricity. After their brief visit, her mother had whisked her home to the coast. Stella would have preferred to stay. To face head on the places where her father had spent his time. The memories were too much for her mother.

"It was all neon signs. Drink specials. Bouncers at the door. Crazy. Every night of the week." Jean walked over to a table and pulled out a chair. "You mind?"

Jean sat and pulled a packet of cigarettes out of his jacket pocket.

Parker slid out a chair across from Jean and sat.

Stella leaned against a chair.

Jean lit a cigarette with a cheap neon-yellow lighter and took a long drag. "When Jimmy opened this place in '87, it was like spring break every night of the week. Fifty-cent shooters. Penny highballs. Bladder busters." Jean took another drag.

"Bladder busters?" Parker asked.

"Yeah. Specials that lasted thirty minutes. Kids would line up at the door to those places. Drink as much as they could." Jean shook the cigarette over a plastic leopard-print ashtray with purple lettering declaring it the property of Cheetahs. "But Jimmy didn't do that. He was all about the music. Brought in big names. Charged at the door. He was crushed when it simmered out."

"You bought it from him?" Parker asked.

"Yeah. He went home. The Sunset Strip. That's why he had all the connections to bring in all those bands."

Stella walked up to the table, pulled a chair out and sat. She settled her boot across her knee and leaned back. "You open every day?" She'd greased him up enough. It was time to get to the point.

Jean shook his head. "Closed Mondays. Don't get enough customers. Gives the girls a break."

"No one was here yesterday?" Stella leaned toward Jean.

"No. Just getting here now to open up. Tuesdays we only have an evening show." Jean crushed the butt into the ashtray. "Girls will be arriving soon. I gotta get things ready. We done here?"

Had he totally forgotten about the body she'd mentioned?

"You're not opening tonight," Stella said.

"I gotta open. I need the money. Girls need the money."

"Well, *Jean,* we got a dead body in the alley, right behind your joint." Stella leaned over the table, hovering close.

"What?" Jean's eyes widened.

He was either playing dumb or simply ignorant.

"Who would leave a body behind my place?" He leaned into the chair.

"That's what we need to find out. We'd like your co-operation," Parker said.

Jean bolted up from the chair. "I don't know nothing about no body. Like I said, my place was closed yesterday. No one came in. Now, I gotta get to opening. Girls will be here soon. Customers count on us. One of the few places open tonight."

Stella stood and looked him in the eye. "New plan, *Jean.* You're gonna greet your girls as they arrive. You're gonna tell them to talk to us. Then you're gonna flag your regulars as they come in."

"Or what?" Jean spat.

"Or we'll inspect those *private rooms* you got over there." Stella nodded at the smaller rooms closed with long curtains. Gold-and-black patterned, like the rest of the place. He'd really taken the cheetah theme far. "I'm sure the girls would love to share what you make them do in those private rooms to keep their jobs." She glanced back at him.

He hesitated. "Fine."

"Thanks." She smirked, then shot a glance at Parker. He nodded.

"Yeah, whatever." Jean walked over to the bar, yanked a bottle and glass from behind, and poured himself a healthy dose. He shot it back, then glared at Stella. "You better not spook any of my girls. My business depends on it."

Parker smirked. Stella moved across the room to face Jean. "You help us out and I'm sure your business will be just fine."

# Chapter 10
# Missy Chrissy Sissy

Stella's head throbbed. A sticky dryness clung to her mouth and throat. She blinked a few times, refocusing her gaze.

Missy...*was it Missy?* She scanned the open page of her notebook. *No, this was Chrissy.* She'd already moved on from Missy to Chrissy.

Chrissy sat, well poised, in the chair across the table from Stella, yammering on in her too-bubbly voice. The gold-and-black drapes provided a background for the show she was putting on. The nauseating leopard-vomit décor was making Stella sick. Or maybe it was the wicked bourbon-soaked hangover that was thrumming in the base of her head and seizing her entire body. Stella pasted a smile on her face and refocused on Chrissy.

"The minute I started my audition..." Chrissy twisted in her chair and waved her milky hand with perfectly manicured hot-pink nails at the cheetah-themed dance floor, adding, "the *second* I started dancing"—she twisted to face Stella—"Jean's eyes lit up. I *knew* I had the job. It was, like, *meant to be.* What's that word?" Her eyes rolled to the top of her head. "Oh yeah. Serendipitous." She chomped a wad of gum a few times. "Of course, it wasn't as nice in here as it is now. Hadn't been redecorated yet." The pink gloss on her lips glimmered as she smiled.

"When did you start working here?" Stella asked.

"The day Cheetahs opened. I'm a lifer."

"And your last shift was when?" Stella tapped her notebook with her pen.

"Three days ago. I get all the Fridays and Saturdays. Senior Rank." She smiled. The pink gloss glistened. "I get Sundays off. And we're closed on Mondays."

"Have you ever seen this man?" Stella slid a photo of the victim, one that focused on his face and didn't show the fleshless hand, across the table.

Chrissy tapped the table with a hot-pink nail and squinted at the photo. "Nope. I know all the regulars. And I'm good at remembering new ones too. Never seen him in here."

It was the same story they'd all told. Lizzy, Sissy, Tami, Trina, Joni, Cheri, Missy, and now Chrissy. Most of them had been working for Jean the entire time he'd owned the place. Apparently, he was a good boss. Despite his image, he treated his staff well. Didn't put up with poor behaviour from the customers.

Jean walked up and leaned over the table. "Is everything OK here, ladies? Can I get you a drink?" His smooth exterior oozed sleaze, yet he'd been surprisingly cooperative—despite the hint of nervousness he'd displayed when Stella had mentioned the private rooms.

"I'll have a Long Island iced tea." Chrissy tilted her face up to him with adoring eyes.

"Water," Stella said. She'd kill for a sliver of the hair of the dog right about now.

Jean saluted, then moved toward the bar. As she watched him walk away, Stella caught a glimpse of Parker. He was involved in what appeared to be quite an engaging interview with a brunette wearing gold lipstick. She snorted to herself. Maybe he wasn't so perfect after all.

"So, we're really not opening tonight?" Chrissy batted her eyelashes. The silver shadow on her eyelids twinkled.

"No."

"Then can I go to the change room? This thing's scratchy as shit." She smoothed her hands over the sequined top clinging to her ample breasts and tiny waist. "The things a girl has to do for her career." She rolled her eyes.

*Yeah. The things a girl has to do.* A string of dead bodies flashed through Stella's mind. "In a moment. What goes on in those rooms?" Stella motioned toward the half-dozen private rooms roped off and hidden by more leopard-print curtains.

Chrissy blushed. "Well, we—the girls—we spend extra time with our top customers."

"Extra favours for extra tips?" Stella eased her shoulders down and smiled at Chrissy.

Chrissy hesitated.

"Don't worry. I'm not here to bust any of you. I'm just getting a feel for this place. Drive out anything that might have had to do with the situation in the alley." She relaxed her expression.

"It's nothing like that. We give them exclusive lap dances, in an intimate setting. We say nice things to them, make them feel special. There's no touching. Jean doesn't allow it," Chrissy blurted in a rapid, bubbly stream.

No one seemed to want to point the finger at Jean. Either they were desperate to keep their positions as dancers at Cheetahs, or Jean really was a nice guy trying to run a decent place.

This wasn't going anywhere.

"OK, thanks for your help." Stella slid a card across the table. "You think of anything else that has to do with this guy"—she tapped the photo of the victim—"you call me."

Chrissy smiled, grabbed the card, and bounced away.

She met Jean on his way to the table and giggled as he handed her a drink. She made her way toward the rear of the place. He continued toward Stella, glass of water in hand.

They'd been here all night. Ever since Jean arrived around nine. It was nearing on two o'clock in the morning. They'd interviewed all the staff as they'd come in for their shifts. Several girls. A bartender. A bouncer. Jean had called in the other girls not on duty. He couldn't get a hold of his back-up bartender and bouncer.

She doubted it mattered. They'd follow up. It was unlikely they'd find anything new. All the stories lined up. None of his staff seemed nervous or on edge. They didn't appear to have anything to hide. It didn't seem that their vic had ever stepped foot in the strip joint he'd been dumped behind. The killer appeared to have positioned the drop-off perfectly when the place was empty.

If there was no connection between the location and the victim, then why here? Convenience?

Jean set the glass of water on the table. "As you asked, Detective."

"That's all the girls?" She took the glass and chugged half the water. The throbbing in her head eased slightly. Her mouth softened with the needed moisture.

"That's all of them. I'll try Jim and Bob again." He walked over to the bar.

Stella slid her hand into her coat pocket, draped over the back of the chair. She stroked the fur of her good luck charm, the rabbit foot. She slid the photo of the vic toward herself and examined his face. The striking emerald of his eyes drew her in. His too-blond hair stuck out. It struck her that if he had been in this place, someone would remember those eyes. And that hair. And if they were all lying about not seeing him, then someone would have been even a little nervous.

Still, the feeling in her gut told her that there was a reason he was dumped behind this place.

# Chapter 11
# Back-Alley Scan

A chill bit at Stella's cheeks as she left the sticky warmth of Cheetahs. Her heels poked sharp darts of sound into the quiet of the night. The strip joint staff were the only ones left. Jean had declared a round on the house to settle their nerves before they headed home. She had to admit, he seemed to care about them. He came across as being committed to his business, and to be sincere about making it work. Perhaps that was why he had been nothing but co-operative.

Parker had pulled out of the parking lot in his obnoxious cherry-red Corvette. They'd compared notes. All the interviews lined up perfectly. She'd pretended to head to her car as she'd watched him round the corner at the end of the block. She wasn't quite ready to leave the scene of the crime.

She turned the corner at the end of the walkway and returned to the alley. One more walkthrough of the dark crime scene was all she could think about it. You never knew if there was some tiny detail that had been missed. She also liked to replay the events in her mind, creating her own mini-movie of what might have occurred. Sometimes, it struck a new thought.

Her heels crunched against wet gravel scattered over the dark pavement. The glow from the streetlamps on the front side of the building simmered out as she moved down the alley. As her eyes adjusted, shadows became inanimate objects. The outline of the building morphed into a brick wall. A rectangular frame transformed into a solid rear door to Cheetahs. A ragged outline shifted into the dumpster that the body had been positioned next to. It had been...*positioned,*

As she approached the door to the strip joint, she halted. From here, she could see most of the way down the alley. She focused on the place where the body had been only hours ago. She slid her hand into the pocket of her leather coat, finding the familiar fur of the rabbit foot. Stupid Sutton for luring her into this *trust your gut* idea.

Although, she couldn't argue that perhaps he was onto something. Didn't they all say that her father did the same thing?

She replayed her version of what had happened here, likely less than twenty-four hours ago. Wouldn't it be easier to drive down the alley, then pull the body from a car? The lack of tire marks led to the conclusion this had not occurred. Had the killer parked out front, then carried the body around to the alley? Maybe. If they parked at the farthest edge of the front of the building, they could have gone unnoticed. But to lift the body and carry it down here...did that seem likely? Having been dead for potentially a week—judging by the decomp—before the killer disposed of the victim, the body would have been stiff and heavy.

She pictured the killer leaning over the body, positioning the limbs. Taking the dead victim by the fleshless hand and wrapping his skinless fingers around the book in some sort of horror-show display. The killer, making sure the book was open to the correct page. The one scrolled with the grisly message of a deranged mind. Giving the victim one last glance.

A sudden gust of wind shook Stella's bones. She crouched and stared at the space that had recently supported a dead body. She scoured the slick pavement with her eyes. There was nothing. They hadn't missed a single piece of physical evidence. Yet, something grabbed at her gut, poking it with cold fingers, telling her that there was something here that she wasn't seeing. Something that was slipping through her fingers.

# Chapter 12

# Familiar Eyes

As soon as she entered Sparky's, Lolita relaxed. Drinks were flowing. Lights filled the room with bright colours from the elevated stage, empty and waiting for the main act. The crowd was growing. Hardcore enthusiasts huddled near the front like a pulsing amoeba, sucking in wanderers, building its mass.

Sparky's used to be one of the most vibrant live-music venues on Electric Avenue. It wasn't Sparky's anymore. Management had changed. The focus had switched from live music to a Caribbean restaurant. But Lolita still thought of it as Sparky's. She stifled the coconut-and-pineapple aromas lingering in the air from the closed kitchen, shut her eyes, and pictured it how she would always remember it in her mind. The elevated performance area. The bar at the back, serving cheap pitchers and shooters. The spot in the corner at the front, where she would hover, hand in hand, with Orson and take in some of the greatest acts to perform in the city.

Lolita sighed, opened her eyes, shot a glance at the bar, then walked away. A drink was the last thing she needed. The cracked pill bottle with her name plastered across a ripped label shimmered through her mind. The bottle she'd crammed into her bag years ago when she'd fled the clutches of her mother, following Orson to her dream life. She hadn't taken any of the oxytocin in a while. Tonight, her drooping lip itched something fierce and her body shook with anxiety, threatening to trigger her internal switch on, taking her to a place filled with shadows that she didn't want to go. She walked to the far end where she hung by the brick wall painted burgundy and blue by the pot lights. Only the occasional live act played here now. Most of them were cover bands. Tonight was grunge night. An ode to the early 90s and a style of music that still lingered in the air waves of specialty stations. A style that was still alive in the bubble of Lolita's petite crooked house.

She'd been locked in her studio for several long days. Sleep had been sparse and troubled. Images of Orson had invaded her dreams. She'd woken several times coated in sweat, her dreadlocks sticking to her back, her nightgown drenched, a feeling of dread in the pit of her belly. No matter how hard she focused on her freshly inked lyrics, she couldn't achieve *the performance.* The one that oozed perfection as she enunciated each syllable of each word, sharing her lyrics. Her rhymes. Her poetry. Her message.

The notion of fleeing, pulling herself from the house that seemed to be closing in on her, shot excitement through her veins. She'd wrestled with the idea, sitting on her couch until mid-afternoon, watching videos and listening to tracks, stewing in her worry. Images of the bright lights of Electric Avenue had flashed through her mind, reminding her of all the places she used to go with Orson, seeking fresh inspiration, then rushing home to their basement studio to succumb to the creativity that seeped from their souls.

She almost ditched the idea of leaving the house and crawled into bed instead. After fulfilling an intense craving for *the video* she couldn't live without, she'd jumped from the couch, ran a hot bubble bath, and started preparing for the evening.

The crowd murmured as a young man with tousled blond hair took the stage. He wore baggy jeans and a Nirvana t-shirt. Lolita leaned into the wall and watched him set up. As he secured his acoustic guitar strap over his shoulder, sat on a high wooden stool, and pulled the microphone stand toward him, his hair slid away from his eyes.

Lolita gasped. She stared into the too-green eyes of the singer. They were almost the colour of tourmaline. Just like Orson's.

In a trance, she slid away from the wall and shuffled up to the front as he spoke into the microphone. As he sung the first words of his first track for the evening, Lolita found herself nestled beside the small crowd hovering right in front of him. He performed beautiful renditions of her favourite grunge artists. His voice was rough and raw at times, yet sweet, almost angelic, at others. As his performance progressed, the grip he had over her swelled. The anxiety escaped from her pores, dissolving into nothing. The rootedness she longed for sprouted, grew, reached through her, taking her where she needed to be.

It was a massive relief.

Maybe there was a way out of her spiralling craziness after all. Maybe she *could* escape from her internal switch and its continuous threat to click *on* and stay there.

She gazed at the singer. His smooth skin. His lips enunciating each word with the utmost care. *His eyes.* Those striking emerald eyes, so much like Orson's.

The oxytocin took its full hold on her. Her trance-like state deepened. The room flickered. Lolita blinked.

She stared up at the singer.

*Orson.*

His words flowed as he reached the end of the line, the tone of his voice like a syrup tinged with a bite. A rough hook pulled at Lolita's gut, just enough to make her want more. Then it retreated, returning to that smooth, lulling sound, feeding her.

As she inhaled, she breathed him in. His words. His essence. It was as if they were the only two in the room.

Why had she argued with him about coming here tonight? Guilt swelled inside of her. She'd argued because she was jealous that she wasn't performing.

As he reached the peak of his performance, her shoulders lowered. She stroked her dreadlocks. A warmth swelled within her, wrapping comforting hands around her. She sank into a trance, staring straight into the emerald eyes of the man she loved.

As his words shot through the room, across the space between them, and straight into her soul, she knew with her entire being that he was going to be big.

She'd tell him again. Tonight. Until he believed her.

# Chapter 13

# Music Fusion

The tiny house curled in, wrapping its walls around the living room. Lolita sprawled out over the plush sofa, watching the video flashing on the television. The entire day had stretched out in an easy flow. Last night had been amazing.

She'd watched Orson at Sparky's, achieving the performance that had been simmering within him for a while.

They'd walked home, hand in hand, under the lights of Electric Avenue. Energy seethed through her veins under the neon signs of the nightclubs and live-music venues. A sense of peace washed through her. As they approached the house, an excitement bubbled through her as they talked about fresh lyrics.

After watching Orson's killer acoustic set at Sparky's last night, she'd followed him into their basement studio to start laying down the tracks. They'd worked until the sun started its ascent, reaching pink fingers through the bay window facing the street. She'd nestled into the crook of Orson's arm and fell into a deep sleep. He only had a few hours before he'd had to leave for work. When she woke, the bed was empty.

She stretched her legs out in front of her, settling her socked feet onto the coffee table. Images flashed on the television screen. *Mama Said Knock You Out.* A dark background. LL Cool J, an epic rhymer of the time, wearing a hoody, face partially concealed. Every word was pronounced to *perfection*. The beat, the flow, drew her in. Her body swayed in time, involuntarily. He was a lyric *king*, in her eyes. Something smooth coated his words, yet his voice had an aggressive edge to it. The voice *was* the rhyme. The lyrics *were* his message. She lost herself in the video, until it came to an end.

Orson kept telling her it would be *their* time soon. She was starting to believe it might be *his* time. Not hers. Lately, it was getting more arduous to rhyme smoothly without a glitch. Sometimes, her mouth felt strange. Her lip pulled at the occasional word. It hadn't happened enough for Orson to notice. Or anyone else in their band. She hoped it would go away soon.

Their next show would be important. Critical to her own success. Orson promised her the lead on several tracks.

She could see it now. Her olive skin shimmering under the purple-and-blue pot lights. Her luscious dreadlocks flowing to the beat. Her own rhymes. None of the creative spark had come from Orson.

She wondered why he wasn't home yet.

She got up and walked over to the stack of VHS tapes next to the television. Even though they were all new releases, you couldn't rely on MTV to play the ones you wanted when you wanted them. She shuffled through the stack, seeking a wild fusion that she had an intense craving for. She smiled as she found the tape, sliding it from the case and into the player.

Fixated on the screen, she lowered herself onto the couch and settled in a cross-legged position. The wheels of the tape clicked as they spun, and the video flashed across the screen.

*Body Count "There Goes The Neighborhood" Body Count Sire Records*

Thrash metal meets rap. A sea of bodies flooded the screen. The badass rapper, Ice-T, thrust his face close. The song, an assault of aggressive rhymes melded with high-voltage guitar riffs, amped her up. It was ahead of its time. Genius. A historical movement in music.

It had inspired her own vision.

In a time when rap was skyrocketing, and the new grunge was taking the world by storm, Lolita saw a prime opportunity. *Electric Skin* would execute her fusion. Rap and grunge. It would be unique. Raw. Honest. Emotional. She'd been slaving over the rhymes, the rest of the band following her lead to hash out the music. Nicky had really come through with killer percussion to match the vibe she wanted. Jud had followed suit with edgy bass lines. Orson had been supportive, providing the guitar riffs that she would usually play.

They were close. The final touches were the hardest, smoothing out the minute details that would take the rhymes from great to over the top.

The last image of the video shimmered from the screen as it came to an end.

She could see it. A crystal-clear vision in her mind. The smooth-as-silk rhymes, like LL himself. The raw edge of the grunge greats like Kurt Cobain.

They could do it.

She had the velvety sweet voice. Orson had the raw edge.

Captivated in this moment, she grabbed her notebook and 2B pencil from the coffee table and flipped through the pages. She lost herself in the tiny tweaks that would take her vision to new heights. Her passion consumed her as she waited for Orson to come home.

# Chapter 14

# Skin

The dark quiet of the room wrapped around Stella like a warm blanket. She didn't even find it strange that the basement room in the morgue was a place of comfort. It seemed fitting somehow. Had her father felt the same? She'd been whisked through a whirlwind of activity since she entered *The Cecil*, hunting knife ready to scare Dirty Joe into a confession, only four nights ago.

The peace of the room halted all the thoughts whirring through her mind. Dirty Joe. The knife sliding into him. His hot blood pouring over the hand of his intended victim. The look in her eyes. Relief. Hope for a second chance. The sinking feeling in Stella's gut as she watched Joe take his last breaths. The question pulsing in her mind like a neon sign: *Was there another way?*

Her crazy metal-booze-sex binge. A weak attempt to make herself feel better. The voice of the metal god filling the depths of Rock Candy. The blur of images streaking the night into a cosmic collage.

Movement in the corner of the room jolted her into reality. She took a heartfelt breath and walked toward the only light bathing the room in a soft yellow glow. The silver streak in Blackwood's dark hair caught in the light as she moved away from her work. The collar of her earth coloured turtle neck clung to her neck, reaching out from the white lab coat clinging to her muscular yet feminine contours. "Mahoney. You look tired." The Medical Examiner's eyes seeped concern.

"Yeah." She *was* tired. She'd only had a few hours of drunken sleep in Seattle. She'd had none since racing to the murder over twenty-four hours ago. "Long night of interviewing Jean's staff at Cheetahs."

"Wow. As classy as it sounds?" Blackwood smirked.

"Oh yeah. Jean runs a real class act. Cheap booze. Scantily-clad dancers. Sketchy private rooms."

"Ready for some post-mortem facts?"

Blackwood was all business. Stella liked it that way. "You got it." She flipped open her notebook.

"I've had time with our vic. No ID yet. Appears late twenties to me. Nothing on him to tell us who he is. No trace of his prints in the system. His information is being verified with missing persons." Blackwood grabbed a folder off a table and walked over to the body.

Stella followed. "At the scene, his skin was greenish, but hints of black were eating him. If he was moving to active decay, you'd think someone was missing him."

"Insides full of larvae. He's already in active decay. Likely been dead a good week. Based on the temperature of the body, he hadn't been in that alley more than a few hours." Blackwood flipped open the folder.

"Keeping him after the kill. What for?"

"Skin fact one," Blackwood said.

Stella swallowed a chuckle. She shouldn't be amused by this, but when Blackwood processed a body, she was like a professor standing at the front of the classroom. It was too cute.

"You with me?" Blackwood raised an eyebrow.

"Yeah." Stella forced a stern expression.

"Skin fact one. It's clean. Washed. Traces of calcium stearate and magnesium stearate. Soap residue, all over his face, arms, legs. When soap mixes with hard water, these chemicals form the residue. The state of the reaction indicates the soap's been in contact with the skin less than forty-eight hours."

"Post-mortem, pre-dump bath. Killer wanted him clean. Wonder how many baths he had." Stella jotted in her notebook.

"Skin fact two. No trace of who washed the body. No blood. No prints. No fluids." Blackwood flipped a page.

"Wore gloves. The right kind." Stella scribbled the note.

"Skin fact three." Blackwood scanned the page. Her eyes narrowed.

Stella wondered about the purple hue to Blackwood's irises. She'd never seen anything like it. She wanted to ask. But she wouldn't pry.

Blackwood swallowed as she walked up to the body and moved a thin sheet away from the right hand. "The hand. The epidermis—outermost layer—was removed in two strips. The palm side. The top. Separately. There's a clear incision separating the two pieces. Seems like they were removed intact. Dermis and hypodermis—the layers underneath—seem intact." Blackwood pointed along the index finger at a scarlet line running along what remained of the flesh.

Stella leaned in and examined it. "Two pieces. Intact. Killer's keeping the skin? Using it for something. Trophy?" Stella jotted more notes.

"You sound like a criminal profiler."

Stella lifted her eyebrow at this comment. Maybe Blackwood knew criminal profilers, like the one Detective Mahoney Senior had worked with.

Blackwood placed the sheet over the skinless hand. "Clothing fact one." She moved over to a separate table lined with the clothing that had been on the victim. It was spread out. The tattered jeans lay flat. Next to them, the long sleeves of the silver shirt shimmered under the overhead light. "Clothing fact one is there aren't any clothing facts. No traces. Nothing. Too clean."

"Killer could have dressed him post-mortem. But how did he get him in the alley without any traces of anything on the clothes?" Stella scanned the items. The silver shirt seemed strange.

"No traces of any human fluids other than his own. No prints. No foreign fibres. No sign of another human being." Blackwood flipped a few more pages.

"What would you do with the skin from a hand?" Stella lowered her notebook.

"Toxicology report is still in progress. Initial results indicate traces of benzodiazepines. Tranquilizer. Likely administered from injection points on his neck." Blackwood swiftly walked over to the victim and pulled the sheet down. She pointed to several red dots in the side of his neck.

Stella took in the face of the victim. His eyes now closed, their striking emerald colour shimmered in her mind. The skin of his face shone under the lighting. A whisper breathed through her thoughts. *What would you tell me, if you could?*

Blackwood settled the sheet over the victim's face. "You got all that?"

Stella nodded. "Yeah. Several injections. Probably used upon initial contact. Make it easier to take the victim. But where?" Stella added quick notes to her notepad.

"COD is unclear. Until the toxicology report is complete, it's inconclusive. The level of exposure to the dermis and hypodermis on the hand indicates that the skin could have been removed days prior to death. It's possible the victim could have bled out. Hydration levels were also dangerously low. Could have been a combination of these factors. Still running tests on the internals." A slight pout pulled at the corners of Blackwood's mouth.

"Drugged. Taken. Kept somewhere. Tied up, likely. Hand sliced, skin peeled away. No water. Probably no food, either." Stella nodded to herself.

"Nothing in the stomach, intestines, or colon. Whatever he last ate was long gone. Dehydration would have had more of an effect." Blackwood flipped through the remaining pages in the folder. "Fingernails. Tiny chips of black were found in the corners of some of the fingernails. Ran a chemical analysis. Formaldehyde resin, camphor, and toluene. Consistent with nail polish. Not sure what to make of that. But that's your realm, Detective." Blackwood snapped the folder on the table.

"Nail polish, got it."

"Book. The pages inside the book appear to be normal paper. Cover seems odd. Book fact one. Cover is composed of sixty-seven white Bristol. Been through a lot of notebooks in my time. Never seen a cover made of cardstock." Blackwood shrugged. "Where it gets good is the page that has writing on it. Book fact two. Words are written in a combination of solvents and pigments, the ink, and the victim's own blood. Appears the two liquids were combined, then applied to do the writing. Real humdinger."

Stella clenched her jaw. A cold chill walked through her gut. Complete skin removal from the hand. Blood. "Victim was right-handed."

"We don't know that. Yet."

No. But he had to be. Skin from the right hand gone and a notebook with writing in blood ink. The victim's blood ink. There had to be a link there. This killer was living out some kind of sick fantasy. What did it have to do with trophy skin and blood ink? Stella was going to find out.

"That's all I can give you." Blackwood moved over to a phone. "Time to bring in..."

The door opened. A blast of light pierced the room followed by a whoosh. A young man in a lab coat entered.

"Doctor Klein," Blackwood greeted, dropping the phone in its cradle. "I was just about to call you."

The man strode toward them, a notebook and a folder stacked in his hand. He was tall, lean, and muscular. His hair was a striking black. Too black to be natural. It was spiked out in multiple directions. Dark, thick glasses perched on the bridge of his nose. Rich, brown eyes contrasted with his pale skin.

He extended a hand to Stella. "Doctor Klein. Call me Bryce." Metal rings adorned his fingers.

Stella returned the greeting. "Detective Mahoney." Would she mind if he called her Stella? Probably not. But she'd worked too hard to get people to use her title to throw that away now.

"Bryce is a forensic chemist," Blackwood said. "He ran extensive analyses on traces we found on the body and at the scene. The traces were small, yet distinct. I knew we needed an expert."

"Traces of what?" Stella asked.

"Thin strands of coated glass fibres. Each a mere eight microns. Smaller than a human hair. Fibre optic cable." Bryce snapped the folder onto the table where Blackwood had put hers. He opened it and spread out several sheets of paper. "Complete report here. A copy for the lab." He nodded at Blackwood. "A copy for you, too, Detective."

"Fibre optic cable?" Stella picked up the sheet of paper and scanned it. PVC. PE. Fluoropolymers. It didn't mean anything to her. What would high-tech fibre be doing on a victim dressed in a silver shirt and dumped in the alleyway behind a strip club?

"Yes. Results are conclusive. GC-MS. Gas chromatography-mass spectrometry. The gold standard for forensic substance identification. It performs a one-hundred-percent specific test to positively identify the presence of a particular substance. It discovered polyvinyl chloride, polyethylene, and fluoropolymers. The chemical compositions blended into the unique formation of fibre optic cable."

Stella put the paper down and scribbled notes in her book. She needed to be able to explain this. "What the hell would this cable be doing on our vic?"

"Precise trace results. Less precise explanation." Bryce's rich eyes were mesmerizing. "I do believe that applications of fibre optics have exploded over the last couple of years. But I'm no expert in that area. I stick to chemicals. You need a tech expert."

She had one. "The case analyst can help with that. But this..."—she picked the sheet up—"can you break it down into normal-people terms?" A slight flush warmed her cheeks.

"Definitely. If you're done here, I've got a few minutes. I can simplify it for you. Make you sound like an expert in the composition of fibre optic cable."

"Anything else?" Stella asked Blackwood.

"No. I'll keep you posted. Next priority is the ID and a more conclusive COD." Blackwood smiled.

Could she read Stella's thoughts? Maybe it wouldn't be so bad to have someone she could open up to.

"All yours." The words shot out of Stella's mouth without warning. That's not what she meant.

Bryce chuckled. "Good." He waved his hand to the door.

Stella started walking, silently yelling at the tingles running down her insides to fuck off.

# Chapter 15
# High-Tech 90s

The scent of stale detective sweat infused with cigarette smoke and cheap coffee tainted the air as Stella wove her way through the cluttered cubicles. Sutton gave her a hard time when she smelled like a low-cost motel room and bourbon. She wished he'd lay off and use some of that hot air he wasted putting his other detectives in line.

She slid her jacket off and settled it over the chair at her desk. The tidiness of her cubicle shocked even her. Her workspace had become her sacred space. Her messy ways hadn't tarnished it. She wanted to keep it that way.

Fibre optic chemical analysis report in hand, she walked over to Jake's desk. Bryce had been a gem. Back in his lab, he'd taken his time to explain the process he used and the results he'd gotten from the tiny particles of glass embedded on the dead body. Alice in Chains rumbled in the background of Bryce's office from a boombox set underneath a rather impressive stack of cassettes. As she approached Jake, she silently prayed he'd be able to whip up some strong leads for her before roll call. Sutton hated it when she labelled his team meetings. She loved getting under his skin.

"Jakey," she greeted as she walked up behind him. Something like pine wafted from his space.

"Stella," he said as he continued typing, eyes glued to the black screen flashing with neon text.

His lime-green sweater vest violated her eyes. "What's with the blinding light of the vest?"

"Very funny. I like colour."

She tousled his chocolate curls. "You're gettin' shaggy. Working too much."

"Not my fault. Detectives are demanding."

"Well...I have further *demands* for you."

He stopped typing, shut down the screen he'd been glued to, and twirled his chair around. "I'm all yours."

"You heard about the new case?"

Jake nodded. "Guy dumped in an alley behind a strip club."

"It's a good one, Jakey."

"Oh great." He rolled his eyes. "What kind of creepy shit are you gonna make me see?" He raised an eyebrow.

"Actually, I got some real tech stuff for you. Computer wiz shit." She set the summary of the chemical analysis on his desk. "Fibre optic cable. Traces of it on the victim."

"Really?" Jake pounced on the paper, devouring the information.

"I need to know how this high-tech fibre would get onto my victim."

"Could be a tough one." Jake continued to peruse the information. "The applications of fibre optics have exploded over the last year."

"What *is* it?"

"Fibre optic cable is composed of a bunch of thin strands of glass fibres."

"Yeah. I know. Coated in..."—she scanned the sheet—"polyvinyl chloride, polyethylene, and fluoropolymers." She shot a proud smile at Jake.

He chuckled. "And the glass particles are *tiny*. When I say tiny, I mean it. *Minuscule.* Each one is about eight microns. Smaller than a strand of human hair." His eyes lit up.

"Bryce said the same thing." Stella pouted.

"Bryce?"

"Forensic chemist. He's the one who did this." She pointed at the paper. "But what *is* it? Like, what is it *used* for?"

Jake sprung into action, wheeling his chair over to another computer on the far end of his desk. He clicked the keyboard, bringing the screen to life. "You see this?" A series of colourful boxes filled the screen, each composed of a series of icons like mini folders. Jake clicked. A new box opened, *Netscape* scrolled across the top.

"Yeah, so? Big deal. Web browser. Search the Internet."

His eyes widened. "But how do you think the data gets from one computer to the next? When you type in a search, data is retrieved from other computers all over the world through a series of networks, using wires. Cables. Fibre optic cable is a high-speed data transmission mechanism. It will change everything about how we use our computers. How we use the Internet. Digitized information is coded and placed onto light pulses for transmission. It travels along the glass fibre at the speed of light—186,000 miles per second. Just think of how fast I can complete searches for you. You should be excited." He smiled.

"OK, cool. Faster searches. That's great. But how the heck would traces of one of these cables get on my victim?"

"Good question." Jake pulled a curl away from his eye. "Most people don't come into contact with the cable. Off the top of my head, you'd have to be manufacturing the cable, or installing it."

"You said this fibre optics is being used for lots of things?"

"Oh yeah. Like I said, Internet communication has gone crazy. More than 150 million users now. Lots of networks being built. Lots of cable needed. But it's also used in cable TV, medical, defence, government, all kinds of commercial applications...tons of stuff."

"So someone could be working in a lot of places either making this stuff or installing it." Stella clenched her jaw. She examined the chemical analysis summary. She'd been hopeful this would lead somewhere. Fast.

"Yeah. Don't give up on the trace. I'll take a closer look. Do a search on local manufacturing and installation. We might get something." He rolled his chair over to the smaller black screen and started typing. Neon-green text flashed across it.

"What about your fancy Netscape?"

"DOS isn't dead yet." He kept typing.

"What?"

"They say the death of DOS is near. This is DOS–command-level prompts." He nodded at the screen. "Less flashy, with a significant amount of control. This is how I directly access a wealth of databases that have been around since before most people started using the Internet."

"Got it." She flipped open her notebook. "I have more for you."

"Of course you do." He continued typing.

"Sixty-seven number, white Bristol. It's like paper. But thick. Card stock, I guess."

"And?"

"There was a book left in the victim's hand. The cover is made of this white Bristol. Book was some kind of notepad. Cover doesn't seem like a typical material for a notebook."

"You want me to find out where you'd buy something like this?"

"Yes."

"On it." He typed another series of searches. Strings of neon text rushed over the screen. "It'll take a bit."

"You need that fibre optics." She chuckled.

"To keep up with your demands, I do." His dimple made an appearance.

"Here. Bristol boards. Folder stock. Can be used in bookbinding. Thicker and more durable than standard paper, thinner and more flexible than other forms of paperboard. I'll see what I can dig up regarding sources of notebooks."

"Dig deep. It's important."

"I always dig deep. Why so focused on the book?"

She pursed her lips. "It was in the victim's hand."

"You said that already." He paused his typing and looked at her with curiosity.

"The skin was missing. From his hand." She pulled a photo out.

He cringed. "No. I don't need to see that."

"It's a photo of the book."

"Better not be a skinless hand." He took the photo gingerly. "You're lucky. If you forced me to see that, I'd ban you from submitting searches."

"You can't do that."

"Well, no. But I can become difficult to work with."

"Doubt it."

He stared at the photo. "There's writing on the page? Some kind of red ink?"

"Blood ink," she said. "Ink mixed with the victim's own blood."

"Geez. What does it say?"

"Here." She opened her notebook and placed it on his desk. He read the words out loud.

*I've been trapped*
*Deep inside the walls*
*Of your love morphed box*
*I've been entranced by your pull*
*Trapped by your dream*
*I'd die to swallow*
*The poison running through your veins*
*To warm your ice-cold body*
*To bring you home again*

"Whoa. What the hell does that mean?"

"No idea."

Jake typed the words into his computer. "I'll see what I can find."

She snapped her notebook shut. "Might mean nothing to anyone but the killer. But it's worth a shot. Could find some obscure source or something."

"I love your positivity. Don't let Sutton see that side of you." He typed rapidly, focused on the screen.

"Whatever. I gotta go." She smirked. "You're a rockstar."

"No, I'm not. I'm a geek in a bright vest. I like it that way."

# Chapter 16
# Time Warp

Warm rays of yellow sunshine reached through the bay window into the little house. White noise cracked over the television screen. Remnants of citrus wafted from a mug half full of cold tea on the coffee table.

Lolita moaned as she rolled over, sunk into the folds of the velour couch.

She rubbed her eyes, opened them, and scanned the room.

What time was it? What day was it?

She sat up and glanced across the room out the bay window. The sun peeked from behind Calgary's downtown towers, looming in the background of a row of houses across the street.

Scratches of white-and-black light etched across the television screen.

Right. She'd been watching videos. All the big ones.

She'd been waiting for Orson. Why hadn't he come home?

Something jolted in her brain, returning her to reality.

He hadn't come home. He wouldn't *be* coming home. He hadn't returned home since that night in 1993. It wasn't 1993 anymore.

Lolita closed her eyes and rubbed circles into her temples. Why did this keep happening to her? It wasn't a dream. It was a wrinkle in reality. She would believe that she was there again. Back in time. Sitting here in their house waiting for Orson to come home.

She was losing her grip.

The condition in her brain was simmering on high, nearing boiling. Was it bubbling over? Reaching its rot into the other parts of her brain?

It had already taken her mouth, causing it to droop, contorting her lip into a grotesque formation. Taking her ability to rhyme with it. Taking her ability to perform.

It wasn't fair.

It wasn't her fault that her mother had continued to consume toxins that reached through her body and into the brain of the fetus growing within her belly. It wasn't her choice that her mother had poisoned her before she had even entered the world. She would give anything to be rid of the fissure in the rear of her brain, lodged in her temporal lobe, deteriorating her rational thought and her emotional control.

*Dammit.* She flung her eyes open, slamming her hand on the coffee table. Tea sprang from the mug and landed on her notebook, exposing the last page she'd been scrolling on.

*Double dammit.*

She grabbed the book, stretched her sleeve over her hand, and blotted the page, trying not to smear the charcoal of her pencilled words.

Carefully placing the book open at the end of the table in hopes that the remaining moisture would dry, she settled into the couch.

It all came rushing back to her in a horrific wave.

It was 1999. Orson was gone. The band was gone.

Electric Avenue had retreated down to a single block.

There were no gigs lined up for her. No audience eager to hear her perform. The bright lights weren't ready to shine over her olive skin. The wild beat wasn't waiting to sync with her rhymes. There was no stage.

The long days in the basement studio rushed through her mind, lined up like an endless, desperate plea to redo her past. To have another attempt. To change history. To create a new destiny.

Panic clawed up her throat. Her stomach churned with pure acid. She swallowed the anxious ball rolling up her insides. She tried to calm her racing mind.

It was too late.

The switch was moving. It was going to switch itself on. Her rootedness would vanish, mere moments from now.

She curled her legs into her chest and rocked back and forth. The contorted corner of her mouth itched. She clawed at it, then gave up and wrapped her arms around her legs, giving momentum to her rocking.

How long it would last, she didn't know.

A thought pierced her mind. A shiver ran through her body. What if Orson was the missing piece? The reason she couldn't achieve the perfect performance in the basement studio. He wasn't coming home.

She reached over and picked up her notebook. The tea left a crinkled corner. As she read through the lyrics, a new wave of belief shot through her.

She bolted from the couch and headed straight for the stairs. This time she would do it. *The performance.*

# Chapter 17

# Dark Instincts

An odour of human sweat trickled up the stairs as Lolita descended into the basement studio.

She ignored it as she scuttled down the creaky stairs. She had a performance to get to. *The performance.*

She reached the basement. The odour intensified. Like someone who hadn't bathed in days. The lights flickered on as she clicked the switch.

Her own switch shuddered as she stared at the man behind the glass separating the recording space from the control room.

Rooted to the floor, she stared. Her internal switch twitched. Her mind wrenched over a series of images flashing through her mind like a disorganized horror flick.

The video on the television screen when she woke up. Body Count. The rap-metal fusion. Her inspiration. In 1993.

Her mind put the pieces together. She hadn't been at Sparky's. She hadn't been watching Orson. They hadn't walked hand in hand along the vibrant Electric Avenue. Electric Avenue was only a low simmer now, crawling toward death. Soon, it would join Orson. Orson wasn't coming home.

Her condition reached rotting fingers through her skull, poisoning the perfect flesh of her face. Contorting her lip. Slurring her words. Ruining her rhymes. Images of full days down in this studio, where she stood now, blurred through her mind. Her. Alone. Trying to achieve that perfect performance as desperation took complete hold on her. The switch inside of her. Taking her mind away. Transporting her total being to 1993. Before it all went wrong.

The man caged in the recording studio stared at her with wild eyes. Eyes that were too green. Tourmaline. His resemblance to Orson was striking. Who was he? Her mind flickered.

She *had* gone to Sparky's last night.

Only, it wasn't Sparky's anymore. It had been grunge night. Covers of her favourites from the early 90s. The whole room shuddered as she realized who she was staring at.

The young man who'd played those covers, his too-blond hair and too-green eyes mesmerizing her. Her switch had flicked to *on;* she'd thought it was 1993. She'd thought she was watching Orson. That they'd walked home together and recorded rhymes all night. *Her* rhymes.

Muffled sounds came from the other side of the glass. Her gaze flung across the room. The man was tied to a chair. A blood-soaked white cloth wrapped across his mouth, stifling his voice. His wild eyes pleaded with her. His dishevelled blond hair stuck out in clumps stained with blood. Sweat poured down the sides of his face.

*How had he gotten here?*

Hot vomit swirled in the pit of her stomach.

*What did she do?*

The vomit surged upwards. She swallowed against the rage. The fear freezing her legs in place thawed slightly. She took a few steps away, shaking her head, her gaze glued to those familiar eyes.

"I...I'm so sooorrry..." her voice shook as tears caught in her throat.

She backed away.

The man's muffled pleas heightened through the gag. His eyes begged her not to leave, to let him go.

She couldn't look at this anymore. Whatever the hell *this* was. She reached the stairs and launched forward, taking them two at a time.

This couldn't be real.

Her stomach clenched. The vile mix of fear and half-digested food lunged. She ran to the bathroom off the main room. As she hurled every last bit of her stomach contents into the porcelain bowl, the images of horror-filled emerald eyes and dripping crimson whirled through her mind in a blood-streaked rainbow. Wiping sour saliva from the corners of her mouth, Lolita leaned over the sink and splashed cold water over her face. She stared into the mirror, into the dark eyes staring at her. The familiar warmth simmered underneath a shiny coat of fear. Her lip trembled. She ran her finger over her mouth, across the contorted droop pulling the left side down.

The memories flooded her thoughts in a barrage of images.

Orson. The last night he was with her. His performance. It had been perfect.

She'd watched, a mere member of the audience. She couldn't perform with him anymore. The fissure in the back of her brain had reached its claws over her face, across her lip, and pulled her mouth into a droop that slurred her words into an incomprehensible blubber. Her rhymes were ruined. Orson's talent shone bright, shooting him up like a star in the night sky.

As she'd watched him shine, a mixture of love and jealousy churned within her.

She might have been able to keep the resulting anger to a slow simmer, hiding it from exposure. If only the afterparty hadn't taken the course it had.

Giggles drifted through Lolita's memories, tainting them with rot. The soft sounds morphed to a sick grinding noise, gripping her mind, clawing through her heart.

She'd watched him perform for the millionth time, pouring her love his way, supporting him in the dream that was supposed to be theirs, not his alone. If only that slutty girl with the perfect mouth and strawberry curls hadn't clung to him at the bar, drinking in his words like they were the last drops of water on earth. If only her face, her mouth, her lips, hadn't been so *perfect*.

If only he hadn't focused on her. Only her. Discarding Lolita after the show as if she'd always be there when he needed her.

If only.

Maybe he'd still be here today.

# Chapter 18

# Night Cap

Stella stared into the glass of bourbon. Its caramel colour taunted her. The sweet fingers of alcohol wove up from the glass, reaching for her nose. She'd just have a couple. Then she'd go home. Sutton had ordered them to get a few hours of sleep. They were already past the first forty-eight, the declared clock for striking up big leads on a murder case. They still didn't even have an ID.

A *typical* murder case.

This one wasn't typical, and she knew it.

She took a long swallow of the indulgent bourbon and relished in the burn in her throat. Two drinks. Go home. Put on some Type O Negative. Try to relive the feeling she had at Rock Candy the other night. The feeling of being in a bubble. No reality. A delightful high from the voice of a metal god. No past. No pain. It was the only way she'd be able to sleep after seeing the victim in the alley, the skin of his hand peeled away in two carefully cut pieces to be used for some grisly purpose.

"Another?" the bartender asked.

Stella jolted. Her glass was almost empty. "Sure." She attempted a smile.

He was cute. But clean. And young. He'd probably get attached if she took him home. And who knew what time he got off shift. She needed to stick to her two-bourbons-then-bed rule.

She swivelled on the high stool and scanned the joint. It was quiet. She'd purposely picked a place she knew wouldn't be packed with the overeager mid-week crowd. She didn't want to be alone. But she didn't want to be surrounded by people, either. Just a slight scattering of other humans to make her feel like she wasn't completely alone in this world. Not tonight.

Sure, there were people in her life who cared about her. Jake. Even Sutton, she supposed. But they were *work* people. They had to be nice to her. They weren't real friends. People who had found her and wanted to be with her. She tried to remember the last time she had truly felt close to someone.

Her father. But he wasn't quite real. Most of her interactions with him were over the phone, and he always sounded so far away, even when he wasn't.

And he *had* to love her.

She dug again into her bank of memories, prying open her mind like a heavy lid on a massive chest. What was inside? Newspaper clippings. Forensic files. Murder victims. Evidence. Investigations. Human monsters.

Friends? She wasn't even sure she'd had real friends as a girl. She'd always felt like an outcast at school.

Boyfriends? Nada. One-night stands. Sometimes with a repeat performance or two. But never going beyond a trio of treat nights before she kicked them to the curb.

She couldn't afford to let anyone in. She had a job to do. She had to prove her worth as a detective. It was what her father would have wanted. Or was it? Maybe she was kidding herself. Maybe it was what *she* wanted.

The bartender placed her second bourbon on the counter and smiled.

"Thanks."

"My pleasure." He smiled wider.

She took a sip of the drink and focused her attention on the counter.

He took the hint and moved away to tend to something else. Relief washed over her. She wasn't in the mood to deal with any human interaction tonight. Even if she was aching for a warm touch, a good feeling to take her away and make her forget about how she really felt.

When she was deep in a case, she could forget everything else.

This case, the Skin Peeler, yeah...the *Skin Peeler,* was a good one. This was the one she'd been waiting for. A redo of the Poison Sisters. A chance for her to show her detective skills. Without going off the rails. Without fucking up. Following protocol. Getting along with others. Including her partner. She grimaced, then took a big swig of bourbon.

She slipped her notebook from her jacket pocket and flipped to the page with the strange message the killer had left. Written in the victim's blood. What the hell could it mean? Trapped. In a love-morphed box. Trapped. By a dream. Poison and an ice-cold body. Had the killer lost someone? And what the hell did the silver shirt mean?

She looked around the joint. The scattered patrons, most of them alone, nursing drinks, avoiding the idea of going home to an empty apartment.

The bartender returned. He leaned over the counter. "Another?"

She didn't have to be alone if she didn't want to. Physically. Emotionally...that was another thing entirely.

"No." She smiled. "The bill, please."

A slight look of disappointment appeared as he politely nodded. As he walked away to get her bill, she settled her sights on her bed and falling asleep to the sounds of metal.

CHILDREN
OF THE
KORN

# Chapter 19

# Jakey

Yellow-tinged pink fingers stretched from the rising sun over the navy sky. Stella stepped on the gas, guiding her Sunfire easily through the empty streets. She'd stuck to her two-bourbons-then-bed rule. The sounds of a metal god had lulled her to sleep in a flash. Nearly five hours later and she felt like a new woman.

This was the day. She was going to be a good detective. She almost snorted as she laughed at herself. What was this? A series of motivations first thing in the morning?

*Oh hell.* The cassette in the tape deck clicked to the next song. *Monkey Business.* She cranked the volume. Sebastian Bach had one of the best voices of rock and metal of *all time. Skid Row* had been in her life ever since the day her mother told her about her father's death. The opening strums teased her, making her crave more. Before she could take a breath, the drumbeat amped up, followed by the guitar, and finishing with the expert wails of a timeless rock god. His primal screams told her she wasn't gonna die even though the freaks were. She felt like she was in the middle of her own monkey business.

As the last bits of his voice drowned her in a metal cloud, she pulled her Sunfire into an empty spot close to the glass doors of HQ. After a long day in the alley followed by a long night in the strip club, topped off by a lengthy stop at the morgue and searches with Jakey that resulted in nothing, she'd put the never-ending day to rest. This was a new day. She was going to find a lead.

As she approached her desk, Sutton came sprinting across the office.

"Mahoney. Good. War room in five," he called as he breezed by.

After settling her jacket over her chair, she went to check in with Jake.

"You get some shuteye?" She leaned on his shoulder.

"I'm not your armrest. And yes, I did as the boss ordered."

"Got anything for me?"

"Nothing earthshattering, but a couple things you might want to investigate." He stopped typing and stood. "We need to go to the war room. I'll fill you in on the way."

"What've you got?"

"We've got over two dozen manufacturing firms here that deal with fibre optics. They all do their own installation. A couple big ones. Mostly smaller companies. You may have to visit them to determine who the employees are that could have come in contact with the traces of fibre optic cable. Could take a long time. Could lead to a big list of names." He shook his head. "Best I could do."

"What about the book?" She opened the door to the war room and flicked on the light. Buzzing followed by a blast of fluorescent light welcomed them.

"Geez. This room smells like sweat. Stale sweat."

"It's the odour of a detective. A whole herd of them." She nudged him with her elbow.

"The book. Now that shows more potential." He walked over to the corner and set up a laptop on the table.

"Wow. Portable computer. New?"

His eyes lit up. "Yeah. Quantex T-1411. It's a power notebook."

"Fancy. How'd you swing approval for that?"

"There are *eight* detectives and *one* analyst. I need extra search power to keep up.

"Maybe they'll hire another analyst. A geek buddy for you."

"Whatever. The book. The sixty-seven white Bristol card stock. Easy to get. Not typically used on notebooks. Couldn't find anywhere that sells a notebook with that type of cover."

"Dead end."

"Maybe. I'll keep digging." He opened the computer and powered it up as he settled into the chair.

The door swung open. Sutton entered, followed by Parker.

"Let's get this show on the road," Sutton announced as he moved to the front of the room, files in one hand, Big Gulp in the other.

# Chapter 20
# Follow the ID

The walls of the room seemed to close in, suffocating Stella with warm, sticky air. She'd rather be out following leads, even if she had to force them, rather than stuck in here for another team meeting. Sutton stomped up to the front of the room, taking control.

"ID just came in." Sutton snapped a folder onto the table lining the centre of the room and sifted through several files. He set a Big Gulp next to it.

Maybe this wouldn't be such a waste of time. Nothing better than an ID to get the history of a victim. History meant leads. Suspects.

"Donovan Goldering. Twenty-eight years old. Male, as we already confirmed. Been living here most of his life. No family. Doesn't appear to be much on where he spends his time or who he spends it with. Might have to start with where he worked: Banditos."

"Isn't that a Mexican restaurant on Electric Avenue?" Parker asked.

"Yeah. You two, go there. Find out anything you can about Donovan." Sutton nodded at Parker, then stared at Stella. "Question everyone at this Banditos. Dig. I want to know what he did in his free time." Sutton flipped through the pages in the folder.

Stella's shoulders relaxed at the release of his stare. She walked toward the pot of cheap homicide coffee.

"What did he do at Banditos?" Stella asked as she browsed the disappointing selection of chipped and faded mugs cluttering the table.

"Cook," Sutton stated.

"White guy cooking Mexican." Stella chuckled as she grabbed a mug that had a dark hue and only a single chip. A faded scene of the city at sunrise plastered the side.

"Well, I wouldn't call a restaurant on Electric Ave an authentic place for cuisine." Parker smirked.

"So not into fibre optics, then." Stella poured coffee into the mug. The aroma of strong beans with a tinge of tin drifted over her face. Not appealing, but at least it would give her a boost.

"Fill me in." Sutton's stern glare made her squirm.

"Traces of fibre optic cable were found on the vic." Jake looked up from his computer. "To come into contact, you'd probably have to be manufacturing the cables or installing them. Most applications of fibre optics, the people are using them, not touching them."

"Doesn't appear our vic was doing either of those things." Sutton's lips pulled into a thin line.

"Doesn't appear so. We can rule it out when we dig into his history." Stella took an extended sip of coffee, grimacing at the tinny flavour. Was it the coffee or the mug?

"Precisely." She almost thought she saw a hint of approval on Sutton's face.

Stella took another long sip, warming up to the flavour. Homicide coffee might be budget-friendly and tinny, but it was strong. Something told her she wouldn't be getting another luxurious few hours of sleep for a while. They were going to have to exert themselves and dig deep to find anything on this guy. Employers weren't as promising as friends and family in terms of really knowing a vic's history.

"Traces could have come from the killer," Stella said.

"How much fibre optic manufacturing and installation we have here?" Sutton asked Jake.

"Lots. Initial search results give me a couple dozen places. Most install their own products." Jake scanned the screen on his laptop.

"Let's keep that on the back burner. Once we find out more about the vic, get any suspects, it might come in handy." Sutton grabbed his Big Gulp and savored a lengthy sip.

"Restaurant isn't far from where he was dumped. Maybe he was taken post-shift, on his way home," Parker said.

Made sense. After spending the night at Cheetahs, there didn't seem to be any reason for the victim to be left behind the place. Maybe it *was* convenience. Grab him on his way home from shift. Dump him nearby. But it didn't explain the week the killer had spent with the victim. It still didn't click.

"We still have a week of unexplained time. Killer would have had to take him somewhere. Couldn't have killed him and left him right then and there. Doesn't line up." Stella leaned against the wall.

"True," Parker agreed. "It's weird he was left so close to where he worked. Wonder if the place the killer took him is close too. Would have made it easier to transport. Especially post-mortem."

Made sense. Parker was already far too useful at such an early phase of the investigation. "Good point." She almost choked on the compliment as it left her lips.

Sutton placed the Styrofoam cup on the table. "Lived alone in an apartment at The Misty. It's on Fifteenth Ave. Downtown. Unit 303. Darlene Drake owns the building. Go see her. Find out if she ever saw anyone coming or going from his apartment. He's been there nearly ten years. If he had anyone in his life, she must have seen something."

Parker jotted in his notebook. Stella sipped her coffee. The victim worked on Electric Ave, was dumped on the outline of the once-bustling party strip, and lived only a few blocks off. Couldn't be a coincidence.

Sutton flipped through the files. "Toxicology report is complete. In addition to the traces of tranquilizer, there's GHB and LSD. Traces of at least one more substance, but too insignificant to be conclusive."

"Tranquilizers and club drugs. You can get those anywhere," Parker stated.

*No shit.* Not a real lead.

Sutton spread the files out across the table. "Nail polish on his nails. Too common to lead anywhere. Soap residue. Washed post-mortem. Clothes appear clean. Too immaculate for the vic to have been killed in or moved in. Message written in his own blood. I've seen this before."

Was he referring to the Glam Boys Case he'd worked with her father on?

"Post-mortem makeovers and cryptic messages take time to crack. None of these clues are gonna jump us ahead fast." He sighed, took a prolonged pull on his Big Gulp, then nodded to Jake. "Jake, stay here, I'll go over all this with you, try to prioritize your searches. Stella, Parker, follow the ID. Banditos. Then the landlady."

Stella nodded as she made her exit. She could feel Parker on her heels.

# Chapter 21
# Children of the Korn

L olita awoke curled in a ball, cocooned in a fluffy blanket on the velour sofa.

Her throat parched, her mind fuzzy, she sat up and scanned the room.

The last images of a video froze on the television set. She pushed herself off the couch and shuffled over to the VHS player. She rewound the tape and clicked play at the start of the video.

A man in a black hoodie carrying a massive boombox walked away from the screen. Letters appeared in the left corner.

*KoRn*

*"Got The Life"*

*Follow The Leader*

*Immortal/Epic Records*

*Director MCG*

A guttural voice emitted primal vibes through the living room. Lolita shook her head, trying to dissolve the cloud of sleep clinging to her brain. The album had been released on August 18 of 1998. She distinctly remembered that day. The song had been a glaring reminder of her failure to be brilliant. When she watched the video for the first time, she could have sworn she felt the fissure in the back of her brain deepen.

Her mind adjusted. It was 1999. She could have sworn it was 1993.

She must have dozed off watching the video. This one packed some serious punch. *Children of the Korn*. Another fusion of genres, similar to Body Count. A creative mix of massive proportions. The fifth track on Korn's album featuring Ice Cube. The punch-in-the-face rhymes of Ice Cube interlaced with the savage vocals of Jonathon Davis reached from the television and grabbed Lolita's gut in a death grip.

It had the same effect on her every time she watched it. Her reaction was a blend of awe at the brilliance of the work, and profound self-loathing sheathed in a layer of anger. It was a reminder that her vision from six years ago was golden, but that she wasn't the one covered in glittery stardom. She'd missed out. And none of it was her fault.

She shuffled her way to the couch and pulled the blanket around her.

Dreadlocks and a black cloak covered the screen as the singer's voice wrapped like a vice around her. Strange images wove a creative tale over the screen. Tall stalks of corn cover provided a background as the singer lunged forward, his voice ravaging her with rough whispers. He begged to be saved as strange corn children were born.

Sadness weighed down her entire body. Children of the Korn had hit the mark. They'd produced something innovative, forward, something that changed music. She would never have that kind of impact. She simmered in her grief. Ice Cube raised his hands in the air as he shot out high-voltage rhymes.

Her mouth twitched. The corner of her lip itched. She rubbed it with her fingers. The left side of her mouth had drooped so severely, she knew it would never be the same. The skin, contorted, grotesque, was a reminder of all she'd lost. Of everything she'd never be. Lately, she felt like she was in a dream. There were gaps of time in her memory. She'd wake, here on the couch, her mind fuzzy and her perception distorted. Panic rose through her. Had her condition progressed? Had the fissure in the back of her brain widened? Had it reached its broken fingers deeper through the rest of her brain?

*No.* This can't happen. Hadn't enough been taken from her? Orson was gone. Electric Skin disintegrated the moment he died. Her vision had been killed along with him. She had nothing left.

She dropped her hand to her side and took a deep breath.

*OK. Relax, little Lola. You'll be fine,* she echoed her mother's words in her mind. Her mother. She didn't even want to think about her right now. The words helped, though. Before her mother became an addict, thrusting poisons into her body at the same time as carrying Lolita in her belly, she must have been a young, innocent woman at some point. Lolita knew it. She saw it in her mother's face, in her eyes, when she crouched down and whispered these words to her. Lolita had been so juvenile then. By the time she was six, her mother had started slipping again, consuming her damn toxins. But before that, Lolita had seen her mother lucid, even angelic. Sweetness in her voice and her eyes. Her mother had been the one person who had understood Lolita's anxiety.

The tender words that her mother spoke to her when she couldn't control her anxiety were hovering in her mind. She clung to them at times like now.

It was all she had.

The sun was setting beyond the bay window. She walked toward the kitchen. She needed some lemon balm tea and a steaming bath. She had to relax, to find her rootedness. It was all she could do to cling to the remnants of sanity she still had.

# Chapter 22

# Banditos

The voice of Jani Lane shot through the car as Stella took a sharp right down sixth avenue. His velvety voice with an edge spoke of getting under someone's skin. Parker clutched the handle on the passenger door as he shot her a glare. The final chords of the track erupted with a hard-edged rock riff as Stella slid her Sunfire smoothly up to the curb. She put it in park and slid the key out of the ignition, halting the fierce wails of the rock god.

"Still a show-off." Parker opened the door and made his exit.

"Whatever." Stella chuckled to herself. She knew he was getting used to her, maybe even liking her. She still couldn't believe he'd requested to work with her on the Poison Sisters case. They'd been partners since, somehow working smoothly together on the series of low-calibre cases that had landed their way.

Stella opened the door. A sign perched above their destination. *Banditos.* The Mexican restaurant their victim had worked in as a cook, before his sudden and unfortunate demise. With no physical trace of the killer left at the scene, close examination of the people in the victim's life was the most promising investigative path.

A neon sombrero flickered off and on above the door. Stella shot a glance at Parker before yanking it open. An immediate assault of refried beans and greasy cheese pelted them. The left half of the restaurant was cluttered with wooden tables and chairs. The right side housed a lounge themed like a beach. Fake palm trees dotted the space between high tables, topped off with a bar along the far wall donned in strands of fake grass and straw. The bar appeared to be closed. The place had opened only minutes ago. A couple patrons sat at separate tables on the restaurant side, wolfing down over-packed tortillas, grease dripping over their hands.

Stella smirked. "Fine dining at its best."

"Greasy does the trick after a late night of partying," Parker said.

"Good point." The joint was located smack in the centre of the core street of Electric Avenue. No one was coming here for an authentic, high-quality meal. They were here for the greasy late-night food to saturate the pool of alcohol in their bellies. And for one last night cap to ensure a solid pass out once they got home.

"So, what? Bar and restaurant in one?" Stella eyeballed the deserted bar plastered in the cheap beach theme.

Parker chuckled. "Not a bad idea down here. Keep 'em drinking. Keep the late night dough rolling in. Give them the feeling like they're on the beach."

Stella couldn't help a smirk. Parker's sense of humour was her style. Maybe she *should* ease up on him a little.

"Guess we start with the kitchen staff." Stella walked across the restaurant side, catching a whiff of the burritos or tacos or whatever it was the two customers were devouring. She'd skipped breakfast. Her fridge wasn't exactly well stocked.

A large man with a bushy beard approached. "Can I help you?"

"Sure. Detective Mahoney." She displayed her badge, letting the man inspect it. "This is my partner, Detective Parker."

Parker presented his badge for an equal inspection.

The man seemed satisfied. "You're here about Donovan?" the man asked, a wave of concern rippling over his face.

"You got it," Stella said. "Who runs the show around here?"

"I do." The man extended his hand. "Jim Colburn. Go by Big Jim around here."

Stella shook Big Jim's hand as she stifled a snort. Big Jim. Big white guy looking like he should be in the mountains running a Mexican bar and lounge on the party strip.

"So...did you find him?" Big Jim asked.

"We found his body. Two days ago," Stella said.

"What?" Jim's face paled. He leaned against a counter housing a cash register and a bowl of shiny wrapped candies. "So, you mean, he's dead?" Jim turned a sickly grey.

"Yes, he is. Are you OK?" Parker stepped toward Jim.

"Yeah." Jim shook his head, composing himself. "What happened?"

"That's what we're trying to find out." Parker said.

"When's the last time you saw Donovan?" Stella asked. Jim seemed sincere. She needed to test him now before he could calculate a response.

"That's the thing. He missed three shifts. The last time he was in was almost two weeks ago." He reached behind the counter, pulling out a calendar from underneath. He flipped it open and spun it toward them, pointing at the dates. "Wednesday. September twenty-ninth. Worked his shift that night. Four till midnight. We stop serving food at midnight. Bar stays open another couple of hours." Jim swallowed as slight colour returned to his face. He stared at the calendar.

"Did he have any further shifts since then?" Parker asked.

Jim blinked. "Yeah, sorry. He usually works the weekend shifts. Friday, Saturday, Sunday. Busiest days. He missed October first, second, and third. Didn't show up for any of them." Big Jim set the calendar down. "Usually, I don't think anything of it when someone doesn't show. Plenty of places around here to grab another job. Something didn't sit right with me when Donovan didn't turn up." Big Jim's lips took on a slight pout.

"Why?" Stella asked.

Parker stood silent, taking notes. He was skilled at waiting his turn to speak.

"Most reliable employee I ever had. He was...*different*. Super friendly. Extra nice. Hard worker. Always came in early and stayed late to help clean up. I wasn't paying him for those extra hours. He wanted this job. I was thinking about giving him a raise." Jim motioned over to a table. "You mind if we sit?"

"Not at all." Parker led the way.

The three of them settled into the rickety wooden chairs.

Jim continued his recap. "Anyways. He missed one shift. I tried calling him. Nothing. Figured he'd be in the next day. When he didn't show, I called him again. Nothing. After the third no-show, I filed the missing person report. I know, it sounds extreme, I'm just his boss at a low-class, fast-food joint on the party strip. But he worked here longer than most. I had a good feeling about him." Jim settled his mountain-man hands on the chipped table. "When he didn't show again last weekend, my gut told me I'd done the right thing."

No nerves apparent. So far, Stella was buying his story.

Parker took charge. "How long have you owned this place?"

"Sixteen years. Opened it in '83 when Electric Avenue was the place to be. Most of the joints along here were nightclubs in those days. Not many places to grab a bite. Now, a greater number of restaurants have popped up, replacing all the drinking joints that have gone under. My business is dwindling. I was thinking of giving the place a makeover." Big Jim scanned the room, wincing at the décor.

Maybe he was like Jean from Cheetahs. Trying to run a decent joint in a low-class location. Serious about his business, despite its appearance.

"You said Donovan worked here a long time?" Parker asked.

"Ten years, just out of high school. He came late 80s. It was still bustling then. He stuck around even when things declined." Jim leaned into the chair. The weak wood appeared ready to give against his substantial stature.

"Couldn't get another job?" Stella asked.

"I don't know. He didn't talk much. Only thing he talked about was his poetry."

"Poetry?" Stella raised an eyebrow.

"Yeah. Poetry. He wrote his own poems. He would read them by heart to us in the kitchen. Rhyming, I think he called it." Jim smiled, big and warm.

Poetry? What the hell? A man in his late twenties settling for a fast-food cook's position, passionate about poetry.

"You know who he hung out with?" Parker asked.

Good. He was leading them where they wanted to be. She was stuck on the poetry.

"Never saw him with anyone. He never talked about anyone. He only came in alone for his shifts. Even when the other staff would joke around, you know, about girlfriends and stuff, he stayed quiet. Think he was just genuinely shy." Jim smiled again. Reality struck him again. Concern riddled his face. "I can't believe he's dead. Everyone liked him."

"From what you're saying, he was a real likeable guy," Parker said.

"Oh yeah. Shy. Friendly," Jim repeated as if in a daze.

"You're sure you don't know anything about who he hung out with? Or where?" Stella asked.

Jim shook his head. "No. I'm sorry. I didn't pry."

"Did he seem particularly chummy with any of the other staff?" Parker asked.

"Not really. Appeared to get along with all of them fine. Never saw any of them outside of work, that I'm aware of," Jim said.

"We'll need a list of your employees," Stella said.

"Yeah, sure. If you can stick around, some of them will be in shortly. We do a lunch special today. And happy hour starts at three." Jim pulled at his full beard. His gaze became distant.

"Sounds good," Parker said.

Jim got up and moved to the counter. "I'll get you the employee list. It's short."

He seemed to be processing the information as if it was news to him. He appeared to really care about the fact that one of his employees was dead. There was nothing suspicious about him or his story. If they stuck around for a while, they could determine whether it was an act or not. Stella's gut told her it wasn't.

"Say, you want some lunch? Chicken enchilada special. Comes with beans, mini gauc, and house-made chips." Jim's eyes lit up.

"Sure, why not?" Stella responded for both of them. If Parker didn't want his, she'd eat it. Hell, she'd even pay for his lunch. Wouldn't that be a boost in partner relations.

## Chapter 23

# Skin

Lolita's brain jolted.

She blinked rapidly. Her heavy breathing whipped through her ears.

Where was she? What happened?

She scanned the room in a manic movement. *The studio.*

The walls of her basement studio closed her in. When did she come down here?

Sensing she wasn't alone, she shook her head, clearing the haze from her mind.

She locked her gaze onto those ever-so-familiar emerald eyes. The colour of tourmaline. They stared at her with wild fear. A white cloth pulled taut over his mouth, suffocating any sound that might escape. Liquid heat trickled down her fingers. Her eyes jumped to her hands.

Fear scratched her throat like a rusty nail sliding along her esophagus.

Blood. So much blood. Running down her trembling hands.

Her fingers gripped skin. *His skin.* The fingers of her other hand clutched a knife.

Sheer terror punctured her heart as she saw her shaking, bloody fingers, gripping a sheet of skin, pulling it away from his hand.

Flesh slipped from her fingers as she jumped back. The knife clattered across the floor.

His half-skinned hand shook. Tears spilled from the corners of his eyes, drenching the white cloth gagging his mouth.

Lolita froze. She couldn't move. She couldn't speak.

How did she get down here? How did *he* get down here?

She narrowed her eyes and focused on the tear-stained face.

His appearance was so like Orson's. But it wasn't Orson. She knew it. Orson had been dead for six years.

The room flickered. Images shimmered in her mind. *Sparky's.* The psychedelic lights glowed in her eyes. Neon signs shimmered through the corners of her brain. Electric Avenue. A crisp walk home. The soothing cool of the studio hitting her face.

The images bombarded her as she tried to piece together the last few days. She shook her head, clasping her hands over her chocolate dreadlocks.

Lolita took several steps backward, frantically scanning the studio. They were inside the recording room. The Orson lookalike, with his too-blond hair and too-green eyes, sat in the chair. Tied to it. The skin half peeled from his hand, exposing bloody flesh and white cartilage.

The microphone perched a ways behind the chair, the familiar scarf flowing down from the silver bulb. Her scarf. The one she'd always tied to the mic when she was performing for an audience. A fresh notebook, opened to a blank page, sat on a stand on the wooden table next to the microphone.

What was this? Had *she* brought this man down here? *How?*

Lolita stood still, hands shaking, blood dripping from her fingers in soft splats on the floor. Her brain buzzed, trying to process the gory scene her recording studio had digressed into. The droop pulling her lip down itched with a fire-like burn. The walls breathed. They closed in on her. The lights flickered. The entire room buzzed. Everything went dark. Light flashed. The room came to life again.

Something cold slithered through her brain, seizing it, taking hold. She blinked several times.

It was *him.* It was Orson. Sitting in front of her. She didn't recognize him at first. She must still be foggy from the deep sleep she'd been in all day. It came rushing back to her in a wave, her mind filling with fresh memories.

Orson. He was here, with her. She'd walked home with him, under the vibrant lights of Electric Avenue. Hitting each other with rhymes the whole way. Co-creating the final lyrics for their big performance. As soon as they'd burst through the door to their crooked little house, they'd run down the stairs into their recording studio, only pausing to grab a bottle of wine from the fridge. He'd sat in the chair, prepared to be her back-up singer. For the performance, she would record as the le ad.

Her mind, her body, her energy clicked into place in a single moment of alignment.

It was time.

For the performance.

All she could see, taste, *smell* was the stardust-coated dream. She stared straight into his sparkling emerald eyes.

"It is time. For *the performance.*" Her voice deepened with a sultry edge. A darkness glimmered behind her gaze.

She inspected his hand, her unfinished work. A click, audible in the pits of her ears, echoed as everything fell into place. As she peeled away his flesh in two strips, she sank deep into a trance. She needed the skin smooth and unbroken. She longed for a fragment of him that she'd never possessed. She needed his ability to write the rhymes that would thrust her up the golden star-dusted ladder to the top of the charts.

She needed it now.

As she tended to her project, peeling away the piece of him that belonged to her, she mouthed the words drifting through her mind. Her lips formed careful pronunciations of syllables and sounds. Her whispers heightened until her voice rose in a raw-edged, smooth flow.

*I've been trapped*
*Deep inside the walls*
*Of your love morphed box*
*I've been entranced by your pull*
*Trapped by your dream*
*I'd die to swallow*
*The poison running through your veins*
*To warm your ice-cold body*
*To bring you home again*

The words came to her from the depths of her being. She poured out her heart and soul. She shared the epic rhymes that had always been hers, that she'd kept from him. The ones she'd written after he'd discarded her, tossing her aside like a tarnished microphone. He'd taken from her everything he could. Her mind was rotting, her lip was drooping, her rhyme was deteriorating. She wasn't perfect anymore. He didn't want her any longer.

She'd holed herself up in the basement studio when he was out, writing her rhymes in her own notebook, the ones that formed themselves on her lips now.

The ones that she'd never shared. Until now.

The ones that would evolve into their fullest form as soon as she had the piece of him she needed to elevate her abilities far past his own.

His muffled pleas broke her concentration. The length of skin rested on her palm in a smooth sheet. Perfect. She walked over to the table where she'd placed the other half. Setting the fresh piece on top of the other one, she lined them up and smiled at her craftsmanship.

The piece of him she longed for.

For the hand of the poet was the sacred vessel through which the lyrics left the mind, the body, the soul, and found their home on the pages of the book. The book that would contain the rhymes so epic that, in the proper hands, with the suitable rhymer, the perfect performance would be achieved.

The path would be shining with glittering stardust.

# Chapter 24

# Land Lady

Paint peeled in strips from the walls of the fading blue apartment complex. A sign better suited to a strip club, or a massage parlour that offered extras, flashed over the front door. *The Misty*. Who lived in an apartment called *The Misty?*

Apparently, their victim had.

Stella chuckled. "Nice place."

Parker smiled. "Oh yeah, maybe I'll ask if they have any vacancies."

Stella walked up to the front door, Parker in tow. As they entered the lobby, an odour of stale cigarette smoke and must engulfed them. She walked up to a keypad and scanned the numbers labelled with the names of the residents. *Darlene Drake. Unit 101.* Stella punched the button. Buzzing followed.

Over the intercom, a hoarse voice was audible. "Yeah?"

"Darlene Drake?" Stella leaned toward the speaker.

"Yeah, who's asking?" Coughing crackled through the speaker.

"Detective Mahoney. We need to talk to you about your tenant, Donovan Goldering."

Loud buzzing echoed through the lobby. A click as the door opened.

Stella shrugged and walked through. Parker followed.

Before they could get halfway down the hall leading to unit 101, a woman emerged from the apartment. Late sixties, at best, wearing a faded floral house-dress and holding a burning cigarette.

"Darlene?" Stella asked.

"You know where Donovan is?" the woman, supposedly Darlene, inquired.

"Yes, we do. We'd like to ask you some questions, ma'am," Parker said.

Darlene motioned to some tattered chairs in the corner of the lobby. "Kid owes me rent. I'd be pissed, but it's the first time in ten years he's been late. Most of the fuckers around here take advantage of an old woman. Not him. So, where is he?" She plunked down in one of the chairs and took a long drag on her cigarette.

Parker sat across from her. "I'm sorry to tell you, but we found his body two days ago."

"Body?" Darlene bolted upright. "Oh god." She indulged in another drag, her hand shaking slightly. "What happened to him?"

"We're trying to figure that out." Parker said.

"You said he's lived here for ten years?" Stella asked.

"Yup. I've been running this joint for thirty. He's the best tenant I ever had. Isn't exactly *The Ritz*." She laughed a hoarse smoker's laugh as she waved her hand around the room, smoke trailing from the dwindling cigarette.

"Donovan was a reliable tenant?" Parker gave Darlene a sincere look.

"Yup." She slapped her knee with her free hand. "You seem like a nice guy." She leaned toward Parker. "I'll tell you something, I don't like people. Nope. I pretend. So I can run this place. I liked Donovan. Paid his rent on time. Always polite. Kept to himself. Quiet."

"Did you ever see anyone come visit him?" Parker asked.

Stella settled into the chair, taking notes. No sense rattling this woman. Parker seemed to be doing just fine using his good-boy charm.

"Nope. Like I said. He kept to himself. I didn't pry. A responsible tenant deserves privacy. Darlene retreated from her hover over Parker and took the last drag on the cigarette. She crushed it out in a cracked plastic ash tray on a table between the chairs as she exhaled the last bit of smoke.

"You're sure, in ten years, he never brought anyone here?" Stella asked.

Darlene eyeballed her. She narrowed her eyes. "Wait. That's not right. Like I said, he kept to himself. Of course, people who come in here and get buzzed in by a tenant, that's none of my business. I don't keep watch. But I never saw anyone come in *with* him. Until a couple weeks ago. Lady. Real interesting appearance." Darlene fished in the pockets of her housedress, pulling out a pack of Luckys.

"Interesting? Can you describe what you mean?" Parker asked.

Darlene flicked a hot-pink Bic lighter and ignited her fresh smoke. After a couple of puffs, she leaned toward Parker as she slid the cigarette pack and lighter into her pocket. "Yeah. Not white. Not too dark, either. Kind of like...*olive* skin. Wild hair." She motioned around her head, pillowing the air with smoke.

"Wild?" Stella asked.

"Yeah. Like woven, you know? Like tight rolls." Darlene rolled her eyes toward the ceiling. She snapped her gaze on Parker. "Dreadlocks."

Stella jotted in her notebook. Olive skin. Dreadlocks. Woman. "You got any security cameras around here?" Stella waved her hand around the lobby and toward the front door. A simple description wasn't much of a lead.

"No." Darlene twisted her mouth into a frown. "Can't afford that. Don't much matter in this part of town anyways." She took a prolonged drag of her smoke.

Stella slid a photo out of her coat pocket across the table. "You ever see Donovan wear this kind of shirt?" The silver sleeves shimmered, even in the photo.

Darlene's eyes widened. She leaned over the table and slid the photo toward her. "Well, I'll be damned. That's Donovan, all right. That ain't his shirt." She coughed and sank into the chair. Taking an extended drag, her gaze became vacant.

"You never saw Donovan dressed like this?" Parker asked.

"Nope." Another drag, her stare remaining distant.

What did this mean? Did this mystery woman have something to do with the silver shirt? Or with his disappearance?

"You don't know who the woman was?" Parker asked.

"The *lady friend*?" Darlene shook her head. "Nope. Saw them come in late. I was on my way down to the laundry room. He waved at me; they went up the stairs. Never saw her again."

"When was that?" Stella asked.

Darlene rolled her eyes upwards. "I do laundry Sundays. Nothing on the tube. What else is an old, lonely lady gonna do?" She chuckled, the hoarseness in her throat hijacking her. She coughed it out, then glanced at Stella. "Sorry. Should cut back, I guess." She took another drag. "Sunday. Let's see...two Sundays ago. What's that?"

"October third," Parker offered.

"Yeah. Whatever two Sundays ago was. I remember. Never saw her again."

"Do you recall the last time you saw Donovan?" Parker asked.

"Yeah. The next morning. Monday."

"The morning after you saw him with his lady friend?" Stella asked.

"Yup. And he wasn't wearing no fancy silver shirt." She pointed at the photo. "Thought it was weird I hadn't seen him around after that. But, like I said, he kept to himself. Think he worked a lot. Not sure. Didn't give it much consideration until he missed his rent. Knocked on his door. Called him. Figured maybe he split. Didn't seem right, but you know, you think you know people, sometimes you're mistaken."

"You didn't believe anything was wrong?" Parker asked.

"Nope. People split from here all the time. Not a word." Darlene inspected the photo, her mouth twisting down in a subtle frown.

Stella didn't know what to make of all this. Another person in the vic's life a long time who knew very little about him. Seemed nice, kept to himself. Nothing else. Until a woman enters his world. The one time this landlady of ten years saw anyone with him. He turns up dead, a week later, wearing a gleaming silver shirt. Had she influenced a new style for him? Was that it? Or did she have more to do with this? There was nothing indicating that. Still, Stella couldn't help but feel a tug in her gut.

# Chapter 25

# Poetry Slam

The cheese enchilada special at Banditos weighed heavy in Stella's stomach. It should have been the optimal choice after a late night at a metal concert and bourbon simmering in her belly. Today, it was only riling things up inside of her more. But her bare refrigerator in her lonely apartment had left her with an angry appetite halfway through the extensive day of interviewing.

A sliver of the moon pierced through the denim sky amidst a scattering of twinkles as the stars poked their way through the final remnants of the day. The day had slipped quickly through their fingers. They'd intensely interviewed all the staff that arrived at Banditos for the lunch special and happy-hour shift. Over half of them present, Big Jim was easily able to call in most of his remaining employees. There were only a few left to follow up with.

The situation was a mirror image of their night at Cheetahs. Minus the sparkly lineup of dancing gems and leopard-print vomit. Like Jean, Jim seemed to be a good boss. None of the employees showed any signs of awareness about their victim except for his mad rhyming skills and lyrical genius.

One of them was able to point them to a place where live poetry slams occurred. Poetry slams. That was a new one for Stella. Tonight happened to be a live open mic. Anyone who wanted to show up and slam could.

"Which street?" she asked Parker.

He seemed comfortable on the passenger side. She'd simmered down her driving speed and her music choice. A little Zeppelin once in a while was a good thing. Most people were fans, whether they realized it or not. As the kick-ass guitar riff of Heartbreaker rumbled from the speakers, Stella shot a glance across the car.

Parker scanned his notebook. "Next right."

"Thanks." Politeness was becoming second nature for her. That was good, right?

"Always loved this album." He tapped his knee with his thumb in time to the building rock riff.

She shot him a look. "Didn't take you for a rock guy."

"Not usually. But no one can deny how legit the classics are. You'd be crazy if you didn't like this." He waved at the speaker blasting the wails of the guitar god from the dashboard.

Stella smiled. *Dammit.* More likeable by the minute. Oh well. Maybe she wasn't so tough to get along with, after all. Maybe she needed the *right* person to get along with. If only he'd stop wearing that damn *Blue Jeans.* The *Versace* cologne that still clung to the tweed strands of her father's coat, despite the thorough scrubbing it had been given at the dry cleaner's.

"Next left. Then a block down." Parker snapped his notebook shut.

"You ever been to a poetry slam before?"

"Nope. Never heard of it."

"Yeah. Me, neither." She contemplated what this would be like. More importantly, she wondered—hoped, prayed to the metal gods—that this place would lead their investigation somewhere.

No one at Cheetahs had ever seen their victim before. Despite the fact that he was dumped directly behind the strip joint. No one at Banditos knew anything about their victim except that he had some mad passion for poetry. *Poetry.* What did that have to do with a strip joint and a low-class Mexican restaurant and lounge combo, both in close proximity to the one party strip in the city?

The hand. The book. Images of the fleshless fingers clutching the book pulsed in her mind like one of the nightclub signs on Electric Avenue. It had to have something to do with the victim's love for poetry. How could it not? Lyrics written in his own blood stained the very page open in the book he clutched in his lifeless hand. It couldn't be a coincidence.

The cold tingles in Stella's gut confirmed it.

# Chapter 26
# The Mint

As the wails of Robert Plant ended, Stella pulled her Sunfire up to the curb. She placed it in park and tilted her face up to the neon-green sign. *The Mint.*

"That it?"

"Yup." Parker opened the door and slid out of the car.

She slipped the keys from the ignition and followed suit.

The cold air was like a slap across her face. Why did it have to be so frigid before the first snow had fallen? She should be used to it by now. She'd left the milder temperatures of the west coast behind years ago. As soon as she was eighteen, she'd slipped from the clutches of her mother's all-consuming grief.

Stella was ready to move on. Her mother wasn't. Stella left.

"Damn that's freezing." Parker tightened his parka closer around him.

"Isn't it early for a heavy winter coat?"

"Nope. As soon as it hits close to zero, I pull out the puffy coat." He smiled.

She hated that she thought he was cute. She made her way up to the black door and yanked it open. The second she walked through, the hot air stifled her.

The room was small. A couple dozen people were scattered throughout, some in chairs haphazardly set in an open space facing a stage, others crowded around a bar lining the far wall. The whole thing seeped a vibe, a feeling, like it might give them the most insight into their victim they'd had since they'd first seen him in the alleyway.

A wiry man in his twenties, with reddish spiked hair, approached them. "Welcome, fellow poets." His voice, excessively enthusiastic for Stella's comfort, roared through the quiet of the room.

"Detective Mahoney." Stella provided the standard scan of her badge. "My partner, Detective Parker." She nodded her head in Parker's direction.

"I didn't know detectives like poetry." The young man's face flushed, matching the colour of his hair.

"We're here about someone in your group. Donovan," Stella said.

"Donovan? Oh my." The man seemed concerned. "Is he all right? He missed last Thursday." He fiddled with a mood ring on his middle finger. It changed from blue green to pure blue.

"Does he usually come every week?" Stella asked.

"Most. Sometimes he has to work. I thought he was coming last week, but when he didn't, I guessed maybe he got called in or something. It's not like him to not show up when he's on the roster." The mood ring altered to amber. "Is he all right?"

"I'm sorry to tell you, but we found his body. Two days ago." Parker's soothing tone seemed to put the red-haired man at ease, despite the shock washing over his face.

The man twisted the ring over his finger several times. It shaded to grey, then went black. "I don't believe it." The man walked over to a chair, sat, and gazed vacantly across the room.

Stella nodded at Parker. They joined the young man, pulling chairs up to sit across from him. A young woman with a shoulder-length, brown bob and thick black glasses walked up to them. Her thigh-high boots clomped across the floor.

"Damian. Is everyone who signed up here?" she asked the man with the reddish hair.

He shook his head. "What? Oh. Yeah, I think so."

"Should I start?"

"Give us a minute." Stella shot the woman a stern look.

Her boots clomped as the woman stomped away, muttering, "Fine. Just wanted to start on time."

"Damian?" Parker asked.

"Yes." The man's focus returned to the room.

"Do you organize this event?" Parker waved around the room.

"Yes. Every week."

"And you said Donovan came most weeks, unless he was working?" Parker asked.

"Yes."

"When is the last time you saw him?" Stella inquired.

"Well, I can check the roster, but I thought he came two weeks ago. Signed up for last week, but didn't show. Like I said, I assumed he had to work." Damian stood. "I need a glass of water." He walked over to the bar.

"What do you make of this?" Parker asked Stella.

"Seems shocked. We need to question everyone here. Find out something about our vic." Stella flipped through her notebook.

"Welcome to Poetry Slam, hip-hop style." The woman with the thigh-high boots and bob stood up on stage, microphone in hand. "Time to get this show on the road. We've got a killer lineup tonight."

The hum of conversation in the room dwindled. People made their way to the chairs, scattering themselves around the room, drinks in hand.

Damian walked over to them. "Sorry about this. I didn't tell her to start."

"What else goes on here other nights of the week?" Stella asked.

"We're only here on Thursdays. Most of the time, it's a laidback lounge, I think. Mostly DJs and cocktails. They might have live music on the weekends. Hip hop, mostly, I think," Damian explained.

The water seemed to have replenished him somewhat.

"Did you know Donovan well?" Parker asked.

Good. Digging in while he's talking, still a little thrown off.

"Not really. I only saw him here."

Same story as everyone else in his life. That they were aware of.

The opening poet of the night, a man in his prime wearing baggy jeans and a tattered t-shirt, stepped up on stage. He took the mic from the woman with the bob and high boots.

"How long does this thing go on?" Stella scanned the crowd of close to two dozen poets.

"Depends. We had six signed up. They go first. After, anyone else who wants to can rhyme. Could be a couple hours." Damian spread his palms over his knees. The mood ring had settled again to an ocean blue.

Parker looked at Damian. "We'll need to talk to everyone here."

"Sure. I could bring them by as they finish."

Considering it could take a few hours, Stella wondered if they should hijack the slam or ease into this Damian's way, increasing the chances of the poets being open with them.

Parker leaned over. "I think we should take this slow. We come down hard, we might not get anything." He examined the crowd, all deeply engaged in the words flying from the mouth of the baggy-jeaned man.

Stella nodded. Take it slow. Wasn't her style. Something told her it was the right way though, if she wanted to catch a killer.

"Sounds good," Parker said to Damian.

Damian settled against the chair, twirling his mood ring around his finger. His mouth pulled into a tight line.

The words flying from the poet's mouth grabbed Stella's attention.

*If only he knew...*

*The one that flew...*

*His path was insane...*

*Not mundane...*

Stella flipped her open notebook to the page with the message from the book left in the victim's hand. She read the words silently to herself.

What did it mean? Were they the words of the killer? Or did they belong to Donovan?

She slipped her hand into her leather coat pocket and stroked the familiar deep-purple fur of the rabbit foot her boss had gifted her. The cold tingle surged in her gut.

With no physical evidence of a killer in their hands, what choice did she have other than following her gut?

# Chapter 27

# Bourbon Numb

Stella stared into the glass of bourbon. The rich colour, the caramel fingers reaching from the glass and weaving through her nose, and the cool of the ice all soothed her. She took a big swig and fell into the numbness that tingled down her throat and arms.

She didn't usually frequent the same place for a nightcap. She preferred to scatter her late-night comedowns at various joints, never becoming a familiar patron for any bartender. Except when she went to *The Cecil*. That was her only exception. For some reason, she'd found her way down to the basement of Three Cheers where she'd avoided the gaze of the cute bartender only last night.

"Another?" the bartender asked. She hadn't noticed him approach.

He was attractive. Young. A bit clean cut, yet he had an edge. His shoulder-length, golden hair had a tousled style. His tight shirt revealed the muscular contours beneath. His amber eyes enticed her. Heat rose from her loins up through her body.

"Sure." She smiled, letting her gaze linger on his long enough for him to reveal the dimple that she knew was there.

He shuffled away to get her drink.

She eyed him from top to bottom. His jeans, tight like his shirt, revealed the manly muscles rippling down his legs. A hot tingle surged through her insides and a cold loneliness grasped her heart. Was she simply depleted of physical touch? Or was there some deeper need within her?

Stella snorted and shot back the rest of the bourbon. What the fuck was wrong with her? She grew increasingly fond of Parker. She took the patient approach at the poetry slam. And now, *this*. Visiting the same bar two nights in a row and contemplating a fling with this clean and boring guy.

"Long day?" The bartender slid a fresh bourbon her way.

*Oh hell, why not?* "You could say that."

"Name's Tad." He leaned over the bar. His musk tantalized her senses.

"Stella." Fuck. What was she doing? In the heart of a murder case. The *Skin Peeler.* Might even be a bona fide serial killer. It was supposed to be two bourbons then bed. *Alone.*

"I've seen you in here before. Last night." Golden locks fell over the front of his shoulders. His musk wafted over the bar.

"Yeah. It's uh…on my way home from work," she stammered. "And you've got good bourbon here." *Don't make him think you made a repeat appearance for him.* She took a swig from the glass.

"What do you do?"

"Detective," the word slipped from her cherry lips.

"Really?" He stood up, face flushing. "Intriguing. Must be dangerous."

"Not really." A knife sliding into her flesh, held by a serial killer disguised as a witch, shimmered in her mind. The scar on her arm itched.

"Guess it depends on what you define as dangerous." He leaned over the bar. His amber eyes intoxicated her.

A fire burned in Stella's internals. She swallowed as she relaxed her shoulders. Sweat trickled down the nape of her neck.

"I get off in a half hour. Can I buy you a round? I know the coolest little place." He smiled. "Real nice bourbon."

Tempting. This was her second bourbon. It was supposed to be followed by bed. *Alone.* Maybe an exception. The case wasn't going anywhere. They'd spent all evening at *The Mint,* taking in the hottest poetry in town. Not a single one of them knew anything about their victim. Nothing. They only saw him there, sharing his rhymes.

A cook at a Mexican joint. A poet in his free time. Everyone liked him. No one knew anything about him. Sutton had told them to get some rest. He'd been working with Jake all day, trying to get something out of the strange brew of clues from the scene behind the strip joint. Fibre optics. Silver shirt. Tranquilizers and party drugs. All of it was too vague to lead anywhere. They'd take a fresh look in the morning, dig deep, find something.

What could it hurt to have one more drink? And perhaps to have a warm body in bed next to her for the night? She could keep it under control.

"Sure. But only one drink. I got an early shift." She took a relaxed sip of the bourbon.

"That's too bad. I was going to invite you to my show." He smiled.

"Show?" She raised an eyebrow.

"Yeah." He glanced over his shoulder. A guitar case covered in band decals leaned up against the wall in the corner. "My band's playing a late show at a little joint. It's close. So is my place." He walked to the other end of the bar.

Stella's insides burst into flames. Sweat drizzled down her back.

Either her loneliness was heightening, or this guy really did something for her. He wasn't her usual type, taking his rock star pedestal, writhing sexually with a microphone stand, and oozing primal screeches that reached into her soul. She glanced at the guitar case. Or maybe he was.

She eyed him up and down. No, not her customary type. But her usual type ended up getting a wild ride at an afterparty, then discarded and forgotten. She was always uncertain if she used them more than they used her.

She focused on the bourbon—and calming the rage of emotion swirling inside of her.

Whatever this was, could it hurt to temper the fire? Besides, she could catch some live music, and she could still stay close to her drink cap. Tomorrow would be a new day, a revamped inspection of a simmering case. She'd be clearer-headed if she released some tension.

# Chapter 28

# Rockstar

A purple-blue haze drowned the stage. The last rumbles of the opening act still hummed through the air. Stella settled into her favourite spot front and centre. A glittery scarf hung from the tip of the microphone stand.

As she took a lingering sip of the bourbon in her hand, something stirred inside of her. Everything about this was so damn familiar, yet something told her the night would be wildly different than anything she'd experienced.

*Stop being dramatic.*

It would probably be boring. She'd heard the humdrum lyrics of the opening act, faint yet decipherable, from the cozy confines of the green room. Tad had poured her a bourbon from his private stash, then introduced her to the rest of his band. A typical four-piece rock 'n' roll getup. She thought the band name, *Purely Purple,* was cool. The names of the members were less spectacular. Jim. John. Brad. *Ugh.*

As she curled into the corner of the couch, fingering the stuffing cascading from the long slash in the velour, she couldn't help but be a little intrigued as they pulled on wild print leggings and pleather, and put the finishing touches on their flawlessly coiffed hair.

A rumbling erupted from the rear of the stage. Percussion pounded through the room, bouncing off her bones. Jim, the guitarist, strode across the stage in his pink-and-purple striped leggings, bare chested, ripping at the strings of his shiny electric guitar like a beast. The riff was rock 'n' roll through and through. It reminded her of the Zeppelin records she'd listened to from her father's collection. She took a deep breath and closed her eyes, willing the butterflies in her stomach to halt.

A rock god wail shot through the room and straight into her soul. The voice sent vein-sizzling electricity through the space. He sounded like Robert Plant. The second the words hit her ears, she knew she was in new territory.

She opened her eyes. Tad walked straight to the front of the stage, holstering the mic in the stand, and owning the entire audience in a single heartbeat. His words seeped from his mouth, weaving tantric fingers through the smoky air, over to her, up her legs, her thighs, and touching the most tender parts of her.

She shook her head. She was the fucking metal queen of ravaging a rock god then leaving him high and dry.

She'd done it a million times. Tonight wouldn't be any different.

As she took a long swig of bourbon, she looked up again, at his mouth, into his eyes.

His amber irises moved across the crowd, up to the front row, then found her.

A gasp caught in her throat. Her heart palpitated wildly.

The minutes flashed by as if they were seconds.

As he launched into the final round of the chorus, he moved to the rear, into a plume of purple smoke. When the haze cleared, he was standing tall, up on the drum set pedestal. The drummer beat savagely. Tad's voice simmered then drifted away.

As the song came to an end, Stella stood stunned, staring at the spot where he'd been seconds ago, his gaze locked on hers.

Before she could recover, a mellow guitar strum echoed from above. Golden curls, wet with sweat, fell around his shoulders as Tad walked forward, an acoustic guitar slung around his neck, his fingers working magic over the strings.

Every nerve ending in her body tingled. Her mind was like mush.

A sense of being in a foreign place took a hold on her. This wasn't like clinging to the lip of the stage looking up at the Zombie King or the gothic leader of Type O Negative. This entire experience wasn't like any other she'd had.

A fire of lust burned within her like never before. Something else pulsed from the pit of her belly. A warmth, simmering through her, caressing her heart.

# Chapter 29
# Back Alley

Lolita fixated on Orson. Why had he made her do this? She crouched and peered straight into his glassy emerald eyes. "Why?"

He didn't answer.

She slid her gloved hand into the pocket of her long coat and pulled out the book. The one that contained the lyrics she'd written with his hand. The ones that had finally enabled her to achieve *the performance*. She could still feel her lips moving in perfect motions, enunciating each word with the utmost precision. She could still hear Orson, with his gritty voice, backing her up, taking his place.

She reached out, took his icy hand in hers, and leaned in close to his face.

"I'd die to bring you home again. But now I'm no longer trapped." Her voice, a raspy whisper, broke the silence. Her breath wafted white wisps through the chill air.

She placed his arm against his body, his hand reaching out. Opening the book to the page with the lyrics, she placed it in the clutches of his exposed fingers. Rising up from her crouched position, she inspected her work. The self-loathing usually bubbling inside of her had been replaced with a warm glow.

The whole *display* felt like a tribute to him.

The chill air swept an icy breeze across her face. Her lip twitched. The left side of her mouth itched.

She knew it was time to go.

She read the words, whispering into his ear.

*I've been trapped*
*Deep inside the walls*
*Of your love morphed box*
*I've been entranced*

*By your pull*
*Trapped by your dream*
*I'd die to swallow*
*The poison running through your veins*
*To warm your ice-cold body*
*To bring you home again*

She kissed his frigid cheek, pushing her lips into his icy flesh.

She crouched and pulled the lid of the amp case closed. Clicks broke the silence of the gloomy alley as she snapped the latches tight. Orson had bought the eighteen-inch deluxe case when they originally formed Electric Skin. She stood, gripped the handle of the case with her hand, took one last look at her Orson, then walked away. As she pulled the case down the alley, the small wheels crunched over oily gravel. The silence cloaked the dark night once again.

# Chapter 30

# Night Recap

The voice of Ozzy vibrated the entire front half of Stella's Sunfire as she yanked the steering wheel and took a harsh right. Amidst jagged riffs, his voice sung of words from a mother, messages from mirrors, and a life in danger. She hoped the warmth tingling in her loins was a sign of no further tears. Tangerine streaks slowly spread from the horizon, painting the denim sky. She wasn't required at roll call for a couple of hours. She laughed to herself at the expression that painted Sutton's face when she called his debriefings *roll call*. He preferred *team meetings*. He was way too square.

She'd stretched the boundaries on her two-bourbon-then-bed rule. The intention of two bourbons had crawled to four under the influence of the bartender. *Tad.* The place he knew about was interesting. The *Poison Room.* Nestled snugly next to the Bourbon Lounge. With a vintage vibe and a compact stage, it was a cool experience. Only, she didn't feel so cool. Every time she thought of Tad during his performance, his voice reaching into her, electrifying every nerve ending, her entire body flushed with a lustful fire. Despite only consuming one bourbon in the green room and one during the show, she couldn't resist going home with him after. His voice, his eyes, his presence possessed a certain power over her. As he'd slid his hand over her thigh, causing an eruption of tingles, he'd locked his gaze on hers and convinced her to follow him to his place. Only a few blocks away.

She couldn't resist. Still stunned at the high-voltage response her body gave to his touch despite the absence of extra bourbon and a manic metal show warm-up, the images of the time with him in his cozy apartment elicited tingles, and foreign feelings, all over again. *Dammit.*

After several rounds of his magic touch, she'd made her departure. But not after he'd fallen asleep. Not by secretly slipping out of his life without explanation.

She'd kissed him goodbye and took the piece of paper he'd scrolled his number on. *Double dammit. What the fuck was happening?*

She didn't know. But she had to admit that she liked it.

After a few hours of solid sleep, she'd left. Criminal profiling books called to her. Her gut told her they had a chance to make progress on the investigation, before a second body showed up. She had to try.

Here she was, whipping down the vacant streets of the city before sunrise, heading to the hot, claustrophobic war room, textbooks in hand, ready to hunt down the *Skin Peeler*.

# Chapter 31
# Criminal Profiling

Stella stared at the photo of the page dripping in blood-ink letters. She'd read and re-read the words a million times. It had to be a poem. It was the only thing that made sense.

All they knew about their victim was that he worked at a cheesy Mexican restaurant in the heart of Electric Avenue, lived close by in a low-rent apartment, and attended the weekly poetry slam at *The Mint*. His body had been dumped in an alley behind *Cheetahs,* which, apparently, he'd never set foot in.

Stella found herself unconsciously stroking the purple rabbit foot in her leather jacket pocket on a growing basis. Something throbbed in the pit of her gut. There wasn't a physical trace of who had killed the victim. The drugs in his system, his clothing, even the message written in his own blood in the book he was clutching in his dead hand weren't leading anywhere. Every clue was eerily specific, yet extremely vague at the same time.

How could a loveable under-the-radar cook writing poetry be the target of a murder? It *had* to be his physical appearance. The distinct colour and style of his hair. The hypnotizing pigment of his eyes. Perhaps even his race, build, stature. The only way to verify a victim type was for another kill to happen.

Anything Stella had to go on was based on the information she'd devoured from the set of books she'd inherited from her father. Her mother had wanted nothing to do with them. She'd gone so far as to scold Stella for taking such an interest in *grisly* reading. Stella had chided her, reminding her she was a detective. It had struck a match under an old argument that was constantly on simmer every time they spoke.

Her mother didn't understand why she'd chosen to follow in her father's foot-steps. Not after all the pain and anguish he had caused them. *Pain. Anguish.* She'd actually used those words. Even after reminding her mother of the unconditional love her father had given to her, to both of them, her mother refused to admit he had any redeeming qualities at all.

Stella took a lingering swig of stale homicide coffee as she shook off the memory. She swallowed down the bitterness and glanced across the war room at the coffee pot. How long had it been sitting there? Whatever. She didn't have time to brew a fresh one.

She leaned into the chair and looked at the page she'd been reading for the millionth time. *Criminal Profiling 101.* The well-worn pages suggested her father had used this one a lot. She ran her finger down the smooth paper, landing the tip of her pointer on the section titled *Fantasy.*

She re-read the section. Slowly. Taking in every word.

The mind of a serial killer is stuck in cognitive immobility, a state that recreates something from the past and can even be focused on a particular event. They relive this event constantly, in their mind, painting a contorted picture of reality. They may believe they are back in the time and place in which it occurred. They are hyper-focused on 'the event.' It is real. It did happen. The places and the people involved did, indeed, exist. How they see the event is a morphed version of what actually took place. Certain aspects will be amplified in the killer's memory.

The event is something traumatic, and ended in a dramatic way, not the way the person in question had planned nor wanted. It altered the killer, permanently. The person clings with the utmost obsession to that moment when their life was irrevocably modified. The killer has recreated the event in their mind and through acts of murder seeks to live it out the way they see it. The act of killing is driven by a need to live out this fantasy that the killer

has created and elicits feelings of euphoria. The
fantasy becomes a fixation, so strong that the person
in question will stop at nothing to recreate this
ideal moment. They keep attempting to live out the
fantasy until it is perfect, which is an impossible
endeavour.

Human beings with the normal set of response
mechanisms would either live in pain or find a way
to move past it. The serial killer will be trapped
in the perfect moment of the fantasy. They will
attempt to recreate the place, the time, the person,
or persons, and to relive the event, stopping at
the euphoric moment. This becomes the playing-out
of the fantasy. It evolves into the person's primary
objective, his or her life's work. [See section 11.b
on portfolio.]

In order for the subject, or subjects, chosen for
the re-enactment of the event to comply, they often
become the victim. The result is usually the murder
of the victim.

The victim type is a key component to the fantasy.
The serial killer chooses victims who are mirror
images of the person, or persons, who were part of
the original event that had traumatized them. [See
section 13.a on victim type.]

Stella took a deep breath. She hadn't even realized she'd slipped her hand into
her leather coat pocket and was now stroking the fur of the rabbit foot. Her guide
to trust her internal sense of intuition was throbbing strong at this very moment.

A flush sent heat over her cheeks and droplets of sweat down her back. She
removed her coat and walked over to a fresh whiteboard at the front of the room.

She popped open a bright-orange marker and sketched out a new strategy. She
was ready to fully share her theory with her team when they arrived. Sutton had
encouraged her to push the limits, given the caveat that he would continuously

challenge her. Parker was more than open to hearing her out. Jakey had his fingers poised at any moment to dive deep into the Internet to find the data she needed.

The clock on the front wall ticked, slow and loud. The stale coffee wafted from the corner. The lights blazed a blinding glow throughout the space.

She glanced at the crime scene wall. The emerald eyes of the victim, glassy and lifeless, stared at her from several of the photos held in place by brightly coloured tacks.

Pressing the marker to the board, she wrote *Victim Type*. Underneath, she added:

1. Green eyes

2. Sandy-blond hair, shoulder length

3. White male, aged 28

4. Cook at Banditos, poet at The Mint, resident of The Misty

She capped the orange marker and uncapped a blue one. She continued to scribe on the whiteboard.

*Trophy*

1. Skin from hand

2. Peeled in two parts, palm and back

3. Represents? [The victim was a poet, wrote lyrics, would need hand; is the skin a representation of the hand itself, or the writing of the lyrics?]

She capped the blue marker, then uncapped a red one.

*Fantasy*

1. Is the killer a poet?

2. Event – look for some traumatic event [would be from the killer's past] that included poetry – a poetry slam gone wrong?

She didn't know what else to write here. They might have some insight into his victim type and trophy, but she was guessing as to what the fantasy was.

Stella stood tall, capped the marker, and scanned her work. It was a start, but even the *profile* she was building was sparse. According to the profiling books, with a lack of physical evidence, examining behaviour could open up investigative leads. However, a certain amount of physical evidence was needed to identify behaviour. It was a chicken-and-egg scenario. The two, evidence and behaviour, could go hand in hand, advancing the investigation faster together than each could in isolation.

The message, the silver shirt, they both seemed so...*specific*. She'd seen this before. It clicked in her mind. An image of a case she'd read about. She bolted out of the stuffy war room, through the clutter of cubicles, and stopped at her own desk. Shuffling through a pile of folders, she found the one marked *Glam Boys Case*. It had been one of her father's. She sprinted to the war room and spread the files over the central table.

Messages carved in the flesh of dead victims. The victims had extreme post-mortem makeovers. Each murder scene had been a recreation of an MTV video. Cinderella. Aerosmith. Guns N' Roses. Skid Row. The wild glam metal and hard hair rock from ten years ago. The outfits and the messages aligned with each carefully chosen track, ending in a grisly display of a message from the killer about his own torturous life—Seth Henderson had been his name.

Could the silver shirt and the message written in blood be a reflection of a specific poem that meant something to the *Skin Peeler*?

Skin. Another click echoed in Stella's mind. She shuffled through a stack of printouts on serial killers that had been studied by the authors of the criminal profiling books she'd been scouring. When she found her desired page, she came to a complete stop.

*Ed Gein.* He had skinned his victims. He'd made a plethora of household items from the flesh. A wastebasket. Chair seats. Bowls. He'd even crafted skin suits. Leggings. Masks. A chill trickled down Stella's neck. The author of one of the books had interviewed dear old Ed. What was her name? Doctor...*Quesnel*. Yes, she was sure of it. What would it be like to stare into the eyes of someone who peeled away the skin from another human being like it was fabric? According to this Dr. Quesnel, it had been like looking into the eyes of a completely vacant being with no soul. Stella shuddered. Ed's father had badly beaten him for years. The blows to the head were believed to be the cause of his lazy eye and speech impediment.

Was she looking at a Seth Henderson mixed with an Ed Gein?

She opened the cap again and added a title over the sketch of a profile.

*Skin Peeler.*

A blast of cool air filled the room as the door opened.

Stella spun on her heel to find herself looking directly at Parker. His shirt pressed, his face freshly shaved, he looked rested and ready. Did sleep really do it for him? Did he ever choose an extra bourbon and a bartender to relax?

"Morning, partner." He smiled as he walked into the room.

"Morning." She wanted to glare but stepped down.

"Whoa. What you got going on here?" His eyes widened as he approached the whiteboard filled with her initial draft of a criminal profile.

He was as nice as he seemed, right? He'd chased her into the forest as she ran after one of the Poison Sisters. When he found her, bloody and hazy, hovering over Viviana Celeste, the younger of the killer duo, all he said was, *You OK?* He hadn't called her out on any of her bullshit, not even her decision to go into that house alone. He had her back. She was sure of it.

"Criminal Profiling." She held up the book and pointed to the cover.

"Hey, yeah, I've heard of this. Didn't think we had any profilers in Canada."

"We don't." She put the book down. "These were my dad's. I think he used them."

Parker walked over to the coffee pot. "This fresh?"

"You know it isn't." She raised an eyebrow. "Physical evidence we have isn't opening any doors. No trace of a suspect. The interviews aren't going anywhere." She looked at her profile sketched on the whiteboard. "Thought I'd try to open a new path."

"Thinking outside the box. I like it." He took a swig of cold coffee from a chipped mug with a faded scene of the Rocky Mountains.

The scene looked as if it belonged to the Overlook Hotel rather than the quaint town of Banff it was supposed to depict.

Parker grimaced. "God, this stuff is awful. No offence. Nice of you to make it."

"I didn't make it. It was here when I got in."

"What? What time did you get here?"

She glanced up at the clock. "Few hours ago."

"Geez. Must be from whoever was in here last night." He put the mug down. "Tell me more." He walked up to the board.

"According to these,"—she waved at the small stack of profiling books—"a serial killer has a certain set of traits. I know we've only had a single victim, but I mean, just look at this." She walked to the wall.

Parker joined her. "Yeah. It's meticulous. Elaborate. And, like you said, whoever did this was careful. Didn't leave us a trace of who they are. Doubt this is their first time."

"Doubt it will be their last," Stella finished the thought. "Time of death was likely sometime October seventh. Body was disposed of early in the morning of October twelfth, the day it was found. If this killer is keeping bodies for five days, we might be looking at another one a couple days from now. Assuming the killer is taking one victim at a time. And there isn't a cooling-off period." Stella scanned the photos, clenching her jaw.

"You've really read up on this." Parker eyed her with approval.

"Yeah, well, what else am I gonna do between murder cases?" Too much information. He was too easy to talk to.

"No, no, this is good." He moved to the board.

"We've bled every possible lead to death. The idea is to examine the behaviour of the killer through the traits he likely has." She pointed at the profiling board. "I was starting with his fantasy. Some type of event that occurred in his life that he is trying to recreate."

"Right. Thus the victim type, someone involved in that event, and the trophy, whatever piece of the victim he is taking that symbolizes that event," Parker said. "Great profiling board."

Profiling board. She was cool with that. "It's just a start. We need evidence to build the behaviour profile. They go hand in hand."

"We could re-examine what we have. With fresh eyes. Go over what physical evidence we do have with a behavioural filter," he said. "At least until…"

"We get another one."

"Yeah." He strode across the room and picked up the coffee pot. "This will *not* do if we're gonna lock ourselves in this stuffy room and examine the behaviour of your *Skin Peeler*." He smiled and walked through the door.

*Skin Peeler.*

With two sets of eyes, what could they drill out that they hadn't already seen? Maybe this partner thing was gonna work out. Stella had to admit that perhaps it already had.

OXYTOCIN
SUFFOCATION

# Chapter 32
# Hot Dog

Stella took a massive chomp of the overloaded hot dog, The condiments drowned the fake meat, soaking the sides of the bun. She wiped her mouth with a thin napkin and chewed loudly, silently thanking the metal gods that she didn't have to worry about smearing the foundation she'd been wearing all week. Her cheek had finally returned to its normal colour.

"Wow. You eat like you play music. Loud and aggressive." Parker took a proper bite of his own dog.

She almost choked as an involuntary laugh caught in her throat. "Don't make me laugh while I'm eating," she responded, her hand in front of her mouth to catch falling bits.

He smirked. "I'm not sure you can call what you're doing eating."

She swallowed the crudely chewed bite. "Whatever." She took another and leaned against the fence next to the hot dog cart. The sharp pain searing her abdomen every time she bent over had dulled to a slight throb. She was almost healed from her encounter with Dirty Joe.

They'd spent the entire morning and part of the afternoon caged in the stuffy war room. Parker's pot of coffee had been amazing compared to the normal brew. He wouldn't tell her his secret. She wondered if he stashed his own source in his desk.

They'd fleshed out the profile of their mystery killer as much as they could with the strange and cryptic bits and pieces they had to go on. When the ideas came to a halt, they'd agreed that hitting the streets and re-examining the crime scene was a wise move. Maybe they'd widen their perimetre of places to go in and grill any inhabitants.

Parker's appetite to keep pushing was impressive.

She wiped her lips and crumpled up her napkin.

They'd re-scoured the alley behind Cheetahs. They'd made another round of visits to any joints, restaurants, bars, and stores in the area. Nothing came of it. The killer had slipped the body into the alley when no one was around. Stella had declared a fuel stop at the precise moment she'd spotted the hot dog cart. What more fitting than cheap meat—if it was meat—to put some fat in their bellies to keep them going all evening. She secretly hoped it would take them all night. She didn't trust herself to restrain from another visit to Three Cheers to see Tad.

The lights of the one remaining street on Electric Avenue blazed bright from several blocks down. A steady hum built as crowds started to form outside the clubs and bars, the eager ones with a low cash flow coming in hot for the drink specials before things got wild.

Stella's murder phone buzzed. She wiped the ketchup and mustard dripping from her fingers with the napkin. She tossed it, along with the empty hot dog paper, into a garbage can and unclipped her phone.

"Mahoney."

"Parker with you?" Sutton barked.

He was in full-on business mode.

"Yeah."

"Good. There's another. Right on Electric Ave. Get over here. Pronto."

The phone clicked silent. She re-clipped it to her belt.

"What is it?" Parker asked as he delicately wiped at the minimal bits of food that clung to his face.

"Another one."

She could swear a hint of excitement glimmered from his eyes. It vanished as quickly as it had appeared.

"Well, at least we might obtain further information."

"True."

# Chapter 33

# Closing in on Electric

Purple, pink, orange, and yellow neon tubes shot flashes of light through the midnight sky, shimmering over the wet pavement. Buzzing from the signs marking the block of nightclubs mixed with the hum of the crowds hovering outside their doors. The one remaining block of Electric Avenue lit up the night.

It had started as the single block still intact. As the party crowds came, it reached its grasp over several blocks in either direction, casting light upon the darkness every night of the week. On the weekend, the mob was so thick the pavement was invisible. It grew until it spanned half-a-dozen blocks of the downtown core.

As the party atmosphere grew manic on Electric Avenue, violence came with it. The vibe sizzled. Nightclubs shut down. The avenue shrank to a single block, the seedling that started the whole thing.

Stella glanced down the remains of the once mini-Vegas and walked briskly toward the flashing blue and red of the cruisers lining the next block over. The crisp air scraped her cheeks. She tugged at her leather coat, making it tighter around her.

It was time to deal with murder.

Stella upped her pace. Fuck, it was cold. She could see Parker pulling his cherry-red Corvette up behind the cruisers.

Sutton waved her over as she approached. "Mahoney." He nodded. "It's around back."

She followed him as he walked by a blinking yellow-and-green sign over the door. *Coconut Rum.*

"What's this place?" Her heels clicked along the pavement as she shuffled to keep up.

"Restaurant. Jamaican. Basement is a lounge. Same theme." Sutton's shoulder-length brown curls fluttered in the icy breeze.

"Weird." What did a Jamaican restaurant and a strip joint have in common?

Sutton took a double turn into the alley. The bright lights of the party avenue simmered. The wind escalated, scraping icy fingers over Stella's face. The hum of the partygoers muffled into a thick silence.

Behind *Coconut Rum* an entirely different scene unfolded.

A series of apartments hovered above the restaurant. Dark windows stared them down like vacant eyes.

They approached the bright-orange rear door to the restaurant. The outline of a figure came into focus, materializing into a body posed against a crudely painted palm tree on a whitewashed brick wall.

A juxtaposition of death and beach vacation.

"First here?" she asked as they approached the body.

"Yeah. You were fast." Sutton nodded. "I saw the techies arriving. Blackwood should be close behind."

Usually they were already immersed in processing when Stella made her entrance. A tinge of excitement wove through her at the thought that she'd get to see the body exactly as it was when the killer walked away.

They approached the figure. A note of rot wafted from the body. Stella leaned in for a closer inspection. Another male. Likely in his twenties—early thirties, tops. Too blond hair. Shoulder length. Striking emerald eyes, glassy and vacant. White. Lean. Muscular. Tattered jeans. Silver shirt.

They'd gotten the victim type right. So far.

As her eyes adjusted, the details came into focus.

"The hand," she whispered.

Sutton unlatched a flashlight from his belt and clicked it on. The light moved over the body, down the arm, to the hand. The skin was gone, the flesh beneath exposed. The bloody fingers grasped the book. Stella followed the direction of the body's vacant gaze. It was as if he were reading.

Stella unclipped her own flashlight and shone it directly over the victim's face. His eyes weren't quite the emerald of their first vic. Slightly bluer. A striking tone.

The hair was so blond it seemed bleached. Just like the first vic. The clothes were eerily similar. Too close for comfort. This wasn't a coincidence. None of it.

She moved the flashlight over the hand. The exposed flesh bloody and grotesque, purple veins and creamy cartilage weaving over the clutched bones of the fingers, the dead hand grasped the book. The flesh was peeled away clean, the same as it had been from the hand of the first vic. Forever in the possession of the obsessive killer who took it. The *Skin Peeler.* That name had to stick now.

The profiling approach appeared to be valid. But would it get them anywhere? Looking at this young man now—dead, poised against a brick wall in a dank alley—he hadn't been helped by the profile she built. Would it aid in finding this killer before a third corpse materialized?

"Dig deep. Take your time. I'm gonna go check on the status of the rest of the team." Sutton started to walk away, then stopped to face her. "Go with your gut." He strode off.

*Go with my gut. Like my father did.*

She focused on the body, hovering the flashlight near the hand. Stella positioned her back to the brick wall and sidled in close, crouching. Moving the light over the book, she saw a message in scarlet scrolled down the open page. Just as she'd expected. The fantasy of the killer was strong. He was replaying exact replicas over and over.

Stella read the words aloud, her voice a mere whisper. Exactly the same words as written in the book that the first victim had been clutching in his dead hand.

Her only inkling was that this was some sort of poem. But who wrote it? And why?

She knew it meant something specific to the killer. She was sure of it. To her, it meant nothing. It wasn't intended for anyone except the killer. And perhaps the person this victim represented.

She twisted her neck and looked into the eyes of the victim. The striking colour was almost hypnotizing.

"What would you say if you could talk?" she asked him in a quiet voice.

Now what? What was she expected to do with this time alone with this dead man? How was she supposed to *follow her gut?*

She stood, stretching her legs. She swept the flashlight at a snail's pace over the victim, from head to toe.

The hair seemed clean. There was no evidence of blood, dirt, or other debris embedded in the shaggy, blond locks. The pale face glowed under the white light. Hovering, she inspected the skin. It appeared clean. Did the killer wash this victim the same way he washed the first one? Likely. Someone this meticulous didn't easily stray from their routine. *The script.* It was labelled in the criminal profiling books as the script of the killer. The lips, a blueish tone with a slight pink tinge, dry and chapped. How long had the killer kept this one for? Was the victim without water, slowly drying away? The rest of the skin on his face was smooth. No marks. No sign of struggle or abuse.

Chatter trickled from around the corner at the end of the alley.

Stella swallowed, sliding one hand into her coat pocket and touching the fur of the rabbit foot. She held the flashlight strong with her other hand, guiding it down the victim's body, over his shimmering shirt. It seemed identical to the shirt on the first victim.

A glint caught her eye. She halted.

Narrowing her gaze, she moved the bulb of the flashlight to the left, then the right.

The glimmer again. Stronger.

She narrowed her gaze. There was something on the shirt catching the glare off her flashlight. She moved the light away just a tad. The item shimmered.

She slid the barrel of the light into her mouth, clamping her teeth around it, as she pulled a pair of latex gloves from her pocket, snapping one over each hand. She could leave it to the techies, but it would be lost in a long queue of traces. Something told her she needed to find out what this was without delay. Retrieving her mini trace-evidence kit from her inside breast pocket, she opened the bag and pulled out the scraper knife and a collection container. She tucked the bag into her pocket. Steadying the light with her mouth, she extracted the minuscule shimmering item from the dead man's shirt. She slid the tip of the knife into the container and tapped it against the side to dislodge the trace, then returned the knife to her pocket, pulled out an evidence seal, and secured the item.

She held the container up with one hand and shone the light on it with the other.

It could be another sliver of fibre optic cable, or something new, something that might shed new light on who the killer was. A hint of behaviour, leading to something concrete that this killer did, leading to the killer himself.

The chatter heightened. Stella glanced down the alley. Sutton led the team, a few techies, Blackwood, and Parker in tow. The techies nodded at Sutton intently, comprehending his instructions. Blackwood appeared stern, focused, her hiking boots splashing in the murky shallow puddles dotting the gritty pavement. Parker, silent and equally engrossed, seemed too clean to be in this part of town. Sutton's curls fluttered with the icy breeze.

Her time alone with the victim was over.

She stared into his striking emerald eyes. His cracked blue lips spoke of depletion, perhaps as he lived through whatever fantasy the killer was trying to make reality. What had the killer done to this young man?

What she wouldn't give to see into his mind. To relive the unfolding of events that took his life. To see what it was like to look into the eyes of a human monster, a being that contorted reality into their own vision, someone who saw their victims as part of their purpose on this earth.

Maybe she would get to look into this killer's eyes. When they caught him. Maybe she'd finally have a chance to talk directly to the kind of killer she'd been wanting to chase down ever since she'd cracked open the case files of the trio of serial killer cases that had led her father to his demise.

Did he die because he couldn't handle it? Could she?

She wasn't sure. But she knew there was no other way. She had to follow her gut. She couldn't turn back. Just as her father couldn't abandon the young girls transformed into horror dolls by a human vampire, she couldn't walk away from this victim now. If he was anything like the picture painted by all the interviewees of the first victim, then he was living a simple life, keeping to himself, following his meagre passions. He didn't deserve to die. Neither did all the others that may be to come. Stella knew a killer like this wasn't going to stop. Someone had to stop him.

They had to find him first.

The group approached. Stella slipped the baggie into her leather coat pocket and stood to join them.

# Chapter 34

# Put the Rum in the Coconut

An assault of hot air and sticky coconut surrounded her as Stella followed Parker down the stairs into the basement of the *Coconut Rum*. Despite their blunt grilling of the restaurant staff, they hadn't drilled out any leads. No one had ever seen the man dumped in the alleyway.

They reached the bottom of the stairs. The place was like the setting for a cheap beach commercial. Massive cans of coconut cream lined the rear wall, evenly spaced across half-a-dozen horizontal shelves. Colourful paper bamboo and palm trees were pasted over the walls and the front of the bar. A record player, perched in the corner, spun an LP. Beach music drifted through the room. Tacky plastic bowls were topped with limes, orange wedges, cherries, and other garish-looking garnishes.

"Wow. Thought the theme went too far upstairs." Parker whistled.

Stella chuckled.

A young woman behind the bar looked up from wiping down the lime-green counter. Her attire forced her to fit in with the theme. She wore a stiff, paper grass skirt over her leggings and a lime-green shirt plastered with an orange *Coconut Rum* logo in cartoonish lettering.

"What can I do for ya?" Her long, sandy-blonde hair fell in waves. Her baggy sweater, buttons open down the front exposing the shirt, appeared out of place for the wannabe beach-vacation stop.

"Detective Parker." He flashed his badge. "My partner, Detective Mahoney." He nodded his head at Stella.

"Detectives?" Concern washed over the woman's face.

"There's been a situation in the alley," Stella filled in.

"Situation?" The woman bit her bottom lip.

"Yeah. Dead body." Stella stared at the woman, analyzing her facial expressions.

The woman paled. She swallowed. "Should I go home?"

"Sure. But we have a few questions for you first." Stella dug into her coat pocket.

"Oh...OK." She sat on a high stool behind the bar.

Was she shaken? Or nervous?

Stella slid a photo of the victim, only showing his face, over the lime-green counter. "Have you ever seen this man?"

The woman leaned over and carefully inspected the man. "No."

"Have you noticed anything unusual over the last couple of days?" Parker asked.

"Nothing." The woman's face remained pale.

"How long you worked here?" Stella asked.

"A long time. Almost six years." The girl swallowed. "Didn't expect to be here that long. Thought I'd be in a different position by now." She bit her bottom lip.

"Oh yeah?" Parker smiled.

The woman returned the smile as her shoulders relaxed. Stella could always count on Parker to bring the charm. Thing is, it worked.

"Yeah. I wasn't planning on being a server in a basement bar on a washed-up party strip." She half-smirked, half frowned. "When I started here, I was a beer-tub girl. Paid well. Plan was to save up and get out. Strip dried up before I had a chance to make enough. Now...well, this doesn't pay as well." She scanned the empty lounge.

"Beer-tub girl?" Parker asked.

Her cheeks flushed. "Yeah. Used to be a real happening place upstairs. Sparky's. Live music every weekend. Both nights. You had to come early to get in."

Live-music place. Exactly like Cheetahs. A tingle wove through Stella's gut. The victims had both been disposed of in alleyways, behind places they had apparently never been in. Was this the missing piece? Did the live-music joints have something to do with each other?

"What kind of acts played here?" Stella asked.

"Moxy Fr 	vous. Crash Test Dummies. Phantoms. Beat Farmers. Jim Rose Circus Sideshow. Barenaked Ladies. Bo Diddley. I could go on."

"Big acts," Stella said.

"Oh yeah," the girl said. "Lots of them weren't famous yet. That was Stan's thing. Bring in the bands that were gonna be big. Or at least the ones he thought would be."

"Stan?" Stella asked.

"Yeah. The guy who owned the place."

Stella ran through the bands in her mind. No specific genre of music. All over the map. All up and coming. Did that have something to do with it?

"Are we opening tonight? Should I go home?" Worry creased the girl's face.

"We have a few more questions. Don't worry, you'll be fine with us here. We'd appreciate your co-operation." Parker smiled.

The girl settled. "OK."

"When was your last shift?" Parker asked.

"Three days ago. Tuesday. Didn't work the last two days. Closed yesterday."

Cheetahs was closed the day before the body in the alleyway was found. It had likely been dumped in the early hours of the morning. Was there a pattern here? Was it nothing but the fact that the places were closed, reducing the risk of being sighted? Or was there a deeper level of connection? Speculation. It was pure speculation at this point. Stella needed more. She needed to connect the dots.

"How many others work down here?" Parker continued.

The girl's shoulders relaxed even further. Her expression joined. "Only four of us. We only have one on at a time. Except happy hour. We have a couple hours of overlap then. But we don't need it. This place never gets busy anymore." The girl shook her head.

"It used to be?" Stella asked.

"Oh yeah." The girl's eyes lit up. "Like I said, you used to have to come early to get into Sparky's. It was crazy. The crowds. The lights. The bands. Even though I had to wear a stupid outfit." She pointed at her grass dress and grimaced. "I mean, it was *small*. We were supposed to look sexy. Sell more beers. But I loved the atmosphere. It was electric."

"The avenue dwindled," Stella said.

"A couple years after I started, Sparky's closed. Kerbie, the new owner, changed it into a restaurant. Kept the lounge down here. Crowds stayed a bit steady for a while, but within a year, they got sparse." The girl pouted.

"Was this"—Parker waved around the tacky beach lounge—"always this way?"

"Oh yeah." The girl rolled her eyes. "Even when it was Sparky's. I have no idea why the tacky theme. Guess the owner thought it was funny. Didn't matter. Drink specials were all people cared about. And he was good at that. After every show there'd be a rum bender."

"Rum bender?" Parker asked.

"All rum drinks for a buck. For one hour. Everyone would squeeze in down here. I liked it. I got to chill upstairs after the show. Serve the ones who didn't go on the rum bender." She giggled.

The girl seemed legit. Her nerves had apparently been due to the situation. Not because she had anything to do with it, but likely because she didn't want to be near it.

"Violence escalated on the strip, after Sparky's closed?" Stella asked. She said she'd been here six years. 1993. Sparky's closed down two years later. 1995. Within a year, the crowds thinned. She was sure that was right around the time of a mob attack on a pair of couples. A series of newspaper articles flashed through her mind. Since she'd returned, without her mother, she'd kept a close watch on everything in the city.

"Oh yeah. That was bad. There was an attack, right on the main strip. Some people visiting. A mob went crazy. I don't really know what happened." She shook her head. "Like I said, I didn't plan to still be here. Without live shows, and fewer places to drink, the crowds got dense. The energy changed. I've been wanting to leave for a while." A frown pulled at the corners of her mouth.

"Well, sometimes our plans don't go exactly how we thought they would," Parker said.

The girl nodded and smiled.

Ugh. Too much cheese. It was one thing to relax the interviewee. But this was an extra coat of cheese Stella didn't need. She caught Parker's gaze and rolled her eyes. He shrugged his shoulders.

"If you think of anything else at all that might help us out, give me a call." Parker slid a card across the obnoxious lime-green counter. "Anything strange, or different than usual, that happened recently."

The girl nodded, taking the card, her gaze glued to Parker. She flushed.

"So, we aren't opening tonight?"

"No," Parker said. "Things will return to normal tomorrow."

"Is it safe to walk to my car?" the girl asked, still fixated on Parker's face.

"I can accompany you to your car," Parker said.

"Oh, thanks." The girl seemed far too excited as she ripped off the paper grass skirt. She moved to the rear of the bar to gather her things.

"Your friendly neighbourhood detective turned personal bodyguard." Stella snorted.

# Chapter 35
# Metal and Chemicals

Tangerine fingers stretched up from the rising sun through the deep-purple sky. Rob Zombie screamed from the speakers, filling Stella's Sunfire with a high-voltage vibe. They'd been at the murder scene behind *Coconut Rum* all night. After a detailed scour of the perimetre, set up to span an entire block of alleyways as ordered by Sutton, Parker had joined her in an extensive questioning of the less-than-thrilled employees of the Jamaican-themed restaurant and lounge.

Blackwood had deduced that the body was left in the alleyway earlier that morning. The lack of sightings of anyone suspicious by the Coconut Rum employees implied that the killer covertly entered and left the alleyway during the hours of closure. Smart. Slip the body into the alley while the entire collection of nightclubs on Electric Avenue were closed. All of the surrounding businesses on the block on either side followed the same hours. Most of their clientele were partygoers wandering in after a drinking binge on Electric Ave.

The last notes of the chorus shot a final manic vibe through the car as Stella pulled into the morgue parking lot. She'd been sent to get a full report from Blackwood. Secretly, she'd been planning a side detour. It was perfect. She could stealthily pass it under the radar without anyone knowing.

Stella swiftly crossed the pavement, through the doors, and down the hall. Nodding at the receptionist, a quick flash of her badge, and she was through. She'd been the main liaison with Blackwood enough times for the receptionists to recognize her.

At a fork in the hallway, rather than opting for a left toward Blackwood's cozy dark room, she veered sharply to the right. She retraced the steps she'd taken when she followed Doctor Klein—Bryce—to his lab to devour his chemical breakdown of the fibre optic cable traces that had been found on the first victim.

His passion for chemical analysis had flowed from every pore in his body as he'd gone to great lengths to help her understand the process and, importantly, the breakdown she'd need to describe it to her team. His equal passion for heavy metal hadn't gone unnoticed. His lab was equipped with a boombox and a rather impressive collection of albums dripping in heavy fonts. She'd recognized them all. When he'd caught her eyeballing the collection, he couldn't help but move the conversation toward the metal greats of the past and the present. Their musical tastes aligned beautifully.

Which was exactly why she hoped she could trust him now.

She reached the door to his lab, hesitated a moment, then knocked. The voice of a metal man hissed through the door. The music stopped. Shoes clicked over the polished floor. He opened the door.

He smiled. "Detective Mahoney." His high cheekbones accentuated his pale skin. Intensity radiated from his rich brown eyes. His wild hair shot in different directions in raven spikes. His aura was as mysterious and soothing as last time.

"Doctor Klein."

"Bryce." He leaned against the door. The sleeves of his black shirt were rolled up to his elbows. His lab glasses rested against his forehead.

"Fine. Bryce." She smiled.

"What can I do for you?"

"I've got a trace." She slipped the container from her pocket and held it up.

He raised an eyebrow. "Same case as the fibre optic trace?"

"Yeah. New victim."

"Rather unorthodox for a detective to come directly to me." He looked at her with equal suspicion and curiosity.

"I figure a fellow metalhead might be open to an unconventional approach."

He moved aside and waved her in.

Closing the door behind them, he led her over to his workspace. "Let's take a look."

She handed the plastic bag to him. He took it, leaned over the desk, and flicked on a lamp. He slid the container out of the bag and held it directly under the white glow. "Small. Glimmers."

"Yeah. That's why I saw it. It was on the shirt of the victim."

"How'd you extract it?" He flicked the light off.

"I carry a mini trace-evidence kit. Scraper. Container. Seal."

"No tainting." He nodded his approval. "You want the standard? Full report?"

"Yeah." She clenched her jaw. "Can you call me directly when it's done?" She slid a card onto the desk.

"You want this between me and you?" He leaned against the desk. His eyes glimmered with total curiosity.

"For now." She pulled at her chin with her pointer and thumb. "I'll add it to my report. I think it's vital. Didn't want to wait for it to be processed in line with the other traces."

He considered her explanation.

"Sure."

"Thanks." Her stomach halted its nervous churn. Her gut told her she could trust him. It also told her there was a reason she had a need to keep this to herself, even if she didn't know what it was yet.

"Hey, got something for you." Bryce walked over to his collection of albums on the far end of the room. He scanned the covers, halting on a specific one.

He slipped it from the shelf and handed it to her. "Had a craving for it after our fibre optic trace rundown. Hadn't played it in a while. Something about it screamed Stella."

She took the album and inspected the band title and the artwork on the front. A white skull oozed over a black background. The album title and band name scrolled over the cover in intricate font. *Sonic Brew. Black Label Society.*

"You heard this?"

"No." He truly was her heavy metal equal. "Thanks."

"No problem. Metalheads stick together, right?"

"Right." She sure hoped so. She needed to trust him right now. And she scarcely put her faith in anyone.

# Chapter 36
# Follow the Drugs

Sutton paced along the crime scene wall. The room was thick with heat and sweat. Stale coffee clung to the air.

"Without any idea *who* the second vic is, we don't have much to go on." Sutton ran his hands through his thick brown curls. "This guy doesn't exist in the system. The only *new* piece of physical evidence is the tox scan. Same things as the first vic. Tranquilizer. GHB. LSD. Now oxytocin. You got anything on that, Jake?"

Jake typed madly at his keyboard as he spoke. "Just got the results, so haven't gotten far on the search. Oxytocin is primarily used to induce labour. Administered directly by doctors."

"Weird," Parker said. "Doesn't really fit with the tranqs and party drugs."

It *was* weird. What would a killer be doing with a labour-inducing drug?

"I'll keep digging," Jake said.

Sutton nodded.

Parker leaned over the long centre table, perusing files. "He was dead twenty-four hours. Tops. No stomach contents. Dehydration. Lost a significant amount of blood, from his hand. So, what? The killer had *two* victims at the same time?" He sounded disgusted.

Sutton walked over to a whiteboard with a timeline etched in bright-blue marker. "First vic dumped October twelfth. Time of death around October seventh. Last seen September twenty-ninth. Missed the poetry slam on the thirtieth. If the killer had him about a week, explains the empty stomach and dehydration. And his general state."

Parker walked up behind Sutton, reading from a file. "Second vic dumped October fifteenth. Time of death likely October fourteenth. To be in the state of dehydration that he was in...probably took a solid week, according to Blackwood.

That would place his disappearance at October sixth or seventh. First vic wasn't discarded till the twelfth.

"Overlap." Sutton moved away from the board.

Stella inserted herself into the analysis. "Seems the vic two was taken right around the time vic one kicked the bucket. Failed attempt. Needed to try again."

Sutton looked at her quizzically. "What do mean, *try again?*"

Stella swallowed. Would he buy her spin on all this? "It's all behavioural. The evidence. The two victims appear almost identical. The silver shirt. The skinless hand. The book. The message. The killer is replaying the same event over and over."

Sutton snapped the cap on the marker, set it on the ledge of the whiteboard with a click, and faced Stella. "Go on."

"Part of his fantasy," Stella spouted the words before she could think.

"You sound like your father." Her eyes widened as the words left Sutton's mouth. "He was into criminal profiling techniques on some of the cases I worked on with him."

So her father had acquired his copies of *Evil Mind Dive, The Mind of the Serial Killer,* and *Criminal Profiling 101* when Sutton was on his team. "Yeah, I, uh, I've got his books." It would have been one thing when the boss was talking about the fantasy of the serial killer, but she was a rookie detective. And she wasn't the boss.

"Let's hear it." Sutton pulled a chair from the table and sat as he grabbed his Big Gulp. "Your theory."

Was he testing her, or interested? Memories of the Poison Sisters case fluttered through her thoughts. He had taken her theory seriously then. Worth a shot now.

"The victims seemed posed. In both cases, the book was carefully open to a specific page, with a message written in the vic's own blood. In the hand the killer had peeled the skin from. It's all played out, to recreate a precise event. Stella paused. "It's too specific to be anything else. Our killer is obsessed with something that happened, and he's trying to recreate it. It's his fantasy."

Parker nodded. "Interesting. Makes sense. Why do you call it a fantasy?"

"That's what they term it." The criminal profilers. It's still in its early stages, behavioural science." Stella licked her lips, then took a sip of coffee. The tingles in her gut told her this was the path they needed to take. She couldn't explain it, she simply *knew*. She wondered if her father had followed the same instinct. From the entries in the book he'd left her, a life-lessons sort of thing, she suspected he had.

"What else?" Sutton drank a sip of Big Gulp.

"I think this won't be the only kill. The killer will do this again. The victims will have similar appearances. The display will be identical. The killer is obsessed with skin, or hands. It's like his trophy from the kill. It means something to him." Stella swallowed down any lingering doubt. She needed to pursue the path that seemed so clear in her mind.

"Parker. Thoughts." Sutton walked over to the grisly display of photos from the murder scene lining the wall. The green rabbit foot dangling from his belt caught her attention. She thought of the deep-purple version in the pocket of her leather coat, the one he'd given her as he told her to follow her gut. That he also needed to continue testing her theories, pushing her to poke holes in them.

"As crazy as it sounds, it's logical. The scene was way too specific for any of this to be random. Who takes the time to wash the person they killed? Who takes the skin off a hand? Who writes a message with the victim's blood?" Parker shook his head. "Whoever did this is not our usual murderer. This is not an emotional, off-the-rails opportunistic act. This looked planned."

Sutton nodded, focusing on the photos of the fleshless hand.

"Besides, we've got nothing else to go on." Parker stood, walking up to the whiteboard. "No physical trace of who did this. And no ID."

Sutton faced the group. "We've got the drug. The oxytocin. Work with Jake. Follow up on *anything* that might lead us to a suspect. *Then* we'll revisit this *fantasy*. I'm gonna push on the ID." He grabbed a folder from the table in one hand, his Big Gulp in the other, and headed for the door.

Stella leaned against the wall and pondered the direction she'd proposed.

As Sutton walked by, he paused. "In my office. Need to talk."

Her gut clenched. Had she pissed him off? Even if she had, something inside of her told her she was onto something. The real serial killer cases she'd been scouring all pointed to victims who were easy to take, wouldn't be missed, and previously unknown by the killer. The ultimate fantasy of the human monster was to recreate some real-life event that had forever frozen them in time. To redo whatever sensational enactment had struck their being and changed them forever, and to do it *right*. To achieve the perfect replay, and thus change the outcome forever.

Impossible. But not in the killer's mind.

# Chapter 37

# Investigative Triangle

S tella knocked on Sutton's door.

"Come in."

She walked in, closed the door, and sat across from him. He didn't say a word. He slid an open notebook across his desk toward her. About halfway down the page, an upside-down triangle had been drawn. In the top left corner, the word EVIDENCE was written. The top right corner was labelled BEHAVIOUR. The bottom tip was designated TRAIL.

"This was your father's notebook."

Her heart pattered as she examined the notebook. She glided her hand down the open page. "What's this triangle?"

"A case I worked with your father had physical evidence that was leading us nowhere. He introduced us to criminal profiling. Added in a behavioural component on top of the physical evidence to open new paths. It led us to catch more than one serial killer." He sighed. "I'm *not* saying that we ignore the physical evidence. That's still our first path. *If* the oxytocin doesn't lead us anywhere, *and* we're stalled on an ID, this *might* open up a path to follow in the meantime." He pointed at the page. "That was his strategy. It worked."

Stella nodded, then stood to leave.

"Take it." Sutton closed the book and slid it toward her.

Her fingers trembled as she picked up the book filled with an investigative strategy developed by the man she most wanted to be like.

# Chapter 38

# Drug Connection

The wheels on her Sunfire squealed, weaving with the primal wails of Layne Staley blasting from the speakers. Electric guitar hammered a background. Stella yanked the steering wheel, taking a hard right. Parker slammed against the passenger door. He glared at her. "We're not on our way to a murder scene. Even if we were..." He steadied himself in the seat.

"Can't hear you," Stella yelled over the screams telling of bones and belief. She pointed at her ear and smirked, shaking her head.

Parker grimaced and sank back.

She loved Alice in Chains. They rocked harder in two and a half minutes of *Them Bones* than a lot of bands did in a lifetime.

Stella yanked the steering wheel left. The Sunfire peeled into a parking lot. She eased up on the gas, drifting the car into an open spot.

"What is this?" The expression on Parker's face was typical for first-time visitors to this area.

Several blocks southeast of *The Cecil*, this was the hood of the hood. It wasn't a place that people chose to spend time in. Unless you were looking to lift or dump a trick. Here, there were a plethora of tricks for sale.

"The seediest part of the city. Where the forgotten dwell." Stella opened the car door and exited.

Parker followed suit, meeting her around the rear of the car. They'd been following potential leads for hours, trying to drum up a suspect list based on the purchase of oxytocin. It was going *nowhere*. It was getting late.

"We need to find Tank." She slammed the door closed.

"Who? What?"

"A drug dealer. Gives me information occasionally." She started walking, hoping he wouldn't be nosy.

"What?" He jogged to catch up.

She picked up the pace, partly to shut Parker up, partly to catch Tank before he crawled into the depths of the city for the night.

"We've been chasing this oxytocin all day. He might be able to tell us more about it." She glanced at him. "Will you be OK? Maybe you should wait in the car."

"No. I'll be fine." He messed his hair up with both hands. "See? Rough."

She chuckled.

They reached the end of a street. Stella guided them to the right into a scene that many would avoid. It was a lot to take. It was the closest thing to a tent city that Calgary had. Stella walked briskly, Parker in tow, past shopping carts full of belongings, tattered tents, and blankets spread on the ground and over still bodies. She reached a corner and peered around. She saw him.

"Let me do the talking." Stella approached a sinewy man in jeans and a leather jacket. His tight tank top rippled over his ripped chest, partially exposed by his open jacket. He looked too clean for this setting. Stella knew it was only because he made enough selling drugs to the half dead living in the gutters, and he spent it as fast as he made it.

Tank nodded at her, keeping his head low and scanning the area.

Stella slid up about a foot away from him and leaned against a crumbling brick wall. "Tranqs. GHB. Easy to get?"

Parker settled next to her.

"Yup. Who's the sidekick?" He glanced at her, then out at the street.

"Partner. He's cool." She shot a glance at Parker. She looked at Tank. He nodded. They both stared straight ahead.

"Ever mixed with oxytocin?"

He smirked. "Rare occasion. That's for crazy motherfuckers."

"Crazy?"

"Yeah. You know, brain damage. Lots of moms around here didn't give up their habit just cause they got knocked up. Fucks with the baby's brain. Those kids, they grow up all fucked up." He waved his hands around his head. "A lace of oxytocin settles that shit. Slows down brain activity. For a bit."

"Where would I lift that?"

He whistled, low and slow. "Round here...not anymore. Used to be able to get this lace. Some of those moms had leftovers. They circulated them for a pretty price. Now you need a note from the doctor. Nobody round here going to the doctor." He smiled, exposing a mouth half empty of teeth.

"You come across it, let me know." She slipped him an envelope, keeping her gaze to the road.

He took it. "Anytime."

She nodded at Parker and started walking.

He stayed quiet. She was relieved. Used to be able to get a nice lace of oxytocin in your street drugs. Now, you needed a prescription. So, what? The killer had a stash from the past? Or they had a prescription?

They reached the car and got in.

"What do you think?" She turned the key in the ignition.

"You've got balls. And valuable contacts. As for the killer, I don't know. If the oxytocin was used for labour, then we have a mother who started killing people. I'm leaning toward someone with brain damage, using it as medicine. Or, could simply be the killer stole it from someone."

He was right. There wasn't a direction conclusion here. She pressed her foot to the pedal and peeled out of the parking lot, cranking the music to maximum volume.

# Chapter 39
# Fix My Brain

Lolita's basement studio had been vacant for days. Every time she opened the door and took a step down the creaky wooden stairs, something cold slithered through the back of her brain. Every time, she retreated to the corner of her couch.

The last few days flickered through her thoughts in a series of fuzzy images. It was as if her mind was an old television set, like the one in her living room, the rabbit ears bent unnaturally, the images concealed in white noise and jagged lines zigzagging across the screen.

She'd played *the video* over and over. Her head rejected the notion of clearing. Her being refused to settle.

Faint pictures flashed through her thoughts. Orson. Up on stage. In the recording studio. His emerald eyes. His lips.

Blood. Skin. Sweat-soaked white cloth across his perfect lips. Flesh oozing from skinless fingers. A constant barrage of images.

Her internal switch clicked madly on and off. One moment, she was looking into Orson's eyes, a glow swelling within her. The next, she was staring into those same eyes, now stricken with fear, sweat drizzling over pale flesh.

Lolita rocked back and forth on the velour couch; her fuzzy blanket crumpled in a pile beside her. Her chocolate dreadlocks were slick with grease.

Her mother's face permanently shimmered through her mind, as if she was with Lolita now. Lolita's brain sizzled every time she thought of the woman who brought her into this world. The poison seething through her mother's veins had seeped into Lolita when she was only a fetus.

Instead of running free in the playground, she'd spent a considerable chunk of her childhood with doctors. Her brain had been scanned too many times. The same conclusion had been come to over and over. A rare event had happened. They had used words like lateral hemisphere, amygdala connectivity, brain, control, and compromised. She had gone numb. The only phrases that stuck in her mind since that day were broken brain and lack of emotional control.

When she finally escaped her mother's clutches, she walked away totally fucked up. Her emotions were a mess. Her memory was all helter-skelter. Her mouth was disformed and grotesque. She couldn't execute a flawless rhyme to save her life.

She had nothing.

She was alone. No Electric Skin. No Orson.

A loud click echoed through the living room as the tape ended. Silence followed.

She'd tried *everything* to calm herself. She'd recklessly blasted through her supply of anti-depressants, tranquilizers, and party drugs. In desperation, she'd dipped into the bottles of oxytocin that she'd stolen from her mother's medicine cabinet. They'd been prescribed to her as a child. Sick roiled in her stomach as she stared at one of the half empty bottles now. She could still taste the vomit on the back of her tongue and feel the hot blood drizzling down her legs from the lining of her youthful uterus.

Lolita had been cautious, terrified of causing a full rupture. Now, as her brain rapidly deteriorated and images of skin and blood dripped through her mind, she knew she had no choice. Besides, there would never be a fetus inside of her. Orson was gone. Forever. She cringed at the thought of a tiny being pulsing in her belly, its deranged brain broken before it came into the world, and its fucked-up face ensuring it would fail.

Her brain buzzed. Blood, flesh, and emerald eyes swirled inside her head. She begged for it to stop. She snatched the half-empty bottle from the table, threw two pills down her throat, and gulped cold lemon balm tea.

DISCO BISCUIT
BOURBON
HIGH

# Chapter 40

# Murder Wall

The sun glowed orange as it dipped low in the sky. Stella stared out the window. Darkness came early at this time of year. The trick-or-treaters would soon be scuttling through the neighbourhoods. Not in her hood. Not on the seedy side of the downtown core.

Zakk Wylde sung to her, telling her to take his hand. A heavy, melodic riff followed, thrusting her into a metal-dowsed trance. *Sonic Brew* had been playing from beginning to end all afternoon. The gift from Bryce. He knew his stuff.

She continued with her pacing along the wall plastered in a homemade murder collage. Back and forth.

For years, it had been a display of the worst serial killers to hit Canada over the last twenty years. At its epicentre, the three human monsters her father had hunted. After the Poison Sisters case, Stella's first bona fide serial killer hunt, she'd let go of the cases that swallowed her father. She'd ripped down the photo of the polished Sargeant Tomlinson, who had derailed the case with greedy intentions, thrusting her father down a path of demise. She'd let go of the photo. She'd let go of the blame.

She'd taken down the entire collage, one photo, one file, one piece of evidence, one clue at a time. The wall had remained clear for a while.

After the Poison Sisters case, nothing big happened in Calgary Homicide. Not for months. The restlessness grew inside of Stella, morphing into an anxious ball. Oppressive in the pit of her belly. She was in search of something. She needed *purpose.*

One day, early for a shift, with nothing better to do, her curiosity took her into the cold case filing storage. She'd lifted a folder, eyeballed the contents, and was immediately hooked. One by one, she'd confiscated folders filled with files describing murders, often in series, who had no suspect. A layer of ice formed over them, freezing the memories of the victims, numbing the information until everyone forgot.

She'd spent her boring nights at home, glass of bourbon in hand, creating a cold case collage, until at least a dozen plastered her wall. The wall was once again filled with pictures of death.

She'd focused on the ones that had gone cold in the early 90s. Old enough to be forgotten. Not too aged to be solved.

When the *Skin Peeler* came into her life, Stella was sure she'd forget about her murder wall. Two victims in, things had stopped. Two weeks and two days had passed since the second victim was left in the alley behind *Coconut Rum*. They'd processed the scene on a Friday night, amidst the bustle of what remained of Electric Avenue, October 15. Now, on Halloween, Stella found herself pacing back and forth within the claustrophobic confines of her apartment, the restlessness within her taking over.

There was nothing to go on. They had exhausted every lead. Even the traces of oxytocin left in the victims was a dead end. In the mid-seventies, it was handed out like candy. Labour was induced freely, viewed as a safe way to ease the strain the baby boomers were exerting on maternity wards. The mid-seventies also saw a spike in alcohol and drug abuse in young mothers. Slowing the activity in the amygdala, oxytocin was a novel approach to treating the resulting damage to the brain of these children. The use of the drug had decreased significantly. However, even with a prescription required, the number of bottles handed out was too vast to lead to a suspect. The only thing that could be deduced was that *if* the killer had a prescription to induce labour or treat a child, then *she* would likely be in her forties. If there was a father involved, he could have stolen the pills. Or, if it was the child who had taken them, he, or she, would likely be in their twenties by n ow.

The similarities between the two victims were striking. The hair colour. The eye colour. The clothing. The post-mortem washing routine. The book. The hand, peeled clean of skin, clutching the book to the open page with the message written in blood. The victim's blood.

Nothing was left behind that would lead to the person who left the bodies.

No one had seen anything. The bodies had been left by a ghost.

People in the life of the first victim didn't know a great deal about him. They still hadn't gotten an ID on the second victim.

Spotless scenes. Searches going nowhere.

Stella's whole being cringed at the thought that her case could go cold. What could be worse than knowing that *she* let a killer run free?

The *Skin Peeler* had killed before. The *Skin Peeler* would kill again.

Stella was left wishing he, or she, would do it soon. A grisly thing to want. But it was better than having a killer slip through her fingers only to resurface somewhere else. Another time. Another place. Leaving authorities stumped and putting the pieces together from scratch. Everything she'd done would be forgotten.

Stella stomped over to the glass coffee table in the centre of the room. She contemplated the bottle of bourbon sitting on the glass coffee table, then changed her mind. It was too early for that.

The track changed. A soul-vibrating riff ripped through the living room. *Mother Mary.* A track like no other. A sense of doom cloaked her. The darkness drowning out the orange glow of the sun through the window, the photos of potential killers plastered to her murder wall, the resonant voice warning her that she might be falling from the track.

All of it was closing in on her.

She plunked down into the well-worn couch and scanned the files on the *Skin Peeler* again. For the millionth time. Sutton had told them to go home, take the day off, stop burning recklessly through hours, and they'd take a fresh look in the morning. She knew it wouldn't be beneficial. They weren't missing anything. There was *nothing* there to miss.

She stood, glanced at the bottle of bourbon, and walked over to the murder wall. She needed something to calm her. None of her heavy metal albums were working. Neither were any of her father's classic rock records. She felt like a caged animal, pacing behind bars, craving a meal. A hunt.

Scanning the series of collages, she rested her eyes on one. Six young women. *Six.* All with curly dark hair and matching eyes. All twenty-two years of age or younger. All of them left on the outskirts of the city, within the boundaries of a city park, yet stretching close to the line declaring the city limits. Made the crime scenes difficult. Part of the perimetre was within the city, part outside of it. Jurisdictional ownership was complicated to define. Co-ordination was required. She'd read the files many times. It didn't seem to her that anyone *wanted* to own it. None of the girls had permanent residences. Some of them had jumped from place to place. Others had been outright homeless for a while. Without anyone breathing down the necks of the authorities, or the papers splashing the progress of a murder case involving a series of young women all over the city, there was a lack of motivation for anyone to further the investigation.

The bodies had stopped. The case had gone cold. Fall of 1990. The files had claimed a lack of evidence to clearly link them. To Stella, the linkage flashed like a neon sign over a nightclub on Electric Avenue.

She scanned down the list of suspects from the files tacked to the murder wall next to the photos of the victims. Then she carefully inspected her private list, the one that she had written and tacked next to the official one.

Their list was a meek attempt to cross-examine anyone directly within the victim's life. People that directly knew her. Spent time with her.

Stella's list was a heightened attempt to drive out that second circle. The vultures that hovered just outside the life of the victim. They were there. But they stayed off the radar as part of the victim's life.

There was one particular vulture all six young women had in common.

His name was Rick Rios. His nickname was *Slick Rick.*

He was still in the city.

She should call Todd. See if this vermin spent any nights at *The Cecil.* Several times, she'd followed him into the *Drum and Monkey.* She could start there. Keep completely off the radar. Not even involve Todd.

She walked up to her murder wall and stared into the eyes of *Slick Rick.* An icy hand reached around her gut and squeezed.

Could she trust herself to pressure him, get a confession, then bring him in?

Her mind plunged to the last night she'd spent at *The Cecil.* Dirty Joe sliding his knife into her abdomen. Joe's next victim, the woman, blood trickling over her hands, trembling as she clutched Stella's knife. Joe breathing his dying breaths.

Joe deserved to die. That's what she kept telling herself. His next victim survived. That's all that mattered. Wasn't it?

She sighed, her jaw clenching, and walked over to the couch. She sat and stared at the bottle of bourbon.

If she listened to her gut now, she knew what she would hear.

None of this was helping.

Her metal music. The murder wall. Being caged up. The four walls closed in on her.

# Chapter 41

# Bea

S tella leaned into the couch, letting her head rest against the worn material. She closed her eyes and exhaled. Tad's face materialized in her mind. His touch, still lingering on her skin from their last night together. The idea of sinking into another night with him sent a thrill through her. It also filled her with a sense of calm. A sense of *everything is going to be OK.*

She sat up and took another longing glance at the bottle of bourbon. Her phone sat next to it. Tad's number scrolled on a crumpled piece of paper flashed through her mind.

Her phone buzzed and rattled across the glass. Maybe it was him.

She grabbed her phone and flipped it open.

"Yeah." It wasn't her murder phone. She didn't have to answer *Mahoney.*

"Stella." The all-too-familiar voice jolted her to the past.

"Mom." Stella's heart plunged.

"I've been trying to reach you. You don't answer."

Stella could picture her mother's face. Despite the years of stress and anxiety, apparently caused by Stella's father, her mother's skin had maintained a natural beauty. Her hair—long, strawberry blonde, curly—had remained untainted by signs of age. If there was any grey, it was unnoticeable. The lustrous shine had been there ever since Stella could remember.

"I'm working a case, Mom." Stella attempted to keep her tone calm. Inside, she was burning with rage. She had avoided the calls. On purpose. She had nothing to say to her mother. Nothing that would help them get along.

"You don't have five minutes for *your mother*?"

The retort stabbed deep. Her mother had always dwelled on the failures of her father. His failure to spend time with them. His failure to choose them over his work. His failure to stay safe, avoid risks, and come home to them in one piece. Alive.

Her mother's unending blame was a direct result of the pain caused by a broken marriage and a dead husband. Ex-husband. Still, Stella had seen it in her mother's eyes when her father died…the authentic love her mother had always felt for her father.

Still, Stella couldn't forgive her mother for her foul words against him. She was too close to him, despite the little time she'd spent with him.

"Yes, I do. Right now." Stella swallowed the bitterness, bit back the attitude clawing at her tone.

"OK. Well…I just wanted to talk to you. To see how you were."

Stella sat up and focused. She needed to put on a good front to avoid further *concern* that would lead them down an argument-fused rabbit hole. "I'm fine, Mom. Really."

"Well, you sound OK. I just…"

"What is it?" Stella attempted to sound pleasant.

"I've had these *feelings*. Like I used to when your father was deep into a case. Like you weren't OK. Like whatever you're working on is eating you up. You know…like it did with him." The sadness seeped from her mother's voice. It had never left.

Stella wondered if it ever would.

The bottle of bourbon tempted her again. She looked away. "Well, I'm fine."

She could hear the hesitation over the phone. Her jaw clenched. Her shoulders bunched.

"You should quit. Now." Any concern in her mother's tone morphed into anger. Fuelled by hurt.

Here we go. "I've told you, this is what I want."

"You're young. You have your whole life ahead of you. Why throw it away like this? Just like he did?"

Stella could picture her mother's mouth contorted into a stern frown.

"I'm not throwing my life away. A homicide detective is a respectable career path." Not the reason at all that she chose it. But she needed any fuel she could grab.

"I'm not saying it isn't. I just don't understand why you want this. After everything. After how your father died." The aging and rotting core of her mother seeped from her pores, over the youthful exterior she'd been able to maintain. Stella could see it, radiant as day, as if her mother were sitting there in front of her right now.

"Stella. Are you there? Are you *listening* to me?"

"Yes, Mom. I'm listening." She rolled her eyes. She needed this to end. She couldn't take it anymore.

"Great. I..." A faint sniffle trickled through the phone.

Stella exhaled as she closed her eyes. "Mom, I get it. You're worried. I understand."

"I'm happy that you understand." Her mother sighed. "You don't know what it was like for me. Without your father all those years. And then...he didn't have to die. I don't want you to choose the same thing."

Silence clung between them. Static echoed over the phone.

How could her mother say that she didn't know what it was like? She'd spent so many nights curled up in her bed, blasting Skid Row on her Walkman, hiding from the world. The world that dangled a father she loved in front of her every time he called or dropped in for a sudden visit, only to whisk him away. The world that took him forever when all he was doing was saving people, some of them teenage girls, just like she'd been then.

"Stella, you need to quit."

For fuck's sake. This wasn't going to end. Ever. "I'm not gonna do that, *Mom.*"

"Don't use that tone with me."

"I'm an adult. I'll decide what I'm doing with my life." Heat rose up Stella's face.

"You're making a misguided decision. For the wrong reasons. He wouldn't want this for you."

"You don't know that," Stella hissed as hot pokers seared her heart.

"Yes, I do. He would not want this. You *have* to quit. Before it's too late."

Enough. She'd had enough. Her head buzzed, her face flaming. "You don't know what he wanted. You never knew what he wanted. You left him. You made *me* leave him. It's your fault he didn't have anyone. It's your fault I didn't even know my father." The words left a foul taste in her mouth. Her heart sank. Her gut trembled. She'd crossed a line she could never go retreat from.

Sniffles crackled through the phone. Thick silence followed.

The phone went dead.

# Chapter 42

# Open Your Heart

Stella's hand trembled as she grabbed the bottle of bourbon and poured it into a glass. She stared at the phone. She couldn't recall the last time her mother had hung up on her. If she ever had.

Usually, they argued. It got heated. But neither of them said anything targeted enough to wound. It was always in the tone and the insinuation. It had never been as crystal clear as the dagger she'd thrown at her mom.

Stella swallowed down the guilt. It wasn't her fault. To say her father wouldn't want her to be a detective. That couldn't be true. Nothing within Stella would believe that. Ever.

She took a sip of bourbon, then grabbed her coat from the corner of the couch. As her fingers brushed the folded square of paper, tingles crept up her arm. She pulled it from the pocket and unfolded it.

She stared at Tad's phone number, biting her lip.

He'd insisted she take his number and call him when she had time to meet up again.

She could still feel his gaze on hers, boring into her. Reading her thoughts.

She could still taste his lips. Soft. A lingering sweetness on her own.

She could still feel the electrifying tingles weaving up her arms, over her entire body, as he'd touched her.

She'd been reliving the evening in her mind, on repeat, searching for a night when she'd felt the same way. She was convinced she never had.

The sound of his voice still simmered through her veins.

Before she could change her mind, she snatched up the phone and punched in the numbers.

It rang. Once. Twice.

"Hello?" His voice made her insides erupt with tingles.

"Tad." Heat rushed her body.

"Stella."

"You have time for a drink?" She bit her lower lip a tad harder.

"Of course."

"Can we meet at the bourbon place, next the Poison Room?" She wanted a direct path to his place. She was barely ready to see him again. She was a long way off from being prepared to invite him over. As connected as she already was, she still needed a getaway.

"I can meet you there in a half hour."

"Perfect."

# Chapter 43
# Close It Up Again

The icy breeze reached fingers over Stella's face. Her long leather coat fluttered open. The frigid air cleansed her. She inhaled deeply, held it, then exhaled in a wispy puff of white.

She'd been playing the routine of detective, trying not to let her desperation show as the *Skin Peeler* case cooled. It was barely warm. They had to come up with something. Fast. Or it would be forgotten. Like the others plastering her apartment wall.

She swallowed against the mixture of anger and frustration clawing up her throat. She amped up her pace and approached the subtle blue glow of the sign. *Bourbon Lounge.*

Her heart raced. Tingles wove through her arms. She approached the place and walked through the door before she could hesitate.

The room emitted a red glow from the lamps dotting the bar and the tables. Red velour covered the chairs. High-end bottles of everything, including bourbon, lined the polished glass wall of the bar. She was satisfied with herself for abandoning the glass of bourbon she'd poured at home. The place was cozy, inviting, and warm.

She scanned the joint. There he was.

The tingles heightened into energetic pricks. She couldn't understand the reaction she had every time she pictured his face. Every time she visualized the other night, replaying it like a forbidden movie in her mind. Her body would relive the aftermath of a fire, radiant, glowing.

This was a good idea.

She needed a release. This had to be preferable to hunting a human.

He waved at her. She forced her legs into motion and walked across the room.

"Stella." He smiled. The dimple took her away.

"Tad." She scolded the flush rising over her neck and face.

"I'm glad you called." He stood, pulled out a chair, and motioned for her to sit.

She plunked down without removing her coat. She could do this. She needed to do this. She had to try to be normal. She had to try to avoid becoming a hunter again.

A waiter approached. Tad ordered them a round of Anderson Club's King Kamehameha, Kentucky Straight. She smiled at the waiter, barely listening to the conversation.

Tad's shoulder-length hair floated around his face. "I wasn't sure if you would call. I've thought about you a lot." Golden threads gleamed under the mellow red glow of the lamps. His muscular arms stretched the sleeves of his dress shirt.

He wasn't her type. Everything about him screamed the opposite of what she usually went for.

But what did she usually go for? Diving headfirst into booze-fuelled nights with the front men of heavy metal bands. Going in hard and fast, knowing she'd be ditched before the night was over. Wishing to be deserted so she didn't have to be the one sneaking out to avoid explanation. To soothe someone's feelings. To make them feel less *used*.

Looking into Tad's amber eyes now, she knew that this *was* completely opposite from everything she'd been doing.

Fear clenched her shoulders. She could back down. She could flee to her apartment. She didn't have to do this. She didn't have to *feel*.

But she wanted to.

"Are you OK?" Tad's suave voice put a hatchet in her thoughts.

"Yeah. Sorry." She shook her head and smiled. "Working on a tough case. It's going nowhere. Needed a break."

The waiter set two exquisite crystal glasses down on the table. An orange glow made them into colourful works of art.

Tad nodded at the server as he left them. He picked up his glass and tilted it toward Stella. She did the same.

"Here's to new beginnings." He took a slow sip.

She did the same. The flavours were incredible, filling her mouth. As she rolled the bourbon over her tongue, clove, cinnamon, and intense berry filled her senses. She swallowed the potent alcohol, a delightful vanilla finish trickling down her throat.

This is what *normal* people did. Go out together, have a nice cocktail, sit and talk.

"Smooth." He put the glass down on the table. "I saw it last time I was here. Meant to try it. Glad I got to try it with you."

"It is. Smooth. Never had it before." She'd never even heard of it. She kept her drinking to the familiar bourbon night after night. Maker's Mark. Just like her father. Maybe expanding her knowledge would be a healthy hobby.

"Tell me about the case." He appeared to be sincerely interested.

"*Skin Peeler.*" The words tasted bitter in her mouth.

"What?" His eyes widened.

"Two murders. Strikingly similar. You haven't seen it in the news?"

He blushed. "No. I don't watch TV. Don't read the paper. I'm trying to keep my mind clear. For my music."

Again, his voice reached right into her soul. The echoes from his show hadn't released their grip on her.

"But I want to hear about this. *Skin Peeler*?" He seemed curious, yet slightly terrified.

"The skin on the victims' hands was missing. Peeled off."

"So they call the killer the *Skin Peeler*?"

"No. Not the media. It's what I call him." She took another sip of bourbon. He actually seemed interested.

"Good name." He nodded. "But you said it's going nowhere?"

"Yeah. Two victims. No tangible suspects." She clenched her jaw.

He chuckled.

"What?"

"Sorry. It's just cute, the way you clench your jaw when you're analyzing something."

She looked away.

"No suspects? This killer, he doesn't leave a trace?" he asked.

"Nope. Nothing that leads to a person. And the victims apparently didn't have a lot of people in their lives. Nothing suspicious. Nothing to indicate anyone that would do this to them." Stella settled against the chair. Heat swelled under her coat. Maybe she should stay for a bit.

"Wow. Fascinating." He was eating it up.

"Yeah, I guess. You said you don't watch TV?" She leaned in and slipped her coat off, one sleeve at a time. She rested it over the chair.

"Keeps my mind clear."

"For your music." She relaxed as she diverted the conversation away from her. It was all fine as he asked her about the investigation. Anything that had been released as public was game to talk about. She didn't want him digging into anything personal.

"Yeah. I write all of the songs, for the band." He blushed.

She clicked her jaw. "Purely Purple. I don't usually go for the classic rock vibe."

"I love the old guys. Zeppelin. Stones. I love a blues edge." He leaned over the table. "I'm trying to bring it back with a modern feel."

"You're doing a hell of a job." A flush ran up Stella's neck. "I've got a great collection of the classics."

"Really? I'd love to see that sometime." His eyes twinkled.

"Sure." She could swallow this intimate exchange with him in a public place. But she had a hard time picturing him in her apartment. That was too close for comfort.

"You like classic rock?"

"Well, I love metal." She smiled. Rob Zombie flashed through her thoughts.

"Really? The hard stuff?"

"Slayer. Sabbath. You know, the usual. But what I really like are the ones that showcase even greater artistic expression. Rob Zombie. Type O Negative." Ian's dark flowing locks fluttered through her mind. His sleek white face followed. The show at Rock Candy had been a killer night.

"Know Zombie. Don't know Type O. Sounds like you're hardcore."

"What can I say? I love my live music." She took a lingering sip of the dwindling bourbon.

"Another?"

"Sure." One more. Then she'd move the night along. A girl could only be expected to do so much talking before getting to the good stuff.

This wasn't so bad. He'd been interested in the *Skin Peeler*. He hadn't gotten all creeped out. He loved music. Classic rock. Despite how tame she'd thought the genre was, he'd given her a brand-new view point the other night. And he wasn't pushy about getting to know everything about her. This could be all right.

She settled into the chair as Tad ordered them another round.

As the waiter walked away, she took her opportunity to direct the conversation.

"How'd you learn so much about bourbon?"

"I come to places like this, I see something interesting, I try it."

"Sounds like a fun education," she said.

"It is. Like music. The more you sample, the more you learn." He took a sip of his drink. "So, why'd you become a detective?"

Good question. "I don't know. I guess I...followed my gut." It was half true. She'd followed her father.

"Anyone else in your family in homicide?"

There it was. Just like that. Why'd he have to get personal? She swallowed. "Yeah. My dad."

"Oh? Is he still on the force?" A sincere question.

Her gut clenched, along with her jaw. "He's dead."

Tad's eyes clouded in an instant. "Stella, I'm so sorry." He reached his hand over the table and brushed her fingers.

She stiffened, but she didn't retreat. "Yeah, well, he got caught up in a case. Out in Toronto."

"Geez. That's rough." He stroked her fingers with his. "How old were you?"

A flash of that day riveted her mind. She pulled her hand away. "Twelve."

A hurt expression dominated his face. *Dammit.* This wasn't about him.

"I'm sorry. I didn't know. I didn't mean to upset you."

"You didn't. I'm fine." She took another sip from her nearly empty glass, willing another bourbon to appear.

The server returned and set two glasses down. She grabbed the glass and swallowed the numbing liquid.

Tad tried to recover the conversation. "Kings County. Peated Bourbon. Thought you might appreciate it." He lifted his glass.

She stared into the bourbon. Images flew through her mind. Her father's face.

*Stella, follow your instincts.*

Her mother's twisted frown.

*Your father wouldn't want this for you. You need to quit.*

The striking emerald eyes, glassy and lifeless. A pale face. Two victims.

*What would you say if you could talk?* She stood, snatching her coat. "Thanks for the drinks. I gotta go."

As she walked briskly from the table, she could feel Tad's stunned expression reaching for her. Why should she explain? She didn't have to.

# Chapter 44
# Chilly Case

Stella burst into her apartment. Heat rushed through her body. She flung her keys into the red glass bowl. A chip flew through the air. *Dammit.* It was already chipped when she'd inherited it from her father's apartment.

She discarded her coat, releasing the heat swelling underneath the leather. She flung it onto the couch as she stomped across the room. Taking a deep breath, she halted and stared up at the rows of LPs.

No hunt. No Tad. No release.

It was barely eight o'clock, and her night was over.

She'd have to create her personal path to Zen. She laughed out loud. She wasn't sure she knew the meaning of Zen. But she could establish a manic metal vibe that would put her into her own version of calm.

She stared at her late father's LP collection. This wouldn't do. She needed something strong. Spinning to face the adjacent wall, she perused her CD collection.

Tad just had to insist on getting to know her.

This case was going cold faster than she could breathe heat into it.

*Dammit. Double dammit.*

Her murder phone buzzed. She unclipped it from her belt. Excitement shot through her. Maybe this would be it. The break they needed.

"Mahoney." A gruff edge tinged her voice.

"Take tomorrow off." Sutton's tone had never sounded this serious.

"What?"

"We're weeks in with no prime suspect. I have to re-organize resources." He was all business. To the max.

What the flying fuck? "Re-organize? What does that mean? What about the *Skin Peeler?*"

He sighed. "I've been ordered to reduce resources. It's out of my hands." He paused, like he wanted to say something else.

"Fine." She flipped her phone shut and tossed it toward the couch. It sailed through the air, bounced off the cushion and landed on the carpet.

She moved over to the CDs. Tears stung the corners of her eyes. Her brain buzzed; skin moistened with fresh sweat. *Re-organize.* How about catching the killer who was peeling the skin from victims' hands?

She exhaled loudly through her nose, snatching an album case from the shelf. Her ultimate favourite. The Zombie King. She snapped the case open, yanked the CD out, strode over to the player, and inserted it. High-voltage blasts of guitar thrust through the living room. Her body vibrated. Her mind buzzed. She required a release. Now. She closed her eyes and drank in the savage song. The first real shot of calm in days trickled through her.

No work tomorrow. No *Skin Peeler.* Fuck the rules.

She walked over to the glass coffee table and poured her first drink of the evening. She wasn't going to count the high-end bourbon she'd had with Tad. This was a clean slate. The evening started now.

She walked over to the murder wall and glared at Slick Rick. She almost gagged. Bourbon sprung from the glass and splashed on her hand as she spun on her heel and stomped toward the coffee table. The *Skin Peeler* files were still spread out over the glass. Her pathetic attempt to *see* something. Something they'd all missed. Something that could ignite this case before it was shoved into the crevices of the storage room at HQ covered in ice.

She'd failed. It was too late.

As the zombie-metal god serenaded her with wild lyrics of ragged ones who kill and super beasts, she polished the glass of bourbon off in three gulps. The glass clanked as she set it harshly onto the table. *Fuck this.*

Her mother's face, skin glowing, mouth pulled into a tight line, shimmered in her mind.

*Your father wouldn't want this. You need to quit.*

An angry claw scratched at her throat. Her mother didn't know anything about what her father wanted. The book he'd left her told her all she needed to know. His words, distant over the phone line, had given her everything she wanted to understand.

Tad's face fluttered over her mother's. His amber eyes. His golden hair. His soft skin, warm smile. The words that killed all of it.

*What had he said?* Her gut told her he hadn't done anything wrong.

The walls of her apartment closed in on her. The grisly collage on the murder wall seemed to pulse, pulling her from across the room. She looked away from it.

She had to leave this place. Now.

# Chapter 45

# Anticipation

The vibrant lights buzzing over the nightclubs painted a neon mural over the pavement. The colours lit up the street like an amusement park. The clubs spanned several blocks. As Lolita walked down the street, she passed by familiar places. A yellow sign buzzed *Three Cheers,* taunting her to take the stairs into the basement bar. She loved that one. The walls closed in like the ones in her misaligned little house, keeping her in a bubble, safe from the world. Not tonight. She had somewhere to be. Somewhere important.

Her heels clicked on the pavement. The neon palm trees of *Coconut Joe's* called to her. She peered through the window, perusing the party crowd dancing on the counters, shooters lining the bar. It was like a tropical holiday in there. Not tonight.

As she passed all the popular joints, she breathed in the excitement simmering in the air. This was the place to be. She was so happy she'd followed Orson here. They'd arrived in Calgary a few months ago. It was 1993 and the music scene was alive. So was the party scene. It centred along this several-block strip of nightclubs she was walking down now. Electric Avenue. It had birthed in the 80s and was thriving by the time they'd arrived.

It had been changing. She could feel it. Every time she wandered along this mini-Vegas in the core of downtown Calgary, its energy fused with hers. She could *feel* its pulse. Lately, the vibe was darkening. The happy-go-lucky, nothing-can-go-wrong, party-it-up-while-you-can vibe was morphing into something progressively manic. There was a desperation to the air. The partygoers were crazed, overeager to get loaded as fast as possible. The love for the pureness of a free night out was morphing into a greedy *need* to go over the top.

Tonight, Lolita wouldn't think about any of that. Tonight was a big night. For Orson.

Something tugged at her heart. She knew that deep down she wished this was a big night for *both* of them. That the shared dream they had when they landed here was still alive.

But she knew the truth.

The condition in her head was simmering at a higher intensity. It was reaching its rot through her brain, across her face, and down her lip. As the droop in her lip deepened and the contortion of her skin evolved, her rhymes deteriorated. She knew it. The band knew it. The expression of awe on their faces when she'd shared her rhymes and they'd declared her lead for those tracks had vanished in sync with the development of the grotesque formation of her skin.

Pain and anger simmered inside of her. So far, she'd been able to mask it. She'd thrown all her focus and energy into supporting Orson. She figured that if he was the one to take their band skyrocketing up the charts, she'd support him. It could still get them to Seattle. Or L.A. By then, maybe her condition would ease up. Maybe her face would smooth itself out.

Besides, she loved him. She really did.

She knew that no matter what, the thing she wanted most was to be with him. To have his captivating emerald eyes staring into her soul.

A clatter of a bottles clinking across the pavement jolted Lolita from her reverie. A group of partygoers high-fived and hooted as they stumbled past her. She was almost there. Just another half a block.

Excitement reached electric fingers up her insides and down her arms. This was it. This would be the performance of a lifetime. This would launch Orson, and their band, to the next level.

The sign pulsed a beautiful blue-purple hue over the pavement. *Vinyl.* This was one of the highest-profile places to perform.

Tonight. October 31, 1993. Tonight was the night she would watch Orson up on that stage, luminous lights blazing over him, silver microphone in hand, crooning his raw-edged smooth lyrics to a packed crowd.

Tonight was the first step of the new journey they'd take down a star-dusted road.

She would be by his side every step of the way.

# Chapter 46

# Ice Air

The crisp air pricked Stella's face. Black tinged the edges of the denim sky. Stars made a meek attempt to glimmer over the city lights. She quickened her pace, walking straight for the neon signs of the one block still claiming its fame as Electric Avenue.

Her mother's accusations simmered in her mind, on the verge of boiling. Tad's face was fading from her thoughts. The *Skin Peeler* slipped through her fingers.

A numbness had overcome her body and her mind.

The neon glimmer of the nightclubs lit up the sky. It was Sunday. It was Halloween. The party strip was livelier than usual. There *had* to be a live show. She could have sworn she'd seen flyers for a few specials to celebrate the holiday. She needed it beyond measure, her desire for a metal god screaming up on his pedestal sizzling inside of her.

Rummaging through the info on the flyers stored in her mind, she couldn't recall anything metal. Or even rock. Most of it was likely dance shit. DJs. Pumping out the tunes to get the partygoers up and ready to blow their wad on drinks.

She perused the flyers tacked to anything they'd stick to as she approached the neon-lit party block. An obnoxious pink paper caught her eye. A trio. Three women. Two metal. One rap. They were doing a special tribute night to the most influential metal and rock gods.

It intrigued her. The fusion had been attempted multiple times. She'd seen something similar. Early 90s. Body Count. Ice-T and Ernie C. The creation to feature the rap lyricist and the metal guitarist. The most up-to-date one that Stella knew about was Children of the Korn. The members of *Korn* and their special guest *Ice Cube.* They'd even performed together at live festivals. She'd only heard it on recordings.

She scanned the info on the flyer. The trio of women weren't a cover band. They had several albums under their belt. Tonight would be a tribute to their greatest inspirations. Maybe she'd get lucky and they'd focus on their metal influences.

Relief washed over her.

Nothing elicited more satisfaction in her than a live and heavy show.

*Nothing.*

She chided herself now for veering off track. For thinking that another night with Tad was the answer. For losing her guts, letting her ability to catch a killer slip from her. For letting Sutton tell her to step back. She should have voiced her disagreements with him to a greater extent.

Was she the only one who cared about the *Skin Peeler?*

Whatever. She shook it off. There was nothing she could do. She needed to blow off some steam.

She rounded the corner. She could see it now. *Vinyl.* A popular place for rock shows. A few groups gathered in front, smoking it up before the show. Some of them looked metal—pleather and chains. Others appeared rather rap, wearing baggy jeans and tight tanks, chains around their necks. It all seemed cliché.

As she neared, she spotted a group of young women huddled in the corner, chatting it up, passing around a joint. They seemed highly captivating. They didn't have a set attire that placed them into a group, a genre, a box. One had red pleather, a t-shirt plastered in a band name foreign to Stella, and a fuzzy fur jacket. Her hair was twisted up into two buns. Her lips were painted black. It was a mix of goth and metal, with her own unique fuzzy spin. Another girl had a short, pleated skirt, long socks reaching above her knees, and bulky black boots, the ankles adorned in chains. Her long pink hair flowed over her shoulders.

Maybe this would prove to be interesting.

Stella eyed the girls as she walked by them. They smiled back.

Yeah, this wouldn't be so bad.

She could already sense the pre-concert excitement enveloping her with energetic vibes. The invigorating air had cleared her mind. No faces or thoughts cluttered it. She wished to keep it that way.

She opened a red door and walked into the tiny entranceway. Stairs led down. Chatter rose from the depths below, along with hot air infused with cheap beer and cheaper hard liquor. Stella smiled.

The red door slammed behind her. Hot aromatic air filled her senses. A blue-purple glow wove up the staircase. She started her descent.

# Chapter 47

# Pure Love

Three stairs down, Stella's mother's face invaded her mind. Smooth, youthful skin, eyes with a twinkle. The pout. The thin line of a mouth contorted into a judging frown, revealing the internal rot, the result of years of pain and h urt.

*Quit. Father wouldn't want this.*

Stella shook her head and focused on the next stair, the pinkish glow from below beckoning her. The rumbling sounds of a sound check pulled her down to thc basement.

Four more stairs and Tad's face flashed, as if he were standing there with her now.

*I'm so sorry.*

He didn't know her.

Stella swallowed against the bile clawing up her throat. She shook off the chilly hand squeezing her heart.

Two more steps and Sutton's piercing eyes shimmered in front of her.

*On hold. Re-organize.*

What hadn't he told her? Was there any fucking way she could still hunt the *Skin Peeler*?

*Stupid girl.* She knew better than that. The numerous cold case files plastered over her apartment wall were ample proof. They were weeks into the *Skin Peeler* case with no prime suspect. She was aware that Sutton couldn't allow them to keep burning up the number of hours they'd been putting in.

A resonant voice beckoned from the basement below. Guitar vibrated then stopped.

She took her time reaching the bottom of the stairs. She didn't want to spoil the surprise fusion of a rap demon and metal god that was waiting below. Waiting to take her away to another realm. If only for tonight.

She leaned against the cold brick of the wall plastered in crude graffiti and dripping in weighty lettering. *Get it together.* She closed her eyes.

A pair of remarkable emerald irises flashed. A skinless hand appeared.

*The Skin Peeler.*

She'd fucked it all up before it had even started.

She knew the *Skin Peeler* would resurface.

The last step appeared as the lights ebbing from the basement dimmed to a soft midnight-blue glow.

Chatter buzzed through the space. Air coated with cheap beer and stinging with alcohol stuck to her face. She breathed it in. The essence of a basement pit that promised to swallow her up for the night.

She walked slowly along the rear wall, devouring the scene with her eyes.

The place was three-quarters full. A good crowd. With room to breathe.

Half the concertgoers were decked in Halloween getups. Women dressed in miniaturized versions of what could be respectable costumes. The scary night a reason, an *excuse* to show off their assets. Find someone to entertain them for the night. The other half were a mix. Some of them wore common everyday attire. Some eased their way through the crowd in black leather adorned with chains. The metal crowd. The rest walked casually around in baggy jeans and tight tanks, gold chains around their necks, matching rings on their fingers. The rap crowd.

This was becoming more interesting than Stella had expected. Desperate for a live show, this was the most promising act for the metal high she was craving.

"Pure love?" a gentle voice, barely above a whisper, said from beside her.

A woman—early twenties, clad in a minuscule cat outfit with black ears protruding from her head over her pink hair—looked at her with affectionate eyes. She pulled a bag from inside her fake fur jacket.

Stella was about to shake her head when her body involuntarily halted. The blue pills were familiar. *Love drug. Ecstasy.* She'd taken her fair share of passion-filled rides from it in her late teens. She wasn't fond of drugs, but for years she couldn't resist the open, loving feeling she got from *E.*

*Quit. Father wouldn't want this.*

*I'm so sorry.*

*On hold. Re-organize.*

*Skin Peeler.*

Thoughts whirled through her mind in an invasive stream.

She nodded, slipped the girl a couple of bills, and let her shake two pills from the bag into her palm. She smiled. The girl winked—glitter on her eyelids shimmering under the orange glow of the room—and walked away.

*Fuck it.*

Slamming her palm to her open mouth, she swallowed the pills before she could think. *Time for a drink.*

She walked slyly up to the bar lining the left side of the room. There might be time for one—even two—shots or double shots of bourbon before the show.

*Perfect.*

Casing the bar, she eyed the bottles lining the top shelf. Cheap. Strong. It would have to do. She'd take the cheapest bourbon in town to be here in this basement pit waiting for a wild ride than sitting in a cozy lounge with Tad sipping expensive shit.

"What's your poison?" A waitress in a black corset, blond curls bouncing around her creamy shoulders, chewed a wad of pink gum.

"Bourbon. Double. Straight up." Stella nodded.

"You got it." The waitress blew a bubble as she mixed the drink.

Stella leaned against the bar, eyeballing the front of the room, picking out her spot. Dead centre, front row, just below the lip, where she could drink in the leader of the wild show.

Body Count was wild. Aggressive. She'd been lured in by the high-voltage guitar riffs. Up there with the wildest metal riffs she'd ever heard. The lyrics had entranced her. Children of the Korn was crazy. She'd wished she could have seen one of the few live performances. These fusions of rap and metal produced some high-voltage guitar-meets-powerful-lyrics combinations. They were explosive. And short-lived.

She swallowed the bourbon. It burned all the way down her throat. Numbness rapidly spread through her arms.

The orange glow over the room morphed into a pink, blue, and purple glow. Golden spots dotted the full cosmic rainbow of lights. A warmth built within her, heating her core, blazing her heart. Tingles of happiness trickled through her. A glow emerged from within, trickling through her pores, shimmering over her s kin.

The waitress chewing the bubblegum appeared just as she was finishing the bourbon. She ordered another double, fully intending to finish it before the show started.

As she sipped the fresh drink, she took in the building crowd, inspecting individual members. She polished off the bourbon, set the glass on the counter, and made her way toward the colourful lights.

# Chapter 48

# Vintage

Lolita descended the stairs into the wild environment below. The heat from the basement seeped up the narrow staircase. Cosmic streams of light followed. She reached the last step and paused to take it all in.

Her eyes darted immediately to the elevated stage. A mist clouded the shiny instruments, glimmers catching off a glittering aqua drum set. Guitars and basses lined racks on both sides, their necks shimmering under the lights. The microphone, encrusted with gems, awaited upon its silver pedestal. The band must have undergone a makeover on their instruments. Lolita didn't recall the aqua glitter coat to the drums or the gems decorating the mic.

The room flickered. She caught her breath.

She scanned the room, regaining her bearings. *Vinyl.* Orson's big night.

Walking along the rear wall, Lolita inspected the crowd. Half of them wore black leather and chains. The other half was split between tattered jeans, tight tanks, and exuberant jewellery, and an array of ridiculous costumes. Right, it was Halloween. By the looks of the crowd, most of them were here for the music, not the party on the spooky holiday. The metal crowd presence was strong. Were these grunge addicts? Or had Orson added a metal edge to his new lyrics? She hadn't been to the last few rehearsals. They had taken an artistic direction without her.

The room flickered once again. It was as if the lights buzzed off then on again.

She shook her head. Maybe she just needed a drink to relax. Flush out her nerves.

As she headed toward the bar, a woman with cat ears approached.

"Pure love?" The woman's voice was nearly a purr. She pulled a bag from her pocket, revealing blue pills.

*Ecstasy.* Lolita had tried it when she was younger. She recalled it taking her into the most inviting dose of rootedness she'd ever experienced. Hell, why not? What was one extra pill in her tranquilizer, party drug, oxytocin cocktail. She needed to dissolve any anxiety clinging to her.

She nodded. Lolita passed her some bills. Sexy kitty placed the pills into Lolita's open palm, grazing her silky fingers across her skin as she pulled away.

Tingles crept up Lolita's arm. The cat woman smiled then walked off.

Lolita beelined to the bar.

A curvaceous woman in a leather corset leaned over the counter, which was slick with alcohol. "What can I get you, sweetie?" The bartender had an edge to her. Slight lines pulled at the corners of her eyes, yet she oozed a sultry, sexual vibe. Her skin was creamy and smooth.

Lolita usually stuck to her lemon balm tea. She bit her bottom lip.

The bartender rested her elbows on the counter, despite how sticky it looked. "How about a slime? Easy on the system. Vodka, soda, and lime." Her blonde curls fell over her shoulders as she chomped on a wad of pink gum. Strawberry perfume wafted across the bar.

"Sure. Thanks." Lolita relaxed her shoulders. A slime and some disco biscuits. She'd be calm in no time.

The bartender winked, then mixed the drink.

The room flickered again. A problem with the electricity? She hoped it didn't affect the show. She leaned an elbow on the counter and scanned the open floor covering half the venue. Front and dead centre. That's where she'd be when Orson made his entrance. Her body buzzed at the thought. She couldn't wait to drink him in.

"Here ya go, sweetie." The bartender slid a drink filled with ice toward her. "Take it easy."

As Lolita reached for the drink, she slid a couple bills across the counter. Her eye caught an earth-coloured birthmark above the bartender's right breast. Her skin was like milk.

The bartender snapped a pink bubble, sucked the gum into her mouth, then moved down the bar, taking her strawberry essence with her.

Lolita slipped the pills from her pocket and settled them on her tongue. She took a sip of the drink. A refreshing wave of citrus and sparkles cleansed her senses. It was like a tropical beach drink without the overwhelming sweetness.

She lingered, watching the stage. The crowd thickened, mostly hanging by the bar. A wiry young man with scraggly hair and tattered jeans moved from one piece of equipment to the next, sound-checking each one. She'd need to make her move soon.

"Another?" A strawberry wave pulled her attention across the bar.

She nodded. She enjoyed the drink. She liked the bartender.

"You be careful out there, sweetie." The bartender smiled as she slid the new drink toward Lolita.

Lolita smiled. "I will."

Drink in hand, she made her way toward the front. The front row was yet to be claimed. A woman in a leather jacket, strawberry-blonde curls falling softly on her shoulders, stood in the centre of the front row.

As the woman spun around, scanning the crowd with her drink in hand, Lolita's breath caught.

That face. Those eyes. She knew them.

It couldn't be.

The room flickered.

Lolita approached the woman, settling in slightly away from her.

She knew the woman. But she was sure the woman didn't know her.

## Chapter 49
# Killer Concert

The lights beamed in yellow and purple streams, stretching their dazzling rays over the room. The silhouette of the building crowd glowed under their reach. A drum beat vibrated, rumbling within Stella's heart. Electrifying excitement shot through her as she nestled at the lip of the stage, dead centre. Her heart soared. She closed her eyes and breathed in the essence of the moments before the show.

A finger brushed her arm. She opened her eyes. A woman with long, dark hair tinged with chocolate and woven into dreadlocks stared at her. Her olive skin glowed. Her rich brown eyes shimmered with golden dust under the everchanging lights. Stella was drawn in. The woman smiled, the skin on the left side of her mouth contorted and rough. Stella wondered what had happened to it as the woman's fingers lingered on her warm flesh.

"Seen them before?" she asked.

Stella shook her head as she returned the smile.

Tingles persisted on her skin as the woman dropped her hand to her side.

High-voltage electric vibes shot through the room with the beginning strums of the first riff of the night. Stella shifted her gaze, seeking its source. A woman, a rock goddess, emerged. Her leather-clad legs rippled with muscle as she made her stealth entrance. Her fingers worked the guitar strings like it was second nature. The riff heightened. The crowd erupted.

The first shot of metal heroine ripped through Stella's veins. A sense of relief followed. If this show didn't deliver, she didn't know what she would do.

In a flash, she was no longer on edge.

She eagerly devoured the guitar goddess as she whipped her luscious, golden locks, her fingers madly eating up the guitar strings, owning them.

An enticing aroma trickled from beside her. The woman with the olive skin sidled up next to her. She was devouring the guitar goddess with her eyes, just like Stella.

The voice. It was so pure. So smooth.

It jolted Stella from the aroma wafting from the woman beside her and forced her attention to the show.

A lean woman with spiked pink hair, chains around her neck, prowled across the stage, diamond-encrusted microphone in hand. Her pale fingers wrapped around the mic, black nails tapping to her rhyme. A roughness tinged the concluding words of each lyric, the smoothness returning on the next line. Nirvana. Pearl Jam. Grunge gods of the past whipped through Stella's mind. This rap-metal goddess rhymed like a grunge rocker. Her lyrics were intricately woven poetry. Stella hadn't listened to a lot of rap, but LL Cool J came to mind.

"Just like Kurt mixed with LL." Spice wafted. Chocolate locks shimmered under the lights.

This woman. It was like she'd read Stella's thoughts. Stella giggled. The aroma tickled her senses. Olive skin glowed. Golden sparkles glimmered. Everything inside of her warmed.

The singer leaned over the lip of the stage. Her pink hair looked delicious. Like cotton candy. Her eyes shimmered with silver. Her candy-pink lips matched her hair. Stella licked her own lips, wondering what the singer's tasted like.

The guitar goddess joined the singer. Her fingers flew, striking a mad riff. The lyrics exploded along with the electric guitar waves rippling through the room. The guitar goddess and the raw-edged rapper teetered over the edge of their pedestal, towering over Stella and the olive-skinned woman.

The pure love stirring within Stella fused with the quick, strong shots of bourbon. The room spun into a psychedelic stream of high-voltage metal with an edge.

The track ended. The crowd went wild.

Stella breathed in the scent of the olive-skinned woman, their arms touching as they both fixated on the show, waiting to devour the next morsel.

The lights changed to a red-orange glow. The lead singer pushed the mic close to her pink lips. She half-spoke, half-sang several lyrics. Her voice floated over the room. The smoothness eased through Stella. The roughness ignited her senses.

A sudden burst of electric guitar wailed through the room, pulling Stella the rest of the way down the metal high she'd been desperate to swallow.

The lead singer demonstrated her skill, weaving her voice in sync with the heightening voltage of the guitar riff. The guitar goddess sidled up to the singer, luscious hair mixing with the pink spikes in a cosmic blur to an orange-red backdrop. The guitar goddess squatted, her cherry-red guitar propped against black leather. The singer looked down at her, devouring the electric strums with her silver shimmering eyes. Sparkles from the diamonds on her rings shot glimmers through the room.

Stella drowned in the celestial array of lights. In the wails of the high-voltage guitar. In the hypnotic lyrics.

A tingle across her arm. The olive-skinned woman ran her nail along Stella's skin. The woman approached, wrapping herself around Stella as she fixated on the rap queen and guitar goddess.

"Another great. I knew he would be," the woman whispered.

*He?* Stella giggled. Her mind was fuzzy. She leaned into the warmth of the woman, the spicy scent hypnotizing her. She took a gulp of the enticing show and the hazy lights. She let go. All of it.

Her mind was free. Her body relaxed. She sunk into the warm arms of a stranger as she slipped into the depths of the wild rap-metal show. Her addiction. Her poison. Her relief.

# Chapter 50

# Strawberry-Whiskey Groupie

A drenaline rose through Lolita. The band launched into the next song. The guitar goddess strode across the stage, hair flowing. Her replacement. Lolita's insides curled into themselves as she watched the new guitarist of *Electric Skin* rip out an amazing riff.

The singer, her voice sweet yet untamed, echoed through the entire space. The woman with cotton-candy spikes walked to the front, clutching the gem-coated mic.

*Wait. Where's Orson?*

The silky voice entranced Lolita. She stood stunned, watching the pink lips move. The singer reached the edge, towered over the crowd, and wove her story through their ears. The guitar goddess sidled up next to the singer, her fingers flying over electric guitar strings. The lethal combination drowned the room in savage energy with a drop of sweetness.

Lolita looked into the singer's striking emerald eyes.

The room flickered.

The yellow, purple, pink, and blue lights blurred into a psychedelic rainbow. Warmth rose up Lolita's body. She closed her eyes and breathed deeply.

She tilted her head back, her face directly toward the show. She opened her eyes. Orson stared down at her, his emerald eyes piercing straight into her soul. His lips formed precise movements, each word a critical piece to a line. Each line essential to the rhyme. His silky voice took on a rough edge at the end of each phrase.

It was an exact replica of how she'd performed it when she shared it with the band. He'd taken it. He'd made it his own.

She should be on fire with rage.

Her disco-biscuit-laced slime ride filled her with love and warmth. He sounded good. Too good. She could have him tonight. As many times as she wanted. She could lose herself in those emerald eyes as she pressed her hot, sweaty body against his.

That's what she wanted. She'd support his dream.

The song ended. Orson stepped to the rear. The guitar assumed control.

Lolita drank the rest of the citrus slime. She glanced to her right. The strawberry blonde stood close, gazing at the guitar goddess. That face. She knew it was *her.*

Images of shows from the past flickered through her mind. The tasty treat, hovering in the front row, drinking Orson in, show after show, buying him drinks.

Lolita should be burning with anger.

Her love-drug-vodka cocktail was taking her on a pure-love wave.

All control gone, her earthy rootedness steered her in another direction. She'd take this delectable treat for one hell of a ride. Orson would love it. He'd love her to a greater extent.

As Orson's voice captivated the crowd, Lolita hung close to the strawberry groupie. She brushed her hip against the groupie's leg. The woman didn't retreat. She returned Lolita's taunting gaze.

Lolita reached out and ran her finger down the woman's arm. The woman's skin, soft to the touch, ignited a spark in Lolita's heart. The woman moved to the music, her strawberry-blonde curls whirling around her. Lolita caught the aroma of flowers and whiskey.

Lolita's body burned with desire. The pills. The vodka. Right. She exhaled, willing her body and her mind to go with the ride.

The show continued. The faces blurred under the psychedelic light show. The emerald eyes the only thing in focus, other than the intoxicating woman beside her.

As the final song came to a close, the emerald eyes ate her up. His words pierced her soul.

*Love-morphed box... I'd die to swallow... Bring you home...*

She slipped her hand into the woman's and ran her fingers over soft skin.

She breathed in the essence of the lead singer, the electrifying atmosphere, and the flower-whiskey woman.

The song ended. The crowd screamed. Lolita pulled the woman's arm gently, leading her across the floor, down a hallway, and toward the series of doors on the backstage area.

She'd create her own destiny. Her dreams crushed, she'd jump on the Orson ride to fame.

# Chapter 51

# Riding the Pure-Love Wave

A luscious apartment spread out in front of her. Lolita caught her breath as she stepped through the hallway leading from the front door into a large living space. It must belong to one of the new members of Electric Skin. She was still jolted by the band changes, but she was intrigued enough to go along with it. Dark-blue paint smoothed over the walls. An elaborate mural etched in gold and silver spread over the entire ceiling. Orange flames licked the walls of a brick fireplace. A creamy fur rug spread out on the floor, concealing the space between several couches and chairs, all clothed in burgundy velour.

The vodka-ecstasy pure-love ride had taken her into a cosmic swirl of movement.

Lolita hung back, scanning the group now. The woman with the golden hair, images of her magic fingers strumming the electric guitar strings in a manic motion as her muscular, leather-clad legs rooted her to the stage. Orson's emerald eyes scanning the room like each and every one of the afterparty guests could be his prey. His pale skin taking on an orange hue as the flames danced wildly in the fireplace. The strawberry-whiskey groupie treat. *Yes.* Lolita could still feel the supple skin of the strawberry-blonde woman under the touch of her own finger as she traced it down the woman's arm. She longed for another whiff of the fruity aura with a smoky tinge. She bet this groupie treat was genuinely sweet with a slight burn. She could understand why Orson succumbed to her, paying attention to her after shows, letting her buy him drinks.

Tonight, the hurt and the anger were gone. She only experienced warmth and pure love. She would be the one to facilitate as the evening unfolded. She would be the one targeted by those striking emerald eyes at the end of the party.

The room filled with a multitude of different visitors. Lolita barely noticed them. She focused on the woman, and Orson. She followed Orson with her eyes as he walked over to a shiny CD player placed on the wall opposite the fireplace. He ran his finger along a selection of CDs lined up perfectly on a shelf and pulled one out. As he slid the silver disc from the plastic case, glimmers of yellow and orange danced off the disc like coloured diamonds. He slid the CD into the player and pressed play. The room came alive in an instant.

It was a special track. One that meant a lot to her. To *them*. Kurt's raw-edged voice ripped through the room.

The partygoers danced, their hands swaying in the air, their hips moving to the beat. Jackets flew around the room, landing on the burgundy-velour furniture. Scantily-clad women slithered over the creamy fur rug.

Orson moved a glass coffee table out of the way, creating a full dance floor.

He seemed so familiar with this space. Had he been here before? Had she?

Her mind contorted slightly. The room exuded a slight flicker.

Before she could follow her thoughts, seeking to put the pieces of this picture together, a wave of warmth surged within her. Tingles of love erupted from her feet, up her legs, through every place of pleasure in her body. The vodka-ecstasy ride heightened, out of control. She giggled and walked over to a table beside the CD player, where the guitar goddess was lining up bottles and glasses. She wasn't willing to surrender this warm, loving feeling inside of her. Not yet.

As she approached the golden-haired guitarist, tingles of pleasure pricked her arms. "This is a lovely party," she managed in a soft voice.

The guitar goddess faced her, her earthy eyes inviting. "We love sharing our space." She smiled.

Lolita's insides melted.

"Drink?" the woman asked.

Lolita nodded.

The woman filled a glass with ice, bubbles, and sweet-smelling alcohol. She handed it to Lolita.

Lolita took a sip. Fruit-filled bubbles tickled her tongue. "Delicious."

"My special concoction." The woman winked.

The guitar goddess mixed herself a drink. She raised her glass to Lolita, took a sip that seemed to last forever, and reached out her hand. "Shall we?"

Lolita let her take her hand and lead her to the makeshift dance floor. Lolita moved to the music, her hips swaying, her free arm flying, her other hand raising the fruity bubbles to her lips every few moments.

Out of the corner of her eye, she could see Orson. He was walking around the room, drink in hand, inspecting the scene. He always did like to be on the periphery, somehow controlling the scene from the outskirts. She felt his eyes all over her. Exploring her body, searching extensively inside her head, trying to read her thoughts. He might be surprised to know what she was thinking right now. She was done with the anxiety. She was deep in this pure-love ride, and her whole body was on fire with desire.

She found his gaze as her body moved to the music, her dreadlocks flowing around her exposed shoulders. His eyes bore into her. She slowed her movements, returning the intensity of his stare. He had her locked in. He reached out his hand and beckoned her to him. She couldn't resist. She didn't want to.

The passionate urge surging up her insides burst into a full-on flame. He led her with his movements, with his mind, out of the glowing room. She followed him down a hallway, into another room.

As she walked through the open door, an exquisite room opened before her. A crystal chandelier hung from a high ceiling painted in red with golden swirls. Another fire burned in a stone fireplace to the right. A private bar spanned the wall to the left, housing crystal glassware and expensive-looking liquors. A bed with intricately-carved posts perched in the centre of the room. A lace sheet fell in delicate folds, creating a separation between the room and the centre of the bed.

Lolita stood, stunned, holding her nearly empty glass.

Orson walked up to her, took the glass, and set it on a side table. He took her hand. Lustful tingles erupted up her fingers, weaving over her arm. She swallowed. She looked into his eyes. The hypnotizing emerald gems that had a hold on her the second she saw them. That seemed like a lifetime ago. Now, they were familiar. They still excited her. Yet, she felt a sense of calm, safety, and comfort when she stared into them.

He led her to the bed, moved aside the lace, and guided her down gently. She fell into the luscious arms of the softest duvet she'd ever felt. It was like a massive cloud, drawing her towards its core. She succumbed.

Orson leaned over her, finding her eyes with his.

She looked into the emerald gems without retreating, physically or emotionally.

He was hers. She was sure of it. The star-dusted dream that had been theirs was now his. But it wasn't his alone. He'd take her with him, wherever he went.

The pure-love wave fuelled by the vodka-ecstasy-fruit-bubble cocktail she'd been drinking in all night swelled within her. She let go, riding it with every part of her mind, body, and soul.

# Chapter 52
# Endless Pure-Love Wave

Orson led her out of the extravagant bedroom, to the living room. The party was alive. It was a parallel to her physical, mental, and spiritual beings. Her entire body was electric with warmth, energy, love. The private show Orson gave her in the bedroom was like no other she'd ever experienced.

She lost herself in his eyes as he explored her body. Yet, he seemed different somehow. Her heart palpitated at the thought that he'd changed. He wasn't going to discard her as her words slurred and her lip drooped. He was going to take her to the top with him.

He guided her into the living room. The attendance had dwindled. A few partygoers danced lazily near the bar, a chill tune seeping from the speakers. The guitar goddess stretched out in an erotic pose over the fur rug. The flames of the fire flickered over her body. Her golden locks and skin shimmered under their glow. The groupie treat sprawled over the couch. Her strawberry-blonde curls spread over the burgundy velour. An invigorating wave of desire surged within Lolita. She couldn't believe she still had lust lurching inside. Not after the performance Orson had just conducted, her body his instrument.

She hovered at the edge of the room, moving toward the bar on the far side. Maybe one more drink would keep her on this ride a bit longer.

Before she could lift a bottle, Orson guided her over to the rug. He nodded at the guitar goddess, then at the whiskey treat.

What was this? He wanted *her* to indulge? He was holding back. For now. He was *including* her. She knew it. He was hers.

Excitement prevailed. Every part of her screamed to touch the whiskey treat. What would it feel like to claim Orson's groupie as hers?

She released her hand from Orson's as she stared into his eyes. She licked her lips. He watched, eyes burning with desire.

She set her gaze on the whiskey treat, willing the woman to pay attention to her.

Blue eyes met hers. She had her.

Holding the gaze of the woman, Lolita crouched on the rug and crawled her way over to the guitar goddess. As she stared into the eyes of Orson's groupie, she ran her hands over the supple skin of the guitarist. The guitarist responded, stretching her arms over her head, writhing against the fur.

Lolita's insides exploded with desire. Not only did she want to know what it felt like to take Orson's groupie, to be in control, she wanted to *feel* the touch of these women. She *needed* to know what it felt like to take them to the utmost place of pleasure.

Lolita lowered her face toward the golden locks and brushed her lips against the guitar goddess's cherry-red mouth. The desire within threatened to burst.

She crawled on all fours over to the whiskey treat, still watching her, lust glimmering in her eyes. Lolita crawled up her body, straddled her, and gently caressed her arms. The whiskey treat responded. Her head fell against the couch. Lolita lingered long enough to ensure control. She retreated, guiding the whiskey treat over to the rug. Rejoining the guitar goddess, whiskey treat in hand, the energy of the three melded.

Lolita scanned the perimetre. Orson prowled, walking slyly along the outline of the rug. Despite the plethora of treats in the room, he devoured her with his eyes. His fixation on her only heightened her sexual hunger. Ravenous for more, she returned her attention to the duo she had brought together. The guitar goddess guided the whiskey treat, laying her down on soft fur. She brushed her fingers over her arms and legs, removing her clothing piece by piece.

Lolita advanced for the kill.

She leaned over and slipped her fingers underneath the outline of the whiskey treat's sheer panties. She slid them down her legs. The whiskey treat pulled her legs into her chest, allowing Lolita to slide the panties down. Lolita tossed them aside. The guitar goddess leaned over, planting kisses up the whiskey treat's arms. Lolita spread her legs and brushed the outline of the whiskey treat's pleasure spot with her lips. The woman arched her back and released soft moans from her pink lips. Her cheeks flushed. She closed her eyes.

Lolita continued to migrate her lips until she achieved the ultimate response from the woman. As she devoured Orson's treat, making the groupie hers, Orson prowled, still devouring her with his emerald eyes.

# Chapter 53
# Sneaky Treat Retreat

Lolita slipped out the door, hand in hand with Orson, casting another glance over the afterparty scene.

The room flickered in and out. The vodka-ecstasy-fruit-bubble ride receding quickly, the world around had started the strange flickering not long ago. She'd awoken, curled in a ball on the rug next to the guitar goddess and the whiskey treat.

She'd prowled through the apartment searching for Orson. He was in the bed in the red-and-gold room.

As the flickering world around her clouded her senses, confusion blurred her mind. Things felt off-kilter. She knew if she could get Orson home to the askew little house, everything would be fine. She'd snuck into the room without waking him and slipped a shot of her tranquilizer concoction into his veins. It would be best if he would follow her home without a fuss.

She clicked the door shut carefully.

Slipping down the hall and out of the building, pulling Orson by his hand, she glanced around the empty streets. It was late. Even the partygoers had all gone to bed. As her shoulders relaxed, she took a deep breath of the chill night air and walked briskly toward her house.

She told Orson how fantastic his show had been. He perked up, sharing her excitement. They talked about the greatest rhymers, fusion of genres, and what they could do.

As the air scraped icy fingers across her face, she narrowed her eyes and contemplated his words. Even after his big performance, could she still feel the limelight too? Could the dream that was supposed to be *theirs* still come true?

As the fissure had cracked, it reached its broken fingers over her brain. She had trouble controlling her emotions. Her face pulled in strange ways. Her lip drooped. Her words slurred. Her rhymes rotted. *Electric Skin* had thrust Orson into the limelight for every track they were laying down on the streams of tape. She felt out of place, even in the basement of her own home, in her own studio.

Her only chance to stay on the star-dusted path was to support Orson with every particle of her being. To be devoted to him and his success. Clinging to the hope that by the time they made it to the big cities, her condition would simmer, her skin would return to its flawless state. Her rhymes would glisten again.

A horn honked, yanking her from her reverie. She jumped back, watching a car speed by. She stood for a moment, getting her bearings. She was only a couple blocks away. She continued walking, letting her thoughts wander again.

That night. The performance. Orson.

Their gazes met, his emerald eyes piercing her soul. He was hers. Tonight, they'd have their own perfect performance.

THRASH METAL
MURDER

# Chapter 54

# The Performance

The basement studio vibrated with the sounds flowing from the control room into the recording space. The tape replayed the rhymes.

Lolita sat within the comfort of the recording space, headphones secured tightly around her ears, pushing away her dreadlocks. Settled in her favourite wooden chair, she tapped her foot to the beat of the rhymes, examining each word as it resounded back to her. Her artistic energy alive and seething through her veins, she slipped her piece of Orson over her right hand.

It fit her like a glove.

Like it was always hers. Like it was a part of her. His hand was now her hand. It was always meant to be, and now it was happening.

She stretched her fingers. The skin, his skin, became hers.

He'd stolen her rhymes, taken the lead, guided *their* band away from her. Despite her all-consuming loyalty, he'd dipped right into that groupie treat waiting for him by the bar, discarding her like she was nothing.

Tonight, she'd felt his power for the first time. She'd made his groupie entirely hers. She licked her lips, the taste of the whiskey treat still lingering. Desire simmered within her body. The power now surging within her dominated, drowning out her sexual desire. It was time to choose control.

Flexing her new fingers again, she picked up a charcoal pencil, opened her notebook to a blank page and began writing. Her fingers flew. The pencil etched line after line, scrawling down the page. The rhymes that were always within her flowed freely. The rhymes that needed the power he'd taken from her to surface.

Several pages in, the words slowed, then halted.

She read them carefully, her lips making overstated movements. It was the best she'd ever written.

It was time for *the performance.*

She slid off her muse and perched it on its designated stand. Examining the stitching down each side, how subtle it was, she admired her work. She grabbed the book and walked over to the microphone.

Orson was finally in his rightful place as her backup singer, where he belonged. The room flickered.

Cotton-candy spikes appeared then disappeared. A young female face—emerald eyes filled with fear—was there, then wasn't.

Lolita shook her head.

The room flickered again.

She blinked hard several times. When she opened her eyes, Orson sat in the chair, hovering over the mic, waiting for his chance to sing. Ready to back her up.

She took a deep breath, refocusing in her basement studio, with her backup singer, prepared to perform her rhymes fresh off the press.

The words hung in her mind. She didn't need the book. She'd set it up anyways. This had to be perfect. After getting it in an ideal position, opened to the new rhymes, she walked into the control room. She leaned over the ADAT controls and pushed *RECORD* four times to cycle through to the FAd4 setting. At just over forty-two milliseconds, the setting allowed for a *slapback* delay to produce a single echo. It made the rhymes sound more *live.* The way Lolita preferred them. She clicked the system to a live feed, then returned to the recording room.

She walked right up to Orson and faced him.

"Get it right this time. It's *important.*" She smiled.

She could swear there was fear in the heart of those emerald gems. Why would he be afraid? Only hours ago, he'd rambled on about the new musical direction as they'd walked along Electric Avenue hand in hand. Didn't he want this?

She refocused her gaze, seeking the meaning behind his expression. His face softened. The wrinkles around his eyes vanished. He smiled. He nodded his head toward her place in the studio.

As she positioned herself, standing in front of the main microphone, she could swear a muffled sound cried in the crevices of her mind. She shook her head again. *No.* She wouldn't let this *condition* that her sorry excuse for a mother had imposed upon her take over. *She* was in control tonight.

After several long strokes of the scarf she always tied to the microphone when she performed, she hovered her lips close to the silver bulb. Letting her body move to the rhythm of the background tracks playing from the control room, she felt each beat, waiting for the right one.

The first word slipped from her mouth in perfect time to the exact beat it belonged to.

The words flowed freely after that. She rhymed like she'd never rhymed before. The lines fell into place, weaving in faultless symmetry to the beat. Every pulse was in sync with her heartbeat. The performance blossomed to perfection.

The skin on the left side of her mouth itched. The droop pulled.

The word forming on her lips slurred.

She froze.

Her eyes snapped open. She willed her lips to keep moving. They did. The words slurred into an incomprehensible blur. Frustration gripped her. Her emotions boiled over.

She snapped her lips closed. She clawed at the contorted skin on the side of her mouth. Grabbing the headphones, she yanked them off, pulling her dreadlocks in a wild toss. She threw the headphones across the room. They crashed against the glass then bounced across the floor. She yanked the mic stand in a wild dance and threw it to the ground. It hit with a deafening *crack,* a fissure forming in the silver bulb.

*Dammit. Broken.* Just like her brain.

"Why?" she screamed, grasping her coiled twists of hair with her trembling hands. She fell to her knees. Hot tears sprung from her eyes, drizzling down her face, searing her contorted skin. Her brain buzzed with a million images, morphing into a flickering horror show, playing the same night over and over.

*Why.* Why couldn't she get it right? It didn't make any sense. The night had been perfect. She'd taken Orson's groupie. She'd taken him. Made them both her own.

She'd taken his hand, made it hers, owning the power within it. The rhymes were perfect.

She wasn't.

# Chapter 55

# What the Fuck?

A gentle ray of sunshine poked through the window into Stella's bedroom. She opened one eye. She moaned.

*What the fuck happened?*

She opened her other eye and rolled onto her back, slipping the covers down to her chin.

*What time is it?*

She tilted her head toward the nightstand. The clock radio said 10:30.

*What day is it?*

Monday. The day she was supposed to back off the *Skin Peeler* case.

She bolted upright. Her head thrummed. Heat surged through her body.

*Vinyl.* The woman with the olive skin and spicy scent. The guitar goddess with golden hair. The cotton-candy-haired rapper. Their faces swam through her mind. She flopped down, her head hitting the pillow.

*What. The. Fuck.*

Of all the booze-sex-metal benders she'd been on, this had to be the most lavish afterparty deluxe she'd ever experienced. She closed her eyes and pieced together the evening. The pills from the cat woman at the joint. The double bourbons. Cheap. Strong. The lights. The cosmic swirl of colours. The killer show. The combination of the guitar goddess and the raw-edged singer taking Stella's live show high into another realm. One she'd never known.

Stella laid down, closed her eyes, and relished in the lingering desire burning within her.

They'd stayed together at the front for the entire show. They'd made their way backstage after the encore. Giggling like a schoolgirl, Stella had walked into the afterparty, arm in arm with her new friend. Like they'd been best friends for life. Something had felt so *right* about it.

Stella chuckled to herself. Of course it did. That's what an ecstasy-bourbon cocktail did.

The olive-skinned woman taking her hand at the end of the encore, leading her backstage. The heat of her touch igniting a desire within Stella that she could barely recall ever feeling.

The afterparty. The den of the guitar goddess and the edgy lead singer.

The woman's lips brushing hers. The genuine, earthy love seeping from her pores, reaching into Stella's.

The touch of the guitar goddess's lips against her skin.

It was wild. Crazy. There had been something dangerous about it. That appearance of darkness in the olive-skinned woman's eyes.

Stella sat up. She was reading too extensively into it. Everything had been closing in on her. Her mother. Tad. Sutton. Her need to blow off steam was on the verge of bursting. She'd gone a bit far. That's all.

She wouldn't let a night of love and desire, something she hadn't felt in a long time, if ever, sour. It was pure. It was honest. It was simply a night of women enjoying music and each other.

A sense of a fresh start simmered within her. The crazy bender was what she'd needed. No more toying with the idea of an off-the-books hunt. No further staring into the dark core of her murder wall.

She slipped out of bed and headed for the shower.

She needed to get her act together. Now.

She had a *Skin Peeler* to catch.

She refused to let the case go cold.

# Chapter 56
# Thrilling Commute

An angelic-metal voice reached every corner of Stella's Sunfire. The vocals mixed with old-school dramatic guitar wails had her heart. *Jet City Woman. Queensrÿche.* It was a track that trickled nostalgia through her veins. As the rock god sung of a woman's face that invaded his every thought, she wondered if Tad was thinking about her. She stepped on the gas, blazing through the belly of the city. Late morning, before the lunch rush in the downtown core, left the streets wide open. The speed at which she was closing in on HQ thrilled her.

She could do this. No more hunting. Stick to metal when she needed a release.

The images of last night simmered in her mind, leaving tingles in her arms, between her legs. What was the harm?

As the glass towers vanished, clusters of industrial buildings appeared along the sides of the freeway. She'd be there in ten minutes. Her mind whirled, already in investigative overdrive.

She refused to let the *Skin Peeler* case go cold. To let a killer run free. To risk another victim appearing in her city with a skinless hand clutching a book. Glassy, lifeless eyes staring at a message written in blood ink.

Sutton ordered them, or at least her, to take the day off. He'd said they would regroup tomorrow. *Regroup. Reprioritize. Reassign.* She wanted none of it.

If she truly cared about catching this killer, she would do everything she could.

She'd re-examine the evidence. She'd revisit her profiling board. She'd go over everything with a meticulous eye. There had to be something they missed. There had to be a way to weave evidence and behaviour into a concrete lead. *There must be.*

Stella settled into the seat and scanned the open road. The next exit would take her to HQ. Anxious about what she'd find there, or who, she swallowed the fear she'd be reassigned. Wasn't she the difficult one? Had it finally caught up with her? Her purple rabbit's foot dangled in her thoughts. Sutton had such a belief in her instinct. He wouldn't reassign her. She'd been the only one to come up with anything that might lead someone on this case. Without any suspects, she was grasping.

She lost herself in the final strums of high-voltage guitar and tried to free her mind of thoughts other than a killer who was peeling the skin off his victims.

# Chapter 57

# Solo Investigation

Stella wove her way through the clutter of cubicles. The majority of them were empty. Parker's desk was vacant. So was Jake's. Maybe she *had* read too much into Sutton's orders. It seemed like he really had told them *all* to take the day off while resources were re-organized.

A faint aroma of anxiety and cheap coffee still clung to the room, despite its lack of inhabitants. It took more than a day to get rid of the odour of detectives.

Slipping her leather coat off, she hung it over her chair. Coffee thermos in hand, she grabbed a folder and her notebook, then headed for the stuffy war room.

After a hot shower, releasing the lingering high of the night before, she'd consumed several glasses of ice-cold water. It cleansed her internals. The thrumming in her head subsided. She'd taken the time to brew a pot of stiff coffee. High-quality espresso. She was shocked to find a bag remaining in the corner of one the cupboards in her kitchen. Today was not a day for budget-friendly homicide coffee.

Reaching the war room, she swung the door open. Slipping the thermos under her arm, she found the switch on the wall and clicked the lights to life. Buzzing followed by a fluorescent glow breathed life into the abandoned room. The detective odour was at a bearable low. She slid a stopper under the door with her foot, hoping to keep the room from closing in on her in a hot flash.

Slapping the folder and notebook onto the centre table spanning the length of the room, she walked over to the corner table, thermos in hand. The mugs were pitiful. She selected a chipped cream-coloured mug with the *Calgary Homicide* logo plastered on the front. The *'o'* and the second *'i'* were missing, leaving *'H mic de'*. It sounded like the name of a rap star. She chuckled to herself as she filled the mug with a healthy pour of espresso from the thermos, then walked over to the crime scene wall.

As she sipped the potent brew, she carefully inspected each of the photos lined up, forming the story of two crime scenes.

After a break, with fresh eyes, the similarities between the two victims remained striking. She hadn't over-amplified it in her mind. Two nearly identical displays. The emerald eyes. The almost bleached-blond hair. The contours of the face. The bone structure. The wiry, yet muscular, build. The clothing. That shiny shirt.

The hands.

If you looked at the closeups of the two separate hands, you'd swear they were the same. The skin peeled away in two sheets, the bloody flesh exposed, white cartilage over bone, clutching the book as if it was the most prized possession of each victim.

A loud ticking interrupted her examination. The clock high on the front wall revealed that it was nearly noon. She had fewer than twenty-four hours to put this together. A deadline that she'd imposed. If she didn't want to be *reassigned,* then she needed to find something to move this investigation forward.

The profiling board she'd created remained intact at the front of the room. She examined it. The victim type was dead on. If a third body appeared, she was certain it would further confirm it.

The first victim had a sparse *history.* His circle of friends was small. Work and poetry slams. The second victim was still unidentified. The situation reminded Stella of the cold cases plastered to her murder wall in her apartment. She'd have to go to the *secondary* or *outer* circle of the first victim to attempt to identify any suspects.

She grabbed a yellow marker, snapped the cap off, and wrote underneath the *Victim Type* details: *Secondary Circle.* She'd return to that.

She moved on to *The Trophy.* Glaringly obvious, it was the skin. She could only imagine what someone would do with two sheets of skin. Was it connected to the writing of the message? The grisly case of Ed Gein resurfaced in her mind. The Butcher of Plainfield. He had a slew of keepsakes made of human skin. She shuddered. The flesh from the hands had to play some critical part in what this killer was doing.

She moved her gaze further down the board. *Fantasy.* The first victim was a poet. He would have written his lyrics with his own hand. The skin was somehow symbolic to the killer. Was the killer a poet? Nothing had come up in the investigation to indicate that anyone in the victim's life had any reason to kill him. The killer might have chosen the victim to replace someone from his past. She'd read about this in other cases. Ted Bundy had a strong victim type. Petite brunettes. Early twenties. All reminiscent of the college girlfriend who rejected him. The Cross-Country Killer, Glen Edward Rogers, was convicted of killing three strawberry-blonde women. As a baby, he would rock himself violently and uncontrollably, falling off chairs and banging his head. His red-haired mother had punched him in the head as a toddler.

Something Tank had said grabbed at her thoughts. Stella grabbed her notes, spread out next to the case file. He'd mentioned brain damage and the use of oxytocin. Ed Gein had been beaten by his father. The blows to his head could have caused his lazy eye and speech impediment. There had also been the Yorkshire Ripper, Peter Sutcliffe. It was suspected that his inherent killer instinct had been sparked by the brain damage he suffered while on an incubator as a newborn baby.

Maybe Parker was right. They could be looking at someone with brain damage.

She clenched her jaw and glared at her profiling board. *Trophy. Fantasy.*

Poetry. Books. Lyrics. What did this have to do with the ultimate event that the killer was trying to recreate? If the *Skin Peeler* was using the skin of the hand, it might have something to do with the writing of the message. If he was trying to replace someone, was this person a poet?

Stella walked over to the wall. Both bodies had been dumped in alleys. Behind places they had never been seen in. Cheetahs. Used to be the Westward. Coconut Rum. Used to be Sparky's.

Stella's train of thought clicked into place. That was it. The message. It wasn't a poem. What if the words written in blood were song lyrics?

Maybe they'd been thrown off by *The Mint* and the poetry slam. Maybe the victims were musicians. Something could have happened at both music venues when they were still thriving.

She ambled over to the files spread over the table. None of the physical evidence had led anywhere. They needed an initial list of suspects to whittle down the hundreds of names of those who had contact with fibre optic cables. The notebook was composed of common paper. The victims had been pumped full of party drugs and other substances that almost anyone could get their hands on. The only one that stuck out was the oxytocin.

She could overlay the musician spin on all of this.

Maybe she should call Jake. She knew he'd come in if she asked him. Sutton might have a problem with that. Stella wasn't sure she should fuck with him now when she was teetering precariously toward *reassignment*.

*The trace. The tiny, shimmering trace.* The one she'd found on the second victim. The one she'd given to Bryce.

She set her coffee on the table with a clank and snapped her phone open. It rang several times. No answer.

*Dammit.* She was on her own. It was up to her to weave her amateur criminal profiling skills with her rookie detective skills.

# Chapter 58

# Walkman

The day had been never-ending, despite the late start.

Fatigue weighed Stella's eyelids. Her brain was grinding to a halt. She was sucked dry of any new ideas. No leads had come of her solo investigation. No suspects.

She walked through the door to her apartment. Stopping herself from instinctively tossing her keys into the red glass bowl, she placed them carefully on the colourful glass. She didn't want anymore damage to it.

As she walked into the living room, she slipped her leather coat off and let it fall onto the couch. She followed it, crumpling into a ball in the cavern worn into the middle cushion. A subtle yellow-orange glow peeked through the window from the streetlight below. The sky had darkened several shades on her drive home. The stars fought to outshine the city lights. It was pretty. Almost tranquil.

Yet turmoil roiled in the pit of Stella's belly. Desperation clouded her mind.

She'd been sure she would find something today that would prevent this case from imploding.

She sighed, eyeballing the half-empty bottle of bourbon perched on the glass coffee table. Her appetite for the caramel-coated numbness had vanished.

With a heavy sigh, she walked over to the shelves of CDs lining the far wall. Minutes passed. Nothing caught her eye. Had her appetite for bedtime metal also dissolved?

If that was the case, things were bleak.

A thought popped into her head.

She walked to her bedroom, flicking off the lights along the way. Her dark apartment settled into a deep quiet. She stepped over to her bed, slid off her pants and her shirt, then made her way to the closet. Crouching, she rustled through boxes in the corner of the closet. Finding the one on her mind, she pulled it out and lifted the lid.

There it was. Right where she'd left it.

The neon-pink Walkman she'd bought with her chore money at Sam's Swap. About a dozen plastic cassette cases in various states of cracked disrepair crowded around it. She pulled out the Walkman and earphones, then shuffled through the cassette cases.

*Skid Row* dripped down the cassette cover in bold red letters. A group of long-haired rockstars walked across the pavement in the dark shadows.

After her mother had sat her down the day her dad died and told her the news, she'd bolted from her mother's reaching arms and ran out of the house. Straight to Sam's Swap. She'd bought the tape, the lettering calling to her. Since that night, metal was the only thing that was a guarantee to relax her. Put her to sleep.

She walked to her bed with the Walkman and cassette.

After settling into a cozy cocoon underneath the soft duvet, she placed the spongy earphones over her ears. She opened the cassette case with caution, not wanting to inflict further damage upon it. She slid the cassette out and into the Walkman. With a series of *clicks,* she manoeuvred the fast forward, rewind, and play buttons like an expert. When she found the beginning of the fourth track, *Piece of Me,* she clicked play.

A punch-you-in-the-gut guitar riff whipped through her insides. The angelic-with-a-rough-edge voice of one of the greatest metal singers of all time, Sebastian Bach, wove through her ears to the pit of her belly.

She laid against the pillow, letting the familiar sounds and words take her to another place. Another time. Back to 1993, when all she did was listen to her Walkman and miss her dad. The idea of becoming a detective didn't exist. She was a teenager on the exterior, an old, wounded soul on the interior.

Not much had changed. Her love for metal. Her fights with her mother. How much she missed her father. Her loneliness.

The only thing different now was that she was a detective. Or trying to be.

And she had the resources to execute the outlets she needed. The metal benders. The hunts. Although, the ability to hunt was vanishing quickly. It might already be gone.

She picked up the case, settled on her duvet, and slid the insert from the plastic. She used to love getting a new cassette. Or at least one that was new to her. She'd bought most of them from Sam's Swap. She would run home, hide in her room, put the tape in, press play, then thoroughly examine the insert. The photos of dangerous-looking metal gods. The artwork. The lettering. The words to the songs, sometimes. The bios of the mystery men crooning smooth metal.

She rubbed her fingers over the thick card stock. Smooth. Heavy.

She bolted upright. Unfolding the insert, she felt the weight of it between her fingers.

It felt familiar. Too familiar. Like she'd had a recent experience with it even though she hadn't purchased a cassette tape for years.

She pressed stop on the Walkman, tossed it aside with the earphones, then leapt out of the bed. Pulling her pants and shirt on in haste, she slid the insert into the case, sprinting to the living room, case in hand.

She had missed something.

Only because she questioned thoughts that kept surfacing in her mind. Thoughts born from the instinct in the pit of her gut.

# Chapter 59

# Late-Night Trace

S tella strode from her Sunfire to the doors of HQ. She'd bolted from her apartment, cassette case in hand. There had been no time for sleep.

It was just after four o'clock in the morning. The sky was dark. The stars were on full blast. The city lights didn't drain them of their power this far into the industrial zone of the city.

She sprinted straight for the evidence room. Finding the two boxes securing the physical evidence from the scenes left by the *Skin Peeler,* she slipped a bag from each. Bags containing the books left in the victims' skinless hands.

The books had been thoroughly processed. They'd been touched by several members of Sutton's squad, searching for clues. Nothing had surfaced.

Now, Stella took the bagged books to her desk. She sat and pulled both from the bags. She lined them up on her desk, next to the cassette insert she'd brought from home. Her desk lamp cast a gentle glow over the lineup. The rest of the office was dark and quiet.

She ran her pointer and thumb down the cassette insert. Then she repeated the same motion along the cover of each book. She was certain of it. The paper was the same.

Why would someone use the same paper used for cassette inserts to cover a book? Was this a custom job by the killer?

She picked up the phone on her desk and dialled. What were the chances a chemist was up at this hour?

He answered the call on the second ring. "Bryce Klein."

"Bryce. It's Detective Mahoney." Relief washed through her. If he was up, maybe he'd be willing to run a rush job.

"Mahoney. I was about to call you. About that trace you left me."

"Really?" Her arms tingled.

"Yeah, I got called in early to do a rush trace. Noticed your results are in. Fe203. Gamma ferric oxide. A magnetic material. And polyester-based plastic."

"Can you send a copy of the report to my analyst Jake?" She knew he'd get on it as soon as he got to his desk.

"Of course."

"Listen, I know it's a lot to ask…" She bit her lower lip.

"I can do another trace."

"It's not a trace. I need a chemical analysis of paper."

"Paper?"

"Yeah. I want to know if it matches the cover on the books left in the victims' hands." She clenched her jaw. Was it a long shot? The manual comparison told her it wasn't. So did the pulsing in her gut.

"Easy."

"How quick?"

"For you? Now. Takes an hour, tops."

"Really?"

"Yeah. The trace I was called in for is processing. Nothing for me to do but wait."

The pitter-patter of her heart slowed. Beads of sweat trickled down the nape of her neck. "Great. On my way."

# Chapter 60
## Fresh Start

As she reached the last stair, Lolita stepped down into her recording studio. After walking home along Electric Avenue, hand in hand with Orson, they had holed up in the basement studio all night and most of the day. Despite his newfound support for her lead role in their innovative musical direction, she couldn't get it right. Every time she rhymed off several lines to perfection, her lip would catch, ruining the total track.

After what felt like a million takes, she had an epiphany. She'd walked right up to Orson and stared straight into his emerald eyes. It was *him*.

She wasn't certain why, but he'd gone silent. He kept missing his beats, failing her as a backup singer. Even when she pushed at his shoulders, he sat there unresponsive.

She was done.

He had to go.

After clearing out the basement studio of the dead weight, she'd taken a brisk walk down Electric Avenue. The brilliant lights and electric energy infused her with fresh vibes and a burst of creative energy. She'd rushed home and come straight down to the studio.

She would do this by herself. The gold-dusted future was wide open in front of her. She would introduce the world to the grunge-rap fusion simmering in her veins.

As she slipped off her coat and set it over the chair by the controls, she relished in the moment.

She walked over to the glass partition, opened the door, and made her way into the recording room. Part way in, she halted. She stared at the beauty of her muse. Her fingers twitched. She ran her pointer down the supple skin, then picked it up and slid it over her hand. As she stretched her fingers out, sparks traveled down her arms and her legs. She walked to the centre of the recording room and sat, then stretched out her legs.

Lolita rested her head against the floor and closed her eyes. She ran her muse-encased hand down the side of her cheek, over her breast, and down to her thigh. Orson's face shimmered, materializing in her mind. He was there. Right there. His hand caressed her body. His fingers traced along her inner thigh. He unzipped her pants and slid his warm fingers inside. Flesh on flesh. Skin on skin. His soft fingers found their way to her spot of pleasure.

Lolita's mind spun, her eyes closed tightly, her mind, her body, her soul, all lost in the moment. Her spine arched and her body trembled as she gave herself to the only man she'd ever loved.

# Chapter 61

# Stopped Dead

Stella peeled around the corner, the tires on her Sunfire squealing as she slid into the parking lot. Her early-morning trip to see Bryce had been a success. The composition of the book covers matched one-hundred percent that of the cassette insert. This had to be it. Both crime scenes were located at places that used to be live-music venues. Both were on the outskirts of the current Electric Avenue, inside the boundaries of the party strip as it was when the music venues were bustling.

Someone using cassette insert paper to cover books and placing dead bodies outside of music venues had to have something to do with the music scene.

A musician?

A producer?

Who knew. It was a new path for them to take on the investigation. Every neuron in Stella's body buzzed with confidence that this would lead somewhere. They would catch the *Skin Peeler*.

She jogged down the hallway straight to the war room. She'd even called Sutton and convinced him to hold their team meeting earlier than he'd intended. As soon as she set the files from Bryce down—the chemical analysis of the cassette insert and book covers, along with the report of the trace from the second victim—Sutton burst through the door

Jake and Parker entered and took their usual spots.

"Reassignment." Sutton dropped a folder onto the table, crossed his arms, and scanned the team. "Stella, you're off the case. Parker, you'll stay. Jake, give Parker what he needs, but pay attention to your other cases. Stella, you know the drill. You're restricted to regular hours and catching up on paperwork. I can't afford to burn resources here. Two full time detectives working around the clock isn't justified."

"What?" Stella blurted as she took several steps toward Sutton.

Sutton looked her dead in the eye. "It's been almost *three weeks* with nothing new. No leads. No suspects."

"The killer won't stop." Stella took a few extra steps forward. "*You* know it." She glared.

Sutton walked right up to her, his breath heating her face. "Doesn't matter what I know. It's out of my hands. You will take orders."

She knew it was warranted for him to come in hot at her. She wasn't exactly the prized squad member when it came to taking orders. "Don't you care?" She raised her hands in the air as she stomped up to the crime scene photos. "*Look* at this. I *do* have something new. The covers. From the books. In the victims' hands. The chemical composition matches that of a J-card, used for cassette inserts. Both victims were left outside of old music venues." Sweat beaded on her face as she pointed at the criminal profiling boards she'd covered in marker. "The message. It's not a poem. It's a *song*." She swallowed, waiting for someone to say something.

Parker frowned, his forehead wrinkled with concern.

Lines of worry etched Jake's face.

Sutton closed the gap between them. "Didn't you hear me? This is out of my hands. Everything you've done here is *speculation.* We need *proof.* A live, breathing suspect." The gnarly green rabbit foot swung wildly from his belt.

She slid her hand into her pocket and touched the fur of her own good luck charm.

She had to salvage this. Now.

"I'll get you a suspect. I need more time. More searches. Focused on the song. The music venues. We need to rewind to the time of the cassette. Before 1993, when CDs started outselling tapes. Someone who would make a book cover out of J-card paper, he's stuck in another time." Stella's jaw clenched. She watched Sutton ponder her theory.

Sutton ran his hands through his brown curls. "Speculation. It's all speculation. We're out of time. I can't spend more resources on this. I have my orders."

Sutton grabbed the folder from the table and headed out of the room. He halted at the door. "I'm sorry, Mahoney. Parker, debrief in my office." He left.

# Chapter 62

# Broken Detective

Her forehead hit the top of her desk with a thud. Her shoulders slumped. A hot tear trickled from the corner of her eye, down the front of her face, splashing onto the desk.

Stella wanted to give up.

She closed her eyes, resting her forehead against the cold desktop, and swallowed the hurt and the anger. Her stomach clenched. Her entire being shut down inwardly. A powerful craving for something to alleviate all of this took over.

Bourbon? Metal?

That wouldn't last long.

Tad? *Tad.* The thought didn't sicken her. Or scare her.

She wished she could find the olive-skinned woman from the other night. A whiff of her spice-infused, earthy scent, the feel of her tender, warm skin, the touch of her lips...all of it would be a welcome escape right now. An escape from the horrid reality that had been thrust upon her. She hadn't *tried* hard enough. She'd been too late in noticing the link between the book covers and the cassette insert. She should have been faster. Smarter. Trusted her gut more.

"Stella?" Jake's voice interrupted her thoughts.

"Go away," she answered in a muffled voice, her lips grazing the desk.

"No." He touched her shoulder.

She leaned into the chair. She examined his dark eyes, his tousled chocolate curls, and his obnoxious lime-green sweater vest. "Jesus. How did I miss *this?*" She tugged at the bright wool.

He smiled. "You were focused. You were onto something. I'm sorry about the reassignment." His lips pursed into a thin line. He ran his hand through his curls.

"It's not your fault. It's my fault. I should have seen it sooner. I should have tried harder. I shouldn't have taken a day off."

"You didn't."

"OK, fine, not the whole day, but…" Her mind jolted. "Wait…how do *you* know I didn't? You weren't here."

"I got the analysis from Dr. Klein."

Oh yeah. The tape trace. Bryce had sent it to Jake upon her request.

"It was the missing piece. I reran the search. Crossed the fibre optic traces with the gamma ferric oxide. Didn't get a chance to share it." He walked to his desk.

Stella stood and followed him. He sat, wheeled over to the screen, and retrieved a series of neon-green strings of text.

"Decipher." Stella rested her elbow on his shoulder.

He shrugged her away, typed something in, then translated strings of new text. "Like I said, the applications of fibre optics have exploded over the past few years. Then last year, especially. But I also told you there were *other* applications. The trace results you came to me with—gamma ferric oxide *and* polyester-based plastic—it's a combination used for cassette tapes. Polyester plastic film with a magnetic coating. It was a long shot, but I ran a cross search. What would use *both* fibre optic cable *and* cassette film?" His expression became smug.

She rolled her eyes and crossed her arms. "And?"

"Alesis Digital Audio Tape. ADAT." His dimple appeared as he smiled with satisfaction. "It's an eight-track recording machine. Eight channels of uncompressed 24-bit digital audio are transmitted over a fibre optic cable. The polyester plastic tape is coated in magnetic oxide particles."

*"What?"* A smile crept across her face. She was spot-on. This killer was in the music business, or somehow hovering around someone who was.

"It gets better." He faced the screen. The ADAT skyrocketed in popularity in 1993. Sales spiked. A lot of smaller recording studios were scooping them up. Taking the power out of the hands of the major labels." He smiled wide. "Your theory holds."

"He's producing music. He's stuck in 1993. Or somewhere around then. Whatever happened, back then, he's reliving it now. Over and over. His fantasy.

He's choosing victims that look like someone that was part of whatever went down." Warmth swelled in her belly. "Jakey. You're a rockstar."

"I'm a geek in a sweater vest. I like it that way. But I'll take your praise."

Her smile dissolved. "So what? We've advanced the profile on our killer. Big fucking deal. I'm not on this case anymore. No one wants to hear this. We don't have a name. A live person. An actual suspect." She crossed her arms and tapped her foot.

"No. But Parker's still on it."

She clenched her jaw.

"Aren't you cool with Parker now? You two seem chummy. Maybe you can *persuade* him to investigate it."

Jake's suggestion made sense.

"Fine. I'll try."

He smirked. "You feed this to Parker, he might find something before he's reassigned too.." He looked up at her, dimple showing, eyes caring. "Just be patient, even though it isn't your forte."

She sighed. He was right. "Fine."

"Hey, Mahoney." Parker approached.

"Oh look, it's the star of the *Skin Peeler* case," Stella chided.

He blushed. "Whatever. No logic to reassignments."

"I'm just kidding." Stella nudged his arm with her elbow.

His face became stern. "Sutton wants us in his office. Now."

Stella rolled her eyes. "Hasn't he had enough kicking my ass for one day?" Her anger had settled and she was actually feeling a mild excitement about Jake's plan. She hated to admit it, but she hadn't lost all hope.

"It's not what you think." He paused. She could swear there was a twinkle in his eye.

"Spill it." She stood tall, her jaw clenching.

"There's another one. A body. Right on Electric Ave. Behind a live-music joint." He leaned in closer. "I was in his office when the call came in. The skin is missing from the hand."

A jolt of excitement shot through Stella. "What?"

"Yeah." Parker smiled wide. "You've been reassigned. Again."

*What in the fuck just happened?* Stella stared at Parker, shock paralyzing her. Parker nudged her with his arm. She wanted to run, scream, jump, but her boots remained rooted to the thin, sticky HQ floor.

"Jakey. We need that summary. Now." She nodded at the cryptic black computer screen cluttered with neon-green text. "Parker, get a move on. We have our orders. Sutton's office. Now." She spun and stomped toward her boss and his gnarly green rabbit claw. On her way, she snatched up the summary of the chemical analysis of the book covers and the cassette insert.

She *knew* the music link was real. It wasn't her music addiction creating a false correlation. It was there. It was real. Chemistry had revealed it. Location further backed it up. Now all she had to do was find the person responsible.

## Chapter 63

# Fucked-Up Murder Scene

S elf-loathing claws scraped their nails up Stella's throat. She choked against the raw scratches. Her eyes electrified with the vivid pulses of the neon sign. *Vinyl.*

*It couldn't be.*

She wished she was in a love drug and bourbon haze. Or that she didn't know what that meant.

The moment Parker said there was another one, she'd felt an unreal sense of relief. Not for the victim. For the next one. Maybe they'd have a chance.

When he said it was in the heart of Electric Avenue, her being froze entirely. She went into autopilot.

Now here she was. Standing in front of the sign she'd walked under two nights ago for the wildest pure-love, metal, bourbon, crazy ride she'd ever been on.

"Behind back." Sutton was in serious overdrive. The *don't you fuck with me* mode.

*Fuck.*

She followed him down the block, double left, into the alley. Hot acid rolled in her stomach. Something wasn't right.

She half ran to keep up with him. Parker was directly next to him. Why were they in such a hurry? Their victim wasn't getting any deader. They slowed. She walked up behind them. Sutton clicked on his flashlight and guided the light up in front of him.

Stella gasped. Her jaw clenched. Her hands balled into fists.

The light revealed the body, poised against the brick wall. Solid black boots up to the ankles. Tight jeans, tattered above the knees. A hand, skinless, clutching a book. Perky breasts. Pink, candy lips. Bright-blue eyes. Glassy. Lifeless. Spikes of cotton-candy hair.

*What. The. Fuck.*

Stella gulped against the revolt surging up her throat from her stomach. She screamed. Not out loud. In her mind. The victim type was male with remarkable green eyes and sandy-blond hair. It wasn't a thin, pale female with pink, spikey hair.

But the hand. The skinless hand clutching the book. There was no denying it matched the *Skin Peeler's* MO.

Sutton and Parker were talking. She couldn't concentrate sufficiently to hear what they were saying.

The spikes of cotton-candy hair, they were real. The pink, candy lips, they were real. The face, it was real. The same face across from her two nights ago as she lay sprawled on a fur rug with a guitar goddess and an olive-skinned woman.

This didn't make any sense. A killer like this, like the *Skin Peeler,* didn't change victim type. Nothing about this was right.

She sidled up against the wall, close to the body. She crouched and shone the flashlight onto the open page of the book in the dead, skinless hand. The light hit the open page. The all-too-familiar words came to life.

Stella nearly choked on the vomit surging up her throat.

"You with us?" Sutton stared at her.

She lowered her flashlight.

"We need to talk."

## Chapter 64

# In Over Her Head

"N ow?" Sutton glanced at Stella. "We have a scene to process."

"Yeah." Stella swallowed as she faced Sutton. "It can't wait."

Sutton glowered, but nodded.

She walked over to the other side of the alley, away from Parker and the techies milling about the scene. Sutton followed.

Her mind whirled. She grasped for the right words. How could she tell her boss, *Sutton,* she'd been with the dead woman sprawled on the pavement? Not just been *with* her, but with her and a group of women at a crazed drug, booze, and *sex* afterparty. Two nights ago.

*Fuck.*

"Well? I don't have all day, *Detective.*" Sutton crossed his arms. The rabbit foot on his belt swung back and forth as he shifted on his feet.

"I know this woman." Her voice was a raspy whisper.

"What?" Sutton shot a glance at the victim.

"I was with her. Sunday night." She clenched her jaw.

"Two nights ago?" Sutton raised an eyebrow.

"Yeah. Here." She nodded at the rear door of *Vinyl.*

"Explain." Sutton's lips stretched into a thin line.

Flashes of the show shimmered in and out of Stella's mind. The cotton-candy-haired singer up onstage. The raw-edged voice hypnotizing Stella. The guitar goddess seducing her with electric riffs from up on her metal-god pedestal.

She shook her head. "I was here for a live show. This woman..." Stella nodded at the victim. "She was the lead singer."

"So? You were at a show. Saw her perform. Fine." Sutton shifted a step away.

Stella grabbed his arm. He spun around.

"No. I didn't just see her perform. I was *with* her." She swallowed the fear clawing up her throat.

His face contorted as he processed the information. "What do you mean *with* her?"

The olive-skinned woman shimmered in her mind. Her aroma still clung to her senses.

She gulped. "I was *with* her. Another woman and I, we went to an afterparty with the lead singer and the guitarist. We went to *their* place."

Sutton raised an eyebrow. "You all partied after the show?"

"Yeah. We partied. We…" She clenched her teeth. Stella's skin was still hot at the thought of the guitar goddess exploring her, the singer circling as she watched. "I might have touched her. There was…sex," she spat it out before she changed her mind. She had absolutely no choice right now. She *had* to be completely honest with Sutton.

He was expressionless. He shook his head. "Go home."

"What?" She shouldn't be surprised.

"Go home. We don't know the last time this woman was seen. You could be a prime suspect."

"You know that's not possible."

"Doesn't matter what I know." He paused. "Your fingerprints could be all over this dead body, Stella. Hell, she could be slathered in your DNA. What don't you understand here?" His face was flushed.

She froze. Her mind refused to comprehend what was happening.

He broke the silence. "Go home. Sit tight. We need to process this scene." He spun on his heel, then paused. "We'll need your statement." He walked away, leaving the words clinging to the air.

She watched him as he walked over to the body. Parker looked at her from across the alley with concern. Sutton approached him. As the two talked, they faced away from her, focusing on the scene.

Stella walked, one slow step at a time, down the dark alley. She couldn't feel her arms or legs. She couldn't think. She couldn't *breathe.* Rapid breaths hijacked her. Heart beating wildly, she upped her pace.

She had to get out of here.

SALIVA BATH

# Chapter 65

# Damning Statement

Stella stared at the officer holding her badge and gun. Officer Preston. Pete Preston. What kind of fucking name was that, anyways? He was young, clean, polished. A rookie. Just like her.

If Sutton was going to kick her out, he could have done it himself.

Her jaw clenched. Her stomach churned.

Officer Preston nodded curtly, then walked to the door. Stella didn't move. Frozen in place, she watched him walk out of her apartment. The door clicked behind him.

Suddenly weak, she fell onto the couch. Heat rushed her body. She swallowed a ball of sick.

*No.* This couldn't be real.

Sutton had sent Officer Preston to get Stella's statement. According to Preston, Sutton thought it would be easier for Stella to give her statement in privacy, away from the office. *Nice try.* Chances are he didn't want to have to deal with her, especially if she made a scene. She'd wrenched her brain, pulling out every morsel of memory from the night at the show. Revealing everything she could recall about her wild behaviour as a hot wave of humiliation rushed through her.

She'd always kept her private life separate from everything else. Even Jake knew very little about it.

Preston's expression had remained blank as he wrote it all down. What little there was. The entire uncomfortable time she'd sat there, watching him take notes, she'd wondered what the hell he was thinking. He revealed nothing.

Sunday night, Halloween, was the last time the lead singer had been seen. Karol Kain. Twenty-two years old. She'd been living in Calgary for less than a year. Since Stella had identified her as the lead singer of the band she'd devoured two nights ago, at the precise place that her body was left, they'd been quick to get a full identification on the woman.

The night was fuzzy. The inventory of who was still there when Stella had slipped out wasn't clear. They'd all been under the influence of an array of substances.

She'd stuck to her guns. One thing she was sure of was that when she'd slipped out of the afterparty, the lead singer was still there.

If only she knew who the olive-skinned woman was. She might be able to confirm that Stella had left while the singer was still alive. Maybe she'd remember something that could narrow down who was last to see the victim.

Running her hands through her strawberry curls, she pulled strands away from her face and stared across the room. She could still feel her hands shaking as she'd handed her badge and gun to Officer Preston. He'd blushed slightly when he asked her for the items. Maybe he was just some poor sucker sent to do the dirty work. Sent to ask her for the indispensable things that she couldn't live without.

He'd assured her it was temporary until the scene, and the body, were processed. It was procedure, nothing more.

Until they could clear Stella from having anything to do with the murder of the lead singer, she was off the case. She was off *every* case. She was just Stella. Not Detective Mahoney.

*Fuck.*

*Double fuck.*

Hands shaking, she reached for the bottle of bourbon in its usual place on the coffee table. She poured, grabbed the glass, and shot it back.

She closed her eyes and exhaled slowly.

She wasn't a fucking *killer*.

Dirty Joe flashed through her thoughts, watching the woman slide the knife into his gut. The sound of his last breaths.

She *wasn't* a killer who took the lives of innocent people. She *wasn't* a crazed *Skin Peeler*.

Was her DNA all over the body? She had no clear recollection of whether she'd fallen prey to the singer's sexual prowess. The images simmered in a constant hum in her mind. The creamy fur rug. The guitar goddess. The earth-and-spice woman. She knew she'd put her hands all over them.

But the singer...she didn't think so. The last she knew, the singer had been circling them.

*Wait.* Was the singer even there when she woke up?

It was useless. No matter how hard she tried, the memories remained fuzzy.

It was absurd that anyone would think she had killed this woman. Peeled the skin off her hand.

There was protocol to follow. She was smack in the middle of it.

All she could do was sit here, like a caged animal, waiting in her apartment.

# Chapter 66

# DNA Profile

S tella shifted on the edge of the couch. Her knee shook. She stared at the notes she'd jotted, an outline of the night of the last *Skin Peeler* murder.

Trapped in her apartment, no badge, no gun, no purpose, she realized how lost she'd be without her detective title.

She had a moderately obvious outline of what happened the wild night of the rap-metal show. Up till the point when she'd sprawled on the fur rug with the guitar goddess and the earthy-spice woman. The lead singer circling them was the last thing she remembered clearly until the evening blurred into a swirl of images.

There were pieces missing. In both her account of the evening and the profile of the *Skin Peeler* that had become her obsession since she'd been sent home.

The buzzing of her murder phone jolted her.

"Mahoney." The weakness in her voice disappointed her.

"Stella, are you OK?" Jake's voice warmed her heart.

"Jake." Her voice shook. "It's good to hear your voice."

"What the hell happened?" She could see him looking around the office nervously, tousled curls falling over his face.

She couldn't get into it now. It was too fucked up. "You mean Sutton hasn't told you?"

"Said you were off the case. For now. Temporarily. That's it. He's being quite secretive about it." She could hear his concern.

"It all happened so fast." Hot tears swelled in her eyes. She forced them to stop. *Not now.*

"Well, this whole thing—you being off the case—doesn't make sense. Stella, talk to me."

"Jake...I..." She swallowed down bile.

He sighed. "Whatever it is, it'll blow over. You'll return soon." He sounded confident. "You pushed too far, didn't you?"

"I guess so." The words stuck to her parched mouth as she forced them out.

"The trace. I brought it up, at the debriefing. Stella, you were correct. I gave a full report. All the info on the ADAT. It *can't* be a coincidence." She could picture him leaning over his computer screen filled with cryptic text, fingers hovering over the keyboard. "All *three* victims outside music venues. Words written in an open book. The cassette paper, used for the book cover. A combination of fibre optics *and* magnetic oxide on the second vic. One of the main applications is a recording device for music studios. Point is, you were right."

A warmth spread through her belly. Her profile was accurate.

"We also acquired an ID on the second victim." Melvin Bradley. No record or a permanent residence. Can't seem to find anyone that knew him. Oh...and you won't believe this. On the last victim, there were traces...of the killer..."

Stella bolted upright, her shoulders clenching. "Prints?"

"Saliva. Doesn't belong to the victim. You can go a long way with saliva. LCN DNA profiling. It's a new technique. It was just approved for application to investigations. You only need a few cells to get an entire LCN profile. A droplet of dried saliva. Wish you'd been here. Sutton gave us the comprehensive rundown this morning." His excitement over the technical advances seeped through the phone.

Normally, she would chuckle at his enthusiasm and tousle his hair. Right now, she froze as she listened to his words.

*Saliva?* Her gut clenched. Whose was it? She swallowed.

# Chapter 67

# Hunt

It was time for *Slick Rick* to pay his dues. Stella slid her fingers along the heavy handle of her knife. Satisfied with its secure position, sheathed in her belt, she slid her hand from underneath her leather coat. Amping up her pace from brisk to manic, she closed in on the *Drum and Monkey*.

She'd been here a few times, stalking cold case killers. It wasn't her usual place to tail a killer. It was a dive, but a tad nicer than *The Cecil*. She pulled hard at the door, un-wedging it from its crooked jam against the doorframe. You really had to *want* to get into this place to enter.

Descending the stairs into the dimly lit heat below, she ran through her last-minute plan.

It had been days since she was stripped of her badge. She'd done what she was instructed to do. She sat tight.

Secluded in her apartment, she'd obsessed over the Skin Peeler. She'd gone through the profile a million times. The evidence had helped her to flesh it out. Without access to searches, she couldn't get the information she needed. She'd hit a wall. Even Jake wasn't answering her calls.

*Fucking Sutton.* He had to know she had nothing to do with a dead woman with a skinless hand. He'd left her stewing alone without the slightest update.

It could only mean one thing.

She was finished. The Skin Peeler case would proceed without her. She'd never be a detective again.

Pacing the perimetre of her apartment, she'd found herself fixated on her murder wall.

She wouldn't catch the *Skin Peeler*. If she had no purpose, she'd find one.

Staring Slick Rick in his dark eyes, she'd silently declared that he was it.

After reviewing her notes from the recon she'd done on him, it seemed most likely that this was where he'd be. She reached the bottom step. Without a hint of hesitation, she walked casually across the room. Blending in was the most important thing here. She had to appear as if she was another patron in a shitty bar needing a late-night drink to drown her sorrows.

With everything that had happened in the last few days, she was sure she wouldn't have a problem pulling that off.

Taking a seat up at the bar, she scanned the room.

*Bingo.*

There he was, in the corner with a young woman.

"Drink?" an older man with scraggly hair and three missing front teeth asked from behind the bar.

He'd seen better days.

"Bourbon. Double. Straight up," she said.

He gave her a crooked smile then went to get her drink.

Tad shot through her thoughts. This old, missing-tooth, scraggly-haired geezer was definitely a different bartender than Tad. Warm tingles wove down her arms. *No.* She forced him out of her thoughts. That was over. No more detective. No more Tad. She'd stick to her hunts, ridding the world of one serial killer at a time. Her own way.

If this was what she was going to do, she definitely couldn't have a *boyfriend* in her life.

The crooked-smiling man returned with her drink and slid it across the bar. She tossed a couple crumpled bills his way, then focused on the drink. Thankfully, he got the hint and stepped away.

Nursing the drink, she snuck glances over at Rick. Sizing up his date, Stella was able to determine that she was a mirror image of the other girls. The ones who had ended up dead in a ditch.

Rick was slick. He was the commonality linking together the string of dead women. If she had anything to do with it, the woman hanging off his arm now wouldn't end up like the others.

Playing it cool, Stella consumed the drink slowly, sneaking stealth glances over at Rick and the woman. She'd been here before. The ideal course of action was to take none until they left. She'd follow close behind until they reached a secluded spot, then strike. It would be over before the woman could blink.

"Another?" the man asked. His voice whistled slightly as air passed through the gap where his teeth should be.

Stella nodded. She hoped Rick would get restless soon and make his departure. After pacing her apartment like a caged animal for days, she needed something to happen. She needed some sort of release of all this pent-up hurt and anger roiling in a toxic ball in the pit of her belly.

A tap on her shoulder jolted her from her downward thoughts.

She spun around. Shock seized her. "Parker?" she hissed. "What the *fuck* are you doing here?"

"What are *you* doing here?" He scanned the room. "You've been paying a lot of attention to that guy in the corner, with the young woman."

"How do *you* know?" She glared.

"I followed you."

"What?" She took a swig of the bourbon and set the glass on the bar, standing. "We can't be here." She pushed past him and walked briskly toward the stairs. Taking them two at a time, she burst through the door at the top.

The cold night air hit her with a slap. She inhaled deeply, watching the white puffs of her exhale.

Parker burst through the door, breathing heavily.

She assailed him. "Why are you following me?"

He steadied his breathing. "I was worried about you."

He seemed sincere. *Dammit.* She hated how *nice* he was.

"You don't owe me anything."

"You're my *partner.*" His face flushed. He pulled his coat closer to his chest.

"Not anymore." She spun, her leather coat flying open on a gust of wind as she took a step away.

He grabbed her arm. Her coat snagged on the handle of the knife. He froze.

"Jesus, Stella. What is this?" He nudged the knife with his hand.

"None of your business." She glared at him.

He released her arm.

"What are you doing *here* with a knife like *that*?" His nostrils flared. His faced reddened. "It has something to do with that guy you were watching. Doesn't it?" He stepped back.

"What's it to you?" she spat. Her heart cringed.

"You're *still* my partner." He ran his hand through his hair. "Stella, I don't know what you're doing here. I'd say you're hunting down some sleazeball." He shook his head. "I didn't *mean* to follow you. I came to your apartment, to check on you. That's it. You were leaving as I pulled up. I figured you were, I dunno, going out to get a bite or something. Figured I'd follow you and catch you when you got there." He put his hands up. "That's it. I swear."

He wasn't lying. She knew it. She doubted he knew how to lie.

"Fine." She twisted her lips into a contorted smile.

"Whatever's going on here, you need to stop. I don't know what happened the other night at the crime scene, but once the air clears, Sutton will *have* to give you your badge back." His face relaxed, along with his stance.

"You don't know that." She swallowed.

"Yeah, I do. So what? You had some kind of heated argument with your boss. Big deal. It'll blow over. You just need to take the foot of the gas a little. Calm down." His lips pulled into a thin line.

Sutton must have been as tight-lipped with Parker as he had been with Jake. Parker didn't know about her wild night. Relief washed through her.

"I was with the victim, the night she went missing." She clenched her jaw. "She was fine when I left. I had nothing to do with it. I was at the show she was playing. Went to the afterparty." She clenched her jaw and swallowed hard. "What if my DNA is on her?"

Parker didn't even blink an eye. "Well no shit you had nothing to do with it. Even if your DNA is on her, like you say..."—his cheeks flushed—"the evidence will lead us to the killer. You're not a Skin Peeler."

She couldn't help but smirk. "No. I'm not."

"So, take that knife and go home. Sit tight."

He'd seen everything. He knew she was hunting down *Slick Rick*. Now he was simply telling her to go home. He wouldn't tell anyone about this. She knew it.

"Fine."

# Chapter 68
# Wild Energy

The icy air seethed through Stella's veins. The neon lights of Electric Ave sizzled her senses. She stood at the end of the street, staring at the one that called to her. *Vinyl.*

The last time she'd looked at the sign, hovering over the destination of her wild bender, she'd been a detective, here to process another murder.

It had gone sour fast, leaving a bitter taste in her throat that wouldn't go away, no matter how many double bourbons she drank.

She'd remained hidden away in her apartment, scouring her profile of the Skin Peeler. The evidence pushed the profile even more. Fibre optics and tape traces clearly pointed to the specific recording device used in the production of music.

Blazing down a trail of her personal research, she'd confirmed a number of things. The ADAT was released in 1993. Recording studios of all sizes and experience levels snatched them up. The supply plunged quickly. They became a prized item for anyone recording music that had even an ounce of quality to it.

The trace had led to a specific, concrete piece to the puzzle. The locations of the murder scenes were all live-music venues in 1993. By 1994, only the most recent one was. It still stood. She stared up at it now.

There had to be something about this place. Something noteworthy enough to make the killer go off the rails with his glaringly specific victim type.

Something told Stella to return to the scene. To relive the night and see if there was anything at all she could remember. She was desperate to feel the weight of her gun in her hand, her badge in her pocket.

If she walked through the place again, she'd remember something that could release her from the de-badged state she was floundering within.

She walked right up to the door and stared at the flashing sign.

*Bzzzt.* A purple glow bounced off her strawberry curls.

*Bzzzt.* As the sign blinked off, the darkness of the night cloaked her.

She breathed white puffs of air in and out, lighting up under the glow of the sign, only to be left in darkness when it flashed off again.

Chatter from behind jolted her. She opened the door and walked through.

# Chapter 69

# Vinyl Uncut

The twisted little house reached after her as Lolita flung herself outside and ran across the lawn. She dashed down the sidewalk toward the vivid lights of Electric Avenue. She ran for several blocks. The cold air seized her lungs. She wheezed in deep breaths.

Slowing the wild palpitations of her heart, easing the icy claws scratching down her throat, she walked around the corner and admired the neon signs lining the street. The *single* street. Electric Avenue was no longer a six-block mini-Vegas. It was one street of washed-out nightclubs and bars.

How many days had she spent living in the world where her mind told her it was 1993?

She wasn't sure.

When she woke up hours ago, curled on her couch in her fuzzy blanket, her brain buzzed. Images flashed in and out. She grasped for control.

After a cup of tea and a hot bubble bath, her thoughts finally settled. She grasped the rootedness reaching its warm hands up her being and held on tight. She closed her eyes, breathed in the citrus of the tea and the lavender of the bubbles.

One image at a time, she sifted through her memories. She replayed the tragic events of that night, in 1993, when Orson showcased a performance of a lifetime. When she stood in complete devotion at his feet, hovering by the lip of the stage. When her soul shattered in a single second as she watched the groupie clinging to him, his emerald eyes fixated on the treat.

The hate, the pain, the desire still lurched within her.

She'd curled into a ball on the couch and flipped through her notebook. The same one that she was sure she'd filled with epic rhymes that would take her to stardom. As she read the same rhyme over and over, the realization that when she'd lost control of her lip she'd also lost her ability to write crushed her soul. She'd tossed the book on the table and retreated to her bedroom, finally deciding to try and calm her nerves.

As she soaked in the bath, she tried as hard as she could to bring her memories of the last few days to the surface. They refused to show themselves. There were flickers of blonde curls, the aroma of strawberry and whiskey, an elegant apartment with crystal chandeliers and red walls with golden swirls. There were whispers of a voice, smooth as silk, with a dangerous edge.

Try as she might, none of the images would come into complete focus. She wasn't even sure when her last clear memory had actually taken place.

After the bath, she'd resorted to her old routine of watching the videos from 1993 in sequence on repeat. The rocking had consumed her body. The twitch pulled the itchy, contorted skin on the left side of her lip. She couldn't take it anymore.

She needed to leave the house. Desperate to escape the bubble that had kept her together for years, that had morphed into a toxic refuge with a vice grip on her sanity, she'd thrust her arms into the first jacket she grabbed and ran from the house.

As she ran, she had no plan as to where she was headed. As her feet slowed, her heartbeat and her breathing eased, and she realized she was heading for the heart of where it all started. *Vinyl.*

She had this strange feeling that she'd been here recently. As she walked through the door, déjà vu descended like the ultimate reality.

This was the place Orson had staged the perfect show. Where he'd discarded her for the whiskey groupie. It was also the place Lolita had ended it all with her own hand.

She walked down the stairs now, wild beats hijacking her heart, sweat glistening on her arms. As she reached the bottom, she stared into the basement pit that had taken her life.

The stage was lit in a soft glow. A young man sat up on a stool, strumming an acoustic guitar and crooning along to the chords. A few people were scattered about the room.

She walked across the empty floor. The young man wasn't there. A woman with cotton-candy spikes of hair gripped a gem-coated mic. Her voice, angelic with a dangerous edge, matched the one that had been floating through the crevices in Lolita's mind for days. A woman with long, golden hair strummed the electric strings of a guitar in a mad riff, merging with the angelic voice. Her face was the one that had been making appearances in Lolita's memory, along with the voice. It was coming back to her now. She'd been here. Recently.

Lolita scanned the dance floor.

Her breath caught. It was her. The whiskey treat.

A woman with strawberry-blonde curls, a leather coat, and black boots stood by the bar.

Lolita looked away, then up at the man with the acoustic guitar. Had the woman seen her? She was the spitting image of that groupie from years ago who sat at this very bar, draping herself all over Orson. It couldn't be her.

She looked again.

The room flickered. A plethora of images flooded her.

*No.* It wasn't her. She was here, watching the cotton-candy-haired singer and the golden-haired guitarist. With her. They'd clung close together, watching the show. Lolita felt the electric shocks all over again, her body being hijacked as desire consumed her. It all returned in a flash. The ecstasy. The vodka. The strawberry blonde. The show.

The afterparty.

It had happened. She could feel herself grounding in the present moment bit by bit.

She needed to talk to her. Maybe this woman would remember the details of the night. If she played this right, she could coax her to reshare the night with her. She could fully grasp the last few days. On the current moment.

She had to play this right.

She watched the singer and took in a profound breath.

# Chapter 70
# Olive Skin

It was mid-week. The atmosphere was chill. A young man in ripped jeans and a baggy wool seater sat on a stool up on the stage, strumming a black acoustic guitar. The smooth body glimmered under the yellow-and-blue pot lights. His angelic voice crooned polished lyrics with a slight raw edge at the end of each line.

Stella paused midway through the room and watched him for a moment. She scanned the joint. She still couldn't wrap her head around the fact that she was here Halloween night, watching the rap singer now resting in the morgue.

An icy hand gripped her gut every time she pictured the ashen face with pink lips, cotton-candy hair framing the dead face.

She couldn't have known.

The victim type changed radically, without warning. Male switched to female. Poet swapped out for a singer.

Stella's brain wrenched. She looked up at the stage, recreating the show from the other night. The singer, weaving lyrics like rhymes along with the guttural riffs vibrating through the room. The voice. Singing. Rhyming. Half spoken, half sung.

Like a poem.

That was it, wasn't it?

Poetry, rhyming, rap…it was all the same to the killer. He was trying to recreate something that stemmed upon someone who rhymed. If he was rooted in the music industry, it was in rap.

The icy hand retreated from her gut. A warmth replaced it. She knew she was onto something. She could feel it.

She walked up to the bar and ordered a bourbon. She needed to sit here, be in this place, relive the other night and see if she could remember anything at all that had been hiding in the crevices of her fuzzy memories. More than anything, she wanted to clear her name and catch the *Skin Peeler*. Before another unsuspecting victim showed up dead with a fleshless hand.

For the first time in days, a calm washed over Stella.

The singer finished his song. The lights dimmed to a rich purple. The modest audience scattered throughout the place clapped unenthusiastically. The singer nodded and smiled, then launched into another song. The acoustic set, nearly empty room, and hushed buzz of chatter was exactly what she needed. She sipped the bourbon and slowly replayed her wild night frame by frame.

She saw herself reaching the bottom of the stairs, accepting the pills from the woman in the sexy cat costume, then walking to the bar. Two bourbons later, she sidled up to the front. This was all clear.

Her first glimpse of the woman with the olive skin was at the lip of the stage. She was sure of it. They hadn't talked. They'd touched. They'd flirted with their eyes. As the band blew through track after track, the night started to blur.

She took a lengthy swig of bourbon, forcing herself to focus on the hazy images of the night as it had progressed.

She'd had no interaction with the singer until the show was over. She had no doubt about it. The woman had taken her hand and led her to the backstage. They were let in. They didn't stay long. One drink. Nothing wild. No touching. Her DNA hadn't gotten all over the singer. Not then.

The singer thrust into a song that was edgier, grabbing Stella's attention. He was good. It surprised her how considerably she was enjoying an acoustic set.

She closed her eyes, letting the voice calm her. She examined the moments after the show. They'd piled into a van. It had sped away into the night. Beers were handed out. It was her, the olive-skinned woman, the guitar goddess, the cotton-candy-haired singer, the wild-haired drummer, and three other women. Their faces blurred.

They'd piled out at the apartment. The drummer wasn't there. Only two of the three other women were.

In the apartment, others trickled in. Stella couldn't remember how many or what they all looked like. They'd continued pouring drinks. Stella had latched onto some bourbon, stayed away from the other substances. The pills had been enough. *Or had they?* She had a slight memory of the woman with the dreadlocks slipping something onto her tongue.

The evening obscured further. She slowed the images of the episode on the creamy fur rug. It became clear. She was sure it was her, the olive-skinned woman, and the guitar goddess. She saw the singer circling, then leaving. She hadn't joined them. She'd gone off to another room. That was it. Stella hadn't touched her.

She had to be patient. She'd be cleared.

Right now, she needed to flesh out the killer's fantasy. One stuck in 1993. One with a rap singer at the centre.

The lights shimmered orange and pink. The singer launched into a smooth song. His voice pulled at her heart.

A woman walked across the open floor, approaching the stage, fixated on the singer. Long, chocolate dreadlocks fell over her shoulders. The lights caught her face. Her olive skin gleamed under the pink glow. The left side of her lip drooped, contorted and rough.

A gasp lodged in Stella's throat. The woman from the other night.

Stella shot back the rest of the bourbon, settled the glass down, and strode toward the woman.

Tingles rose up her legs and over her arms. Her heart thrummed. Sweat trickled down her spine.

Now was the time, particularly at this moment, to take cautious steps.

She watched the woman and played her words over in her mind.

# Chapter 71
# Worlds Collide

Stella walked slyly up to the mysterious woman. Her mind whirled.

She *had* to play this right. The woman would recognize her, without a doubt. After the time they spent together. She *must* know about the murder. It had been all over the news.

Weak claps filtered through the room as the singer finished a song. He leaned into the microphone and declared, in his silky, angelic voice, that he had one more song.

Stella reached the woman.

The woman welcomed her with a friendly smile. Her insides swirled.

Before Stella could say a word, the woman reached out and ran a finger down Stella's arm. "Hello."

"Hi." Stella smiled and tried to appear relaxed. "Quite a show the other night."

"It was." The woman gazed at the singer. "Knew he'd be big."

Stella frowned as she clenched her jaw. Those words seemed so familiar.

"I told him." The woman was fixated on the singer.

"I'm Stella."

The woman faced her. "I'm Lolita."

"You come here often?"

"It was my first time. The other night." Lolita's aroma wafted between them.

Stella's arms tingled. "That was a crazy party." She plastered a smile over her face despite the nerves revolting inside her.

"Yeah." Lolita licked her upper lip.

"Did you hear about what happened?"

A strange expression rippled over the woman's face. She shook her head. "What do you mean?"

"To the singer, from the other night?"

"The singer? The singer." The woman focused on the performer. The rough patch of skin on the left side of her lip twitched.

Cryptic.

"You left the party before I did. Do you remember who was there?" Stella asked.

The woman's gaze drifted vacantly across the room. "Us. Of course." Suddenly the woman met Stella's eyes. "Do you want to come over? For a drink?" She smiled. Everything about her relaxed.

"Sure."

Lolita slid her hand into Stella's and lead her out of *Vinyl*.

## Chapter 72
# Earth and Spice

The chill air bit at Stella's face as she tried to keep up with Lolita. The citrus-and-spice scent wafting through the air between them was as intoxicating now as it had been the other night.

"It's just around the corner."

Several blocks off the main strip of Electric Avenue, they took a hard right and walked down a street lined with small houses. Three houses down the block, Lolita strolled up to a crooked-looking blue one with a yellow door. She dug in the pocket of her coat and pulled out a key. It turned in the lock with a loud *click*. The door opened with a *creak*. In Lolita went. Stella followed.

The room was bathed in a cozy orange glow from a series of candles perched on antique tables. Stella breathed in deeply. The aroma of the room was comforting. Intoxicating.

"Please, sit." Lolita gestured at a cozy couch upholstered in earthy tones.

Stella nodded and sat. The scent in the room made her head swirl. Her senses were in overdrive. She was sure she hadn't had that many bourbons. Was it the candles pulling her into a haze, or was it Lolita? Maybe both. The couch was comfortable. She had a sudden urge to settle into it but resisted, perching on the edge.

"The drinks." Lolita disappeared from the room.

From the edge of the couch, Stella scanned the room. Shelves covered the side wall from top to bottom. The higher shelves held rows of LPs. Cassettes stuffed the lower rows. It reminded her of her own apartment. On the front wall, beside a bay window, a small television sat, a VHS recorder underneath. There were stacks of tapes next to it.

Lolita returned with two crystal goblets. She gave one to Stella.

"Thank you," Stella said.

Lolita settled on the couch close to Stella, their hips touching. A warmth wafted from this strange woman. Stella wondered how to proceed. She *needed* to know what Lolita remembered about the night at *Vinyl*.

"Our collection." Lolita pointed at the rows of albums.

*Our?* "Impressive," Stella said. She lifted the goblet to her lips and smelled it.

Lolita took a generous sip.

She approached the stack of VHS tapes. She traced her finger down them, stopping when she found the one she wanted. She slid it into the machine and clicked play.

A guitar strummed through the living room.

Warmth seeped from Lolita's rich brown eyes as she walked toward Stella. Entranced, Stella stared.

A drumbeat joined the guitar. Lolita hovered over Stella as she reached for her goblet.

A voice emerged from the television. A rough, raw voice. The first lyrics of the song shot through the room.

Lolita's eyes flickered. Stella could swear the warmth that was there only seconds before vanished. Lolita stared her down with cold eyes.

Stella clenched her jaw and focused on the woman's face.

Lolita took the goblet from Stella's hand and placed it on a coffee table. Lolita leaned over and slipped Stella's jacket off. She traced a finger down her bare arm. Chills crawled down Stella's spine.

*Skin. The Skin Peeler.* The words flashed through Stella's mind.

A sexual desire mixed with terror churned in the pit of her belly. Lolita sat and sidled up to Stella, her scent infiltrating Stella's senses, hijacking them, clouding her thoughts.

Stella pulled back. She was here to find out what Lolita knew about the other night. Not for a repeat performance.

"What's wrong?" A hurt expression clouded Lolita's face. Panic dripped from her eyes.

"Nothing." Stella smiled. "I just...I need to ask you what you remember about the other night." Stella glanced at the side of Lolita's mouth, wondering what had happened to her skin.

"The other night?" Lolita smiled slyly.

"Yeah. The show at Vinyl. We went to the party after. When you left, who was there? The guitarist? The singer?"

"The singer." A strange look washed over Lolita's face.

She didn't *seem* intoxicated. Yet her behaviour was erratic. Warm and inviting one second, odd and eerie the next.

Lolita stared at the television. "Told him he'd be big."

A music video played out.

Black lines zigzagged across the screen, distorting the image. The tape had stuck. It clicked free. The picture cleared. Kurt Cobain stared out from the screen. His gravelly voice broke through, singing of being locked in a heart-shaped box. Strange images of a field, a cross, and an old man flashed across the screen. His raw voice seeped sorrow, singing of being drawn into a magnetic trap. A grungy guitar riff ripped across the living room.

A cold claw grabbed Stella's gut.

Kurt stared at them with emerald eyes. His too-blond hair hung in matted tangles around his shoulders. A silver shirt shimmered over his arms. He lunged at the screen, the words slipping from his mouth, singing of a debt that would last forever.

Stella clenched her jaw, then glanced at Lolita. Lolita was in some sort of trance, mouthing along with the words.

*Trapped. Heart-shaped box.*

*Magnetic trap. Entranced by your pull.*

This song. The words. The book, clutched in a skinless hand, blazed through Stella's brain. The image of the blood-ink letters on the open page glared at her.

*Love-morphed box.*

*Trapped by your dream.*

They were a distorted version of those in the video. The victims had the same green eyes and blond hair. They were dressed in the same silver shirt fluttering across the screen now. All to recreate some sort of demented fantasy. She was convinced of it.

Lolita's chocolate dreadlocks rested on her shoulders as she leaned over the couch. The landlady in the housedress, *Darlene* at *The Misty,* appeared in Stella's mind. Her words, describing the one lady friend she'd ever seen her dead tenant with. *Long dreadlocks. Olive skin.*

It all clicked into place.

*Speculation. No proof.* Stella needed proof.

The video came to a sudden end. Lolita snapped her gaze on Stella. "You *need* to finish your drink." Her cold eyes narrowed as she handed the goblet to Stella.

Amidst the clutter on the table, Stella spotted a pill bottle. *Oxytocin* was scrolled on the label. Her stomach seized.

Lolita slid so close her hot breath shot spice into Stella's nostrils. "You don't want to be forgotten, do you?" Lolita clutched Stella's upper arm. Her nails dug into Stella's skin.

Stella swallowed.

Lolita kept her grip on Stella's arm as she leaned in close. Darkness seeping from her eyes, Lolita brushed her lips against Stella's. Tingles erupted down her legs.

Lolita pulled away, a crazed look in her gaze.

Instinctively, Stella's hand slid down to her belt. *No gun.*

Something flashed in her mind. Pages she had read in her father's notebook. *To beat the deranged mind of the serial killer, you must join them in their fantasy.* Her gut told her that the video and the dreadlocks were no coincidence. She could leave empty handed. Or, she could find something that would help her save this fucked-up case. She *needed* to know if Lolita was the *Skin Peeler.*

Words rushed through Stella's mind. *Lyrics written in blood. Peeled skin. Ed Gein. His brain injury. His wandering eye. His slurred speech.* Stella reached out and stroked Lolita's arm. She crawled her fingers over the woman's olive skin, up her neck, and delicately touched the contorted skin on the side of her mouth.

Lolita smiled. She ran her hand along Stella's face, her fingertips down Stella's arm, stopping at the scar. Stella didn't resist. Lolita's lips found hers. Stella took in the luscious kiss, losing herself in the taste of Lolita's tongue.

*Saliva.* What had Jake said? They could get an entire DNA profile from a drop of saliva.

He'd also said they had DNA from the last victim. The singer Stella had been watching, nights ago, with the woman she was now passionately kissing.

Her gut swelled with warming, a knowing. She had to follow it.

She had to play this right.

# Chapter 73
# Killer Sex

Lolita led Stella from the living room. They wove through a hallway into a bedroom. The room was comforting. Like the warm hug that Stella had needed for a long time.

Lolita's gaze intoxicated her. Tiny electric shocks rippled through her entire body, morphing into a gut wrenching ball of sick. The hot desire swelling within her astonished Stella. How could her body respond this way when she suspected this woman of grisly acts? She had to keep control of the situation.

Lolita led her to the bed. Muffled music floated after them. The orange glow from the other room dimmed to a faint golden haze.

It was like they were in a time capsule. As in the living room, there were no newspapers. Only stacks of magazines. Stella caught a glimpse of an issue of Rolling Stone. It was dated July 13, 1993. 1993. The year stuck in Stella's mind.

*Think, Stella, think.* What was her move? The pill bottle might have Lolita's full name on it. Surely, she'd be dripping in Lolita's saliva if she maintained this game. She had to *play along.* As Lolita lowered her onto the bed, a renewed wave of desire surged within her. Would she be *playing?* The darkness and the scent of this woman were too intense.

Stella grasped at the trail of logic simmering in her mind. She let herself sink into the bed. The pine-coloured duvet felt like a bed of soft leaves.

Lolita hovered, straddled her, then traced fingers up both of Stella's arms.

Stella swallowed. It took everything within her to concentrate, not to lose herself in the earthy comfort of the room, the cloud of spice permeating from Lolita, the dark eyes probing every part of her.

Lolita ran her tongue along Stella's arm.

Stella moaned, then bit her lower lip.

A flash of an ashen face jolted Stella. An image violated her mind. Skin peeling away from a hand. Screams of terror.

Stella gasped. Her eyes flung open. Lolita smiled slyly.

Forcing a smile, Stella explored the rich, brown eyes of this strange woman.

As Lolita hovered over her, pausing from her exploration of Stella's body, the warmth in her eyes chilled.

Words from the other room lingered in the air. *Wooden box. Love-morphed box.*

"Please, don't stop," the words jumped from Stella's mouth in an attempt to reach the warm Lolita. The one who didn't twitch erratically.

Lolita's inviting smile returned.

Stella breathed a sigh of relief.

She had to play this right.

What was right?

She cleared the images and thoughts from her mind. She relaxed her body. She focused on Lolita.

As Lolita directed her entire attention to Stella, Stella's body responded accordingly. Turmoil swarmed her as she let it happen, questioning the degree to which she was playing along. Every touch ignited sparks. It felt genuine.

At the same time, Stella grasped to keep control of her thoughts, to retain her focus on what she had to achieve.

Stella stared at Lolita's fingers as they glided down her own body, wondering if those same fingers had peeled flesh. Her senses in overload, she focused on Lolita, on her expression, on her demeanour, adjusting every reaction to keep Lolita's attention while she figured out her next move.

Despite the sensory overload drowning Stella, the weight of her gun in one hand and her badge in the other called to her. Her Mahoney instinct was screaming that there was a connection between Lolita and the *Skin Peeler.* She *had* to find out if she could trust her gut. As she touched the rough skin on the side of Lolita's lip, the image of her own skin peeling away shot through her mind. Clenching her jaw, she focused on every minute movement she made.

# Chapter 74

# Getaway

S tella stared at Lolita from across the bed, watching her chest rise and drop. She'd waited half an hour for Lolita to fall asleep. She'd even tried to slip out to use the bathroom, but Lolita had tightly gripped her arm and insisted she stay. It was time for her move. Another inspection of the pill bottle was imperative. She tiptoed from the bed with the utmost caution. She couldn't disturb Lolita. Not now. Not this close.

With silent steps, Stella walked from the bedroom to the living room. She picked up her leather coat from the couch, slipped her hand inside, and pulled out her mini trace-evidence kit.

Lolita's hot breath still warmed her skin. The press of her tongue lingered on Stella's arm.

Stella took a swab from her arm, right where Lolita had left an ample trace of saliva. She carefully inserted the swab into a plastic container then tightened the cap. She picked up the pill bottle. *Oxytocin. Lolita Salim.* She dropped the bottle on the table, grabbed her coat, then walked toward the door.

It had creaked when they entered the twisted house. She opened the lock, turned the knob, and pulled the door open an inch. Silence.

She opened it slowly. A creak erupted from the rusty hinges. Stella froze. Silence.

She pushed a little further, eased through the wedge between the door and the frame, then closed it in a single motion.

A white puff of air escaped her nostrils as she exhaled. It was the middle of the night. The icy air scraped fingers down her arms. The moon glowed overhead, casting long shadows over the empty street.

Stella walked with haste down the dark, deserted street, clutching what could be the *Skin Peeler's* saliva sample in her hand.

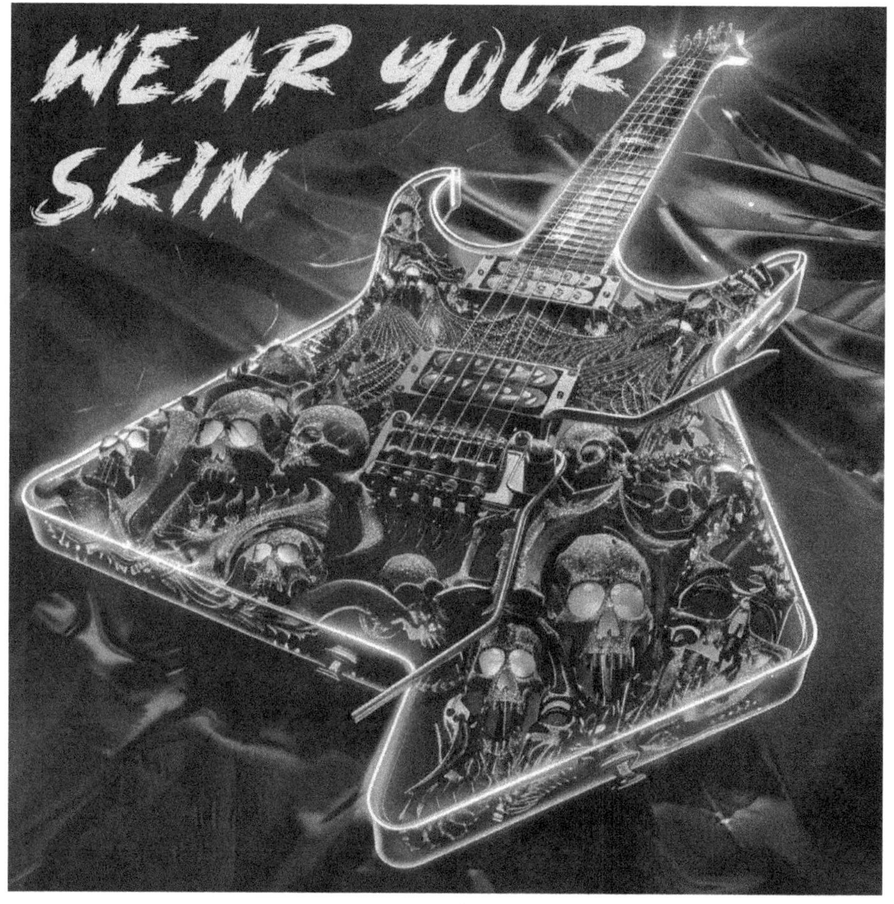

WEAR YOUR
SKIN

# Chapter 75

# Back on the Case

S tella's boots clicked along the pavement as she kept a fast pace down the sidewalk. Scanning the streets for a taxi, she flipped open her phone and dialled.

It rang. Once. Twice.

"Sutton."

"It's Stella." She'd be nice and use the name he preferred.

"Detective Mahoney. I tried calling you." His voice was stern with a soft edge.

"I'm sorry. Listen, I think...I think I found the killer." She gave him a moment to adjust to the situation she was throwing at him.

He sighed into the phone. "OK. Spill it."

"She was at the afterparty with me, the night I was with the victim." This felt weird. It was no time to worry about that. "I returned to Vinyl. Where the victim was found. I was trying to piece it together. I ran into the woman who was with us, who took me to the afterparty. She said some weird shit. I went home with her. It was *her. She's* the *Skin Peeler.* I've got proof." She waited for him to linger on the part where she *went home with* this woman.

She walked faster, the chill air stinging her lungs. The neon lights of Electric Avenue beckoned. Surely, she could catch a ride on the party strip.

"What proof?" he asked.

"Saliva." She waited. "I need that LCN profiling you told the team about. Pronto." She bit against the fear bulging in her throat. "It could match the DNA on the last victim."

Sutton breathed into the phone. "How do you know about that? Have you forgotten that you are *off this case?*"

"Jake told me." *Shit.* "It's not his fault..."

Sutton cut her off, "No, it's not. He didn't know the extent of your...I kept your situation on a need-to-know basis."

Somehow, that didn't surprise her, not with Sutton. She waited.

Silence over the phone.

"OK."

"Really?" She breathed a sigh of relief.

"Yeah. And none of your DNA was on the victim. You've been cleared."

She could feel him smiling through the phone. "Thanks, boss."

# Chapter 76

# Saliva

Her heels clicked along the polished floor, echoing down the vacant hallway. Stella shuffled the words through her mind, trying to put together a convincing explanation for how she'd obtained the saliva sample, in case she was questioned. Sutton had called ahead, requested an expedited LCN profile on the saliva. He ordered her to get here, *pronto,* and put a patrol on Lolita's house.

She could still hear his voice over the phone telling her that the third victim of the *Skin Peeler* was clean of any DNA belonging to her. Absolutely spotless. It gave her an immense sense of relief to know that her ecstasy-bourbon-rap-metal binge hadn't tainted the victim of the serial killer she was hunting. Her two worlds had collided a great deal lately.

She took a hard right down another hallway. This place was like a gleaming sterile maze.

The lab was adjacent to Blackwood's stomping grounds. She wondered how Blackwood was. It felt like a long time since she'd seen her. Since she'd seen any of her team. They really were becoming a part of her life, whether she liked it or not. Jakey. Blackwood. Even Parker.

She reached the door labelled *Crime Lab*. She chuckled. They kept it simple around here. She knocked. The door flew open. Familiar, dark eyes stared at her.

"Detective Stella. I was told you'd be stopping by, and that I should be all set for you," Bryce said. His dark hair contrasted with his pale skin. There was something alluring about his goth look.

"I need a rush DNA profile." She swallowed the building nervousness.

"You got the sample?" he asked.

"Yeah." She presented the container holding the swab from her coat pocket and offered it to him.

He took the sample, moved aside, and motioned her in. As he clicked the door shut, he continued his questioning, going straight down the path she'd feared. "So, you singlehandedly obtained a saliva sample from the Skin Peeler?"

*What?* Had the name caught on? She smiled.

"Parker told me about your profile. Sutton told me you have a DNA sample that you have no doubt belongs to the killer."

"Uh, yeah," she responded.

"How'd you get it?" He held the evidence bag up to a light and inspected it.

"Does it matter? I mean, will it affect the profile?" She clenched her jaw.

He raised an eyebrow. "Unlikely." He paused. "If there are any other traces, human or otherwise, they can be separated out. Even a tiny sample will still give us a full profile."

"Well, not that it matters, but I lifted it from skin." The heat in her cheeks heightened. "My skin." She swallowed the guilt in her throat. Complete honesty was the only way. She needed to do everything she could to avoid fucking up this case any more than she already had. "She...well...her saliva got on my arm."

"She?"

"Yeah."

"Well, if you're right, then we've got ourselves a female serial killer. The *Skin Peeler.*" He whistled as he snapped on a fresh pair of gloves.

Bryce removed the swab with a long set of tweezers, placed it into a plastic vial, and added a few drops of something.

"Polymerase. It's an enzyme. Causes your saliva droplet to reproduce the hell out of itself. Should give us a full DNA profile." He smiled at her. "We just have to wait."

Her shoulders relaxed. She let go of the breath she hadn't realized she was holding in. "How long will it take?"

"Since your boss is breathing down my neck, it's my first order of business." He set the vial into a holding container. "Seems warranted, given the acts of this killer. Grisly case."

Olive skin and long, chocolate dreadlocks drifted through Stella's mind. The intoxicating aroma lingered in her nose. "Yeah. It is. Grisly." Her mind wrenched trying to put together the earthly love wafting from this mysterious woman and the scenes that had apparently been left by her. The bodies, posed, the skin peeled from their hands. It didn't fit. Yet, all the pieces clicked together. The lyrics of that song. The too-blond hair and too-green eyes of the singer. The silver shirt. The message in the books left in dead hands. It was a contorted version of the words reaching from the television set in the strange house. The way this woman, Lolita, had changed, something ominous clouding her eyes, her demeanor became threatening. She *had* to be the killer.

"If the sample is high-quality, we'll have a profile we can compare to the DNA that was all over the third victim within a day or two," Bryce spoke, jolting her back to the crime lab. "I'll call you as soon as it's done."

"Thanks." Stella walked through the door and down the hallway, images of the woman floating through her thoughts.

# Chapter 77

# Muse

The basement called to her. The rhymes within were begging to surface.

Lolita tugged her fuzzy blanket in closer around her and shut her eyes. She wanted to go downstairs to her recording studio and lay down some tracks. Words whirled through her mind, scrolling themselves on an open page in her notebook.

She couldn't fully explain her hesitation.

After the night with the strawberry whisky treat, Lolita had secluded herself inside her house, watching videos on the scratchy TV screen. She knew it was 1999. The memories of that fateful night in 1993 at *Vinyl* pulsed in her mind, as clear as the day they happened.

Orson had displayed the show of a lifetime. She had found him at the bar draped in a whiskey-doused groupie. The fury had raged inside of her. She'd fled to the green room and in a panicked state her actions had spun out of control.

She'd ended it all.

She could still feel her hands trembling as she'd crushed the pills and slid the powder into a vial she'd found discarded in the garbage can.

She'd approached him at the bar with a sweet smile. Playing along, she'd woven sugar-coated words into his ears. Pretending everything was ideal, she'd distracted him and his slutty side treat.

She could still feel the fake giggles erupting from her vocal cords, the sick ball of hurt pulsing in the pit of her belly, the icicle piercing her heart. As vivid as if it had happened last night. She could hear the click as the cap popped off, the fizz as she poured the contents into his drink. His emerald eyes had been so fixated on his slut, he hadn't noticed a thing.

The fury-laced triumph still sizzled inside of her as she pictured him sitting there, not even noticing her slip away, sipping at his toxic drink.

When they found him in the alley behind *Vinyl*, the conclusion was a no-brainer. Pumped full of a lethal concoction, he'd ridden the after-show high like a champion. He'd gone hard. Too hard. The LSD and disco biscuits had been his own doing. She'd added in the oxytocin, putting him over the edge.

Orson Cruz. The star who should have been, but never was. Another case of rap, drugs, and death.

Of course, she'd delivered a flawless performance. A contorted lip wasn't a problem when it came to flowing tears, slurred words, and snotty sniffles. A drooping mouth was an asset in that situation. The last anyone saw of her, she was the devoted lover, staring up at him as he performed. As usual, no one gave her a second thought.

Now, the images came sharper and sharper into focus, making her nauseated. Had she been in control of her actions? Had her switch clicked into overdrive, taking reality down a blurry path? She didn't know. She couldn't remember.

All she knew was that now, she wished none of it had happened.

She would give anything to have him here now. Gold-star-dusted dreams or not, it didn't matter. Her heart ached for those emerald eyes to find her.

She smoothed her dreadlocks with her hands. The rhymes within her itched to live and breathe. Something prevented her from descending into her recording space. In the pit of her gut, a feeling pulsed. She couldn't explain it, but she was afraid to see what was in her studio.

Reaching over to the coffee table, she picked up a mug, warm with tea. She cupped it in her palms, breathing in the citrus scent. In her ultimate rootedness, she had to think that this wild fear was unfounded. What could possibly be in her studio besides strings of tape wound over plastic wheels, the ADAT, her scarf, and her headphones?

She took a deep breath, put the mug on the coffee table, and stood. Walking across the room, she reached the door to the basement. Without hesitation, she flung it open and descended the stairs. The wooden planks moaned and creaked under her weight. Close to the bottom, she found the switch and flicked it on.

The lights buzzed and shimmered, bringing the space to life. Neatly stacked tape cases sat beside the ADAT. Her notebook, closed and on its designated table, waited for her to open it. The controls were primed, quiet, unlit, for her next live session.

Her shoulders relaxed. Her mind settled. Her lips remained still. The fear had all been a result of her anxiety. Her overactive mind responding to the fissure in the rear lobe of her brain.

She lifted her gaze to the glass separating the recording space from the quiet control room. The lights shimmered overhead. A subtle buzz echoed through the room. Something caught her eye. She narrowed her gaze and sprinted a few steps.

She froze. Her hand shot to her mouth. Her finger grazed her contorted skin.

Time stopped.

Gasping for breath, not realizing she'd been holding it, she coughed and stared at...*them.*

Skin gloves. There was no alternative way to describe them. Three gloves, from what appeared to be human skin, perched upon stands, on display, like triumphant trophies.

The room flickered in and out several times. Lolita fell to her knees.

It hit her like a lightning bolt. The clear images of the past few days were one view into reality. The view she had when she was rooted. When her switch was off. All those gaps in time she'd experienced all these years, it had happened again.

A horrifying image formed on the opposite side of the glass. The cotton-candy, spiked hair framing the pale face. The face of a young woman. The singer. Her eyes filled with tears and terror. The skin peeled from her hand, blood dripping from exposed flesh.

Lolita gagged as she keeled over onto the cold floor.

She tilted her face up to the ceiling, unable to breathe, to think, to function.

The world whirled around her into a black hole.

# Chapter 78
# Reunited

The chipped walls of the war room loomed in a claustrophobic hold. Fluorescent tubing buzzed, bright enough to sizzle tired eyeballs. The smell of sweat and cheap coffee clung to the hot air. It was obnoxious and stifling. It felt familiar. It felt like home. Stella loved every bit of it.

She walked into the overheated space, the door clicking shut behind her, closing her in with a blanket of stiff, moist air. Coffee wafted from the corner table. She walked over to it, pleasantly surprised that someone had brewed a new pot. Selecting an appropriately cracked, subtly weathered-red mug, she inspected the blue lettering. It was supposed to say *Calgary Homicide,* but the letters were worn away enough to leave a mere *'gary H ide.'*

She chuckled, filled the mug, and took a long swig of the coffee that she didn't even realize she'd missed. The truth was, it was this place that she missed. It was her team.

The door swung open, allowing a short burst of less odorous air to sweep through the front of the room.

"Stella," a gentle voice reached for her.

"Jakey." The sea green of his sweater vest made her smile.

"What? You don't like it?" He smoothed his sweater with his palm.

"I do. It's calming. Like an ocean."

He rolled his eyes. "Whatever. You're just being nice cause you need me."

His tousled chocolate curls bounced as he walked over to his corner and set up for the meeting.

"I've missed you." She lingered over a sip of coffee.

"We all missed you, too." A curl fell over his eye. He brushed it away, then pushed his glasses up the bridge of his nose.

Every tiny mannerism made her realize how profoundly she appreciated Jake. He was beyond just the data analyst on murder cases to her. He'd had her back, every time.

The door swung open again, allowing another burst of slightly fresher air to reach them. Parker walked in, appearing well-rested and wearing a pressed shirt and crisp jacket as usual.

"Detective." He nodded at her, smiling wide.

She had to admit, she wanted to be his partner. The night at the *Drum and Monkey*—when he confronted her, asking her what she was doing there with a hunting knife, looking like she was stalking a man in the bar—flashed through her mind. He'd told her to go home. He didn't press her. He didn't say anything to Sutton. She didn't realize how far he'd go to be her partner. He was there for her, one-hundred percent of the way. Maybe she hadn't appreciated him enough.

"Parker." She nodded.

"Good to have you back." Parker grabbed a mug and filled it with coffee. "Just what I needed. A fresh cup of homicide tar." He took a swig and grimaced.

Stella laughed.

"Guess we're all here 'cause you found the *Skin Peeler.*" Parker pulled a chair from the long table lining the centre of the room and sat.

"Yeah. Well, hope the evidence lines up." She clenched her jaw.

Sutton burst through the door. "Mahoney. Parker. Jake." He stormed to the front of the room. "Got your results, Mahoney." He snapped a folder on the table and looked straight at her. "The saliva sample you obtained provided a complete DNA profile. Matches the dominant DNA all over the last victim." He smiled.

She couldn't believe it. She wasn't certain if she was shocked that the sample was valid, or that it matched the DNA on the victim, or that Sutton was smiling at her. Full-out smiling.

"Standup job. You trusted your instincts. You found us a prime suspect." Sutton flipped through the files in the folder. "Enough to search her place and bring her in. It's showtime."

A warmth spread through Stella's gut. She couldn't believe that Sutton put her directly back on the case as if she'd never been off it. Not wanting to lose her badge again, she'd fought the urge to question him. He was right, she *had* followed her gut. The moment Lolita spoke those words about *telling him he'd be big,* the feeling had started. When they entered the tilted house, something felt *off.* The second the video started playing from the TV in Lolita's living room, she knew. When the words drifted from the screen, Stella could see them morphing in the mind of this woman, scribing themselves in blood down the open page of a book clutched in a skinless, lifeless hand. Everything clicked in her mind. The sensation in her gut told her to go all in.

She did.

Sutton threw out stern orders outlining the approach they'd take to descend upon Lolita's little off-kilter house and take her into custody.

Stella's stomach churned. She knew this had to happen. It was the only way. The lust still trickled through her as she thought about Lolita, her dark eyes, her olive skin, and her chocolate-tinged dreadlocks. The tingles immediately roiled into a sick ball in the pit of her belly when she thought of the skinless hands and the blood-ink messages. How could she have been so intimate with someone who could do this? How could her instincts be *so right* and *so wrong* at the same time?

Her entire team trusted her. She needed to trust herself.

She wondered what it was going to be like to look Lolita in the eyes as she clasped cold steel around her wrists.

Chapter 79

# The Afterparty

Something rustled outside. Lolita stood from the couch and walked up to the bay window. She opened the curtains and scanned the quiet street. Leaves crackled as a gust of wind lifted them from the front lawn. The branches of the poplars swayed in the breeze. The denim sky dripped with the haze of Electric Avenue as it reached its neon fingers over the row of houses.

Lolita moved away from the window and settled onto the couch. Orson would be home soon. Tonight was a big night. It was her time. Orson was behind her all the way. They'd attain their star-dusted dream together.

The screen on the TV flickered. Text flashed on the bottom.

*Nirvana "Heart-Shaped Box" In Utero DGC Records*

Of all the rap videos topping the charts, many of them gripping her every time she watched them, this one had the strongest hold. The second it appeared, she couldn't look away. *Grunge.* The raw emotion that emanated from the singer—his voice, his face, his eyes, his being—it was as if he were speaking from her soul. This was the inspiration for the fusion she'd created with her rhymes.

Transfixed, she sank into an intense state of rootedness.

The door smashed open. Cracks erupted. Wood flew through the room.

Lolita jolted, hitting the back of the couch.

*Strawberry whiskey.*

The strawberry-blonde woman, the very one who had been in Lolita's bed only days before, stood by the shattered door, gun pointed straight at Lolita.

The woman's mouth moved. Her words blurred through the room, incomprehensible by the time they reached Lolita's ears.

The room flickered in and out.

Was this real? Was her mind completely rotted?

The woman approached, gun pointed, lips moving. Her steps slow and cautious.

Lolita pressed into the couch, her body and her mind frozen. The woman closed in on her. A sweet scent ignited the memory of the creamy fur rug. Lolita's insides sizzled as she remembered the woman's skin under her lips.

Radical flickers seized the room.

Bodies piled in. Vests marked in bright letters loomed at her. Guns pointed at her face. The night air extended its frigid fingers through the space, vaporizing the heat from the flames blazing in the brick fireplace.

The cold gripped Lolita, cooling her skin, her heart, her soul. Whatever *this* was, her mind couldn't comprehend it.

The woman approached her, speaking distorted words. It was like the woman's voice was travelling through deep water. Everything seemed slow motion. Lolita didn't resist. She had no control over her mind or her body. Pulled to her feet, her arms wrenched behind her, cold steel clasped her wrists. She moved her feet to keep up with the forced yanking of her limbs. As her bare feet touched the icy walkway, a shudder ran through her. The grip of the crooked little house refused to let go, forcing her into the living room stuck in 1993, down the stairs to the studio filled with recording tapes. The strong tug made her halt. The strawberry-whiskey policewoman with a gun dragged her from the grasp of the house, the time box, the comforting glowing space that caged her in 1993.

Shoved into the rear of a car, her bare arms wrenched behind her back stuck to the cold plastic of the seat. The door slammed. The world went silent.

# Chapter 80
# Off-Kilter

The smoothness of Lolita's dreadlocks against Stella's hand sent a shudder up her arm. Stella pushed Lolita's head down as she pressed her alternate hand against Lolita's back, guiding her into the cruiser.

Stella closed the car door with a click. She stared into the window. Lolita recoiled, dreadlocks falling away from her face. Stella could swear there was authentic fear in Lolita's eyes. The takedown had felt completely out of balance, the same way the little house seemed so off-kilter.

It was still conceivable Lolita's DNA was all over the victim's body as a result of the lustful afterparty. The images of that night had continued to sharpen over the last few days. Stella was convinced she'd seen Lolita and the lead singer, the victim, leave the room. When they returned, Lolita led Stella onto the fur rug.

Whatever Lolita and the singer did during that time could have left traces of DNA. It didn't lead to the clear conclusion that Lolita killed the woman.

Tears trickled down Lolita's face, over the contorted skin pulling the left side of her mouth into a droop. Stella couldn't help but wonder what had happened to her, how her skin had been damaged.

Lolita's lips moved as she mouthed the words *help me.*

Her behaviour had been peculiar during the whole arrest. Her expression was filled with shock, fear, disbelief, confusion. It could all be an act. Something about the look in her eyes seemed heartfelt. It bothered Stella, nagging at her gut.

Lolita continued to plead with her through the window.

Stella swallowed. She couldn't watch this. There was nothing she could do to help this woman.

She spun on her heel and walked toward the house.

Sutton talked to a techie. He paused as she neared. "Mahoney. Take your time. Go slowly." He stroked the gnarly rabbit foot dangling from his belt and nodded at her.

She nodded. "Got it, boss."

As she reached into the pocket of her SWAT vest, she fondly touched the rough fur of her beloved rabbit foot and walked toward the house. She thought of all the clues clicking into place. The video that Lolita played as they sat on the couch drinking glasses of cheap wine. *Heart-Shaped Box.* The lyrics so similar to those written in blood ink. One of the most legendary and unforgettable music videos of a time past. 1993. The same year stamped on the stack of music magazines she'd seen on Lolita's table. The same year that found The Westward, Sparky's, and Vinyl as prime live-music venues on Electric Avenue.

Pushing the rabbit foot further into the pocket and sealing the velcro closure, she stepped into the house. There was a hive of activity buzzing inside. Techies scattered over the room, hands gloved, snapping photos, taking samples. Parker was on the far side of the room, examining the extensive album collection, talking to a techie. She inspected the scene, deciding where she should start.

Lemon citrus rose from the table cluttered with teacups. She walked around the room, weaving around techies, re-inspecting everything she had noticed the night she was here. The stack of magazines, still on the same table. She snapped a latex glove over each hand, then sifted through the magazines. All of them displayed a rap or grunge musician in a wild pose on the front. Every issue was from 1993. She walked over to the television and watched the video flickering over the screen. The same video Lolita had played when Stella sat in this exact room with her. As the concluding chord was strummed, the singer looked directly at her. His emerald eyes piercing and cold. She was dying to know what happened to Lolita in 1993.

She strode through the living room and into a kitchen. There was a door on the opposite side. Stella opened it and peered down a flight of stairs into darkness. A basement. This had to be it. What would someone who imprisoned victims, peeling the skin from their hands, do in a basement?

She was going to find out.

Stella unlatched a flashlight from her belt and took a step onto a creaky stair.

# Chapter 81

# Recording Studio

The stairs creaked and moaned under Stella's boots as she descended into the dark basement. Lolita's face flashed through her mind. Lolita's scent clung to the air. At the last stair, she saw a switch on the wall. She clicked it on.

Buzzing echoed through the silent space. The intense lights sizzled her eyes. She blinked vigorously several times, adjusting to the onslaught.

The basement was unlike anything she'd ever seen before.

It was some sort of recording studio.

The *Skin Peeler* was affiliated with the music industry. According to Stella's profile.

Clearly, Lolita recorded her own music.

Stella walked into the rear of the room. A control panel lined the wall separating the two halves. Examining the cryptic knobs and switches, the entire board appeared pristine. As if it had been polished. Stella's stomach plunged as her hope of finding traces diminished. She moved to the rear of the room. A series of equipment lined the wall. She approached the display, trying to piece together what it all was. Striving to find something that would close the investigation with an iron-clad lock.

A stack of rectangular cases caught her attention. She walked up to them, picked the topmost one off the stack, and clicked the case open. Inside, a rectangle of durable plastic nestled, the internals exposed through clear squares. Two wheels wound shiny black tape into tight circles. *Tape.* Stella's mind clicked. *The ADAT eight-track recording system.* The trace she'd lifted from the second victim in the alley behind *Coconut Rum.*

She closed the case and set it on top of the stack. It was clean and polished. Not much chance of there being a trace of human on this.

Stella spun on her heel and looked toward the control panel. A substantial pane of plastic or glass separated this side of the room from the other half. A stool sat alongside a microphone stand. The bulb of the mic was tilted upwards, a scarf tied around its neck, flowing down the body. A hefty set of earphones perched on a table next to the microphone. Lolita's face shimmered on the other side of the window, her lips brushing the silver bulb of the mic, her olive-skinned hand stroking the silky scarf.

Stella shook her head.

*No.* Not now. *Focus.* She replayed Sutton's words in her head. "Focus. Take your time." She could see his rabbit foot dangling from his belt. She had to listen to him. He'd taken her seriously despite her wild actions. It was time for her to take him seriously.

There was a door on the right. She strode over to it. As she opened it, a cloud of sweat, body odour, and metallic copper hijacked her. She swallowed against a gag, composed herself, then walked through the door.

Whatever was on the other side, she was ready.

Stepping into the warm space, Stella inspected the rest of its contents. A table held another stand, thrusting an open book high. As she approached, the cover came into focus. It looked just like the books that were in each of the dead victims' hands. The cover made of the same paper used for cassette inserts. She moved to the other side of the book. The same words, written in scarlet ink, dripped down the page.

A trace of the ink could reveal blood. *Whose blood?*

She flipped through the book. The pages were filled with the same rhyme, over and over.

More. There had to be more. All of this, pieced together, painted a clearer picture in Stella's mind. Was there anything completely *conclusive?* She'd seen it before, evidence that seemed airtight ripped apart in court. With sufficient doubt, without complete conclusion, a jury could waver.

She slid her hand into her vest and touched her rabbit foot. Inhaling fully, she felt the warm pulses in her gut. There was something else here. She knew it. Spinning on her heel, she rescanned the recording space.

Something in the corner caught her eye. She halted and narrowed her eyes.

A large, black case sat on its side on the floor. She crouched, released the silver clasps, and opened the lid.

The reek of rotting flesh and metallic blood burst from the case in a rush.

Stella teetered on her heels, swallowing against a surge of stomach acid. She steadied herself, unclipped her flashlight, and shone the luminous beam into the box.

She'd never seen anything like it.

Four skin gloves perched, each on its dedicated stand. *Skin gloves.* There was no alternative way to describe them. Each crafted from two strips of flesh sewn together with meticulous stitching up each side.

Lolita's face shimmered from the box. Lolita's hand, wearing a skin glove, stretching the fingers, grasping a writing tool, scribing lyrics into an open book.

# Chapter 82
# Stella's Skills

Stella flung her leather coat over the chair at her desk. She'd give anything for a cup of coffee, even if it was low-cost homicide brew.

It had been a tiring day processing the house and the grisly recording studio. Lolita had been transferred to an interrogation room. A rush job had been pushed through on the skin gloves. Three should belong to the victims. The fourth...she couldn't fathom a guess.

The barrage of images wouldn't leave her alone. Lolita's olive-skinned face on the opposite side of the cruiser window, her dark eyes pleading for help. The contorted skin on the left side of her mouth. The askew little house. The feeling of *off-kilter* that seeped from the living room. The scarf fluttering down the sleek silver body of the microphone. The headphones, pulling away chocolate dreadlocks.

The skin gloves. That was the worst image of all. From any case Stella had ever been on. The rotting flesh with its copper-tinged odour clung to Stella's nose even now, hours after she'd found them. A shudder shook Stella's shoulders. She couldn't think about it. It was too much, even for her.

The most distressing part of it all was that the very hands that had peeled human skin had touched her own flesh. Only days ago. A disgusting, sick feeling churned in her stomach as the thought glared in her mind.

"Mahoney." Sutton's voice jolted her.

"Yeah." She cleared her throat and straightened from her slumped position in the chair.

"I need you in the interrogation room." His lips pulled into a thin line.

"What?" She stared, eyes wide. "We have human skin gloves. I'll be damned if the DNA doesn't match our victims."

"It does. The first three. The fourth matches the DNA of an Orson Cruz. Died in 1993. Found in the alley behind *Vinyl*. Declared a drug overdose." His eyebrows furrowed. "Your gut was spot on. He was the lead singer of *Electric Skin*. He had blond hair and green eyes. Lolita was the guitarist. Your *Skin Peeler* is stuck in 1993." His expression softened. "You know the procedure. We need a statement from the suspect."

"But I don't have to be the one to take it." Her jaw clenched. Lolita's face shimmered over Sutton's. She swallowed the anxious ball of bile clawing up her throat at the thought of looking into Lolita's mysterious eyes. Being in the same room as her.

"I know. *I* need *you* to take the statement." He stared, waiting.

"Why?" She'd been *with* this woman. He knew that. She'd nearly destroyed a crime scene because of it. Was he crazy? "I shouldn't even *be* on this case."

Sutton ran his hands through his hair as he sighed. "No-one knows that you were *off* it. I mean, besides me, and Officer Preston."

"What?"

"Gut instinct. I *knew* you had nothing to do with last victim. I *knew* you'd be cleared. I *needed* you on this. I've seen cases like this before when I worked with your father. Only way to catch a killer like this is to follow your instincts. You're the only detective I've got that can do that."

She bit her lower lip and stared right at him. "I *am* like my father, aren't I?"

"Yeah." He cleared his throat. "Listen, *you* need to question her. You have a connection with her. And you know what's occurring inside her head better than anyone. *You* created the profile. *You* were *right*."

She sat up straighter, placing her right boot on her left knee.

"If you have any Mahoney in you, which I know you do, I mean, *Christ*, it's seeping from your pores, then *you* have a natural ability to use your connection with a suspect."

She sighed. "She's ... the *Skin Peeler*." Her jaw clenched tightly.

"Yeah. She is. You need to discard any doubt in your instincts. You had a connection with her. You can use that. Get her to talk." He stroked the rabbit foot dangling from his belt. "I've seen your profiling. You know this type of killer.

We have a chance to find out anything we can. Were there others? What really happened to Orson?" He swallowed. "*You* are the one who can find out."

Her boot shook as it rested on her knee.

Her father had done it. She'd read all about it. He'd visited the serial killer that he'd put behind bars, repeatedly, looking him in the eye, pretending to be his friend. He'd played him. He'd gotten along with the exact man who had carved lyrics into the flesh of his victims. It had paid off. It resulted in a lead that took them directly to a serial killer on the loose, hiding in the belly of the hot desert.

"Detective?" Sutton stared down at her, urgency masked with patience.

The words from the book that her father had left her, words of wisdom from one detective to another, echoed in her ears. *Listen to your instincts, Stella. You have the Mahoney instinct. You must follow it.*

Stella exhaled. "OK. But, what about Preston?

"Don't worry about him. As far as you're concerned, you returned to the scene, followed a suspect, got a DNA sample. Report says it was lifted from a glass. Now we have a warrant, and a high priority search to conduct. Got it?"

"Got it."

# Chapter 83

# Elevator of Doom

Stella walked down the hallway, notebook in one hand, coffee in the other. Her shoulders and jaw clenched tightly. Her mind buzzed.

She could do this.

She could trust her instincts.

She replayed Sutton's words. *If you have any Mahoney in you, which I know you do, I mean, Christ, it's seeping from your pores.*

He was right. She knew it. If there was any time at all to listen to her boss, it was now.

He was telling her the same thing her father had, when he called her on the phone from the depths of a murder case, when he wrote the words in the book he left her, and most of all, when he looked at her with complete belief in his eyes.

How she still had a badge and the title of *Detective,* she wasn't entirely sure. It felt right. She didn't want to lose it again.

She had no doubt that she could *play* someone, guide them, coax them to tell her what she needed to hear. She'd done it many times before. Staring into the eyes of a killer and guiding them to tell the truth was second nature to her. When she hadn't drowned in a lust-filled party with them.

Taking a sip of coffee, she rounded the corner and headed down the final hallway. She was almost there, at the elevator that would take her to the basement.

While interrogation came naturally for her, this was different. She could still feel Lolita's lips brushing her own skin, her own lips. The ripples of the contorted skin pulling the side of Lolita's lip down still tickled her own fingertips. The sensation spun her stomach in a wild turn, causing a wave of nausea to surge up her throat. This was *fucking crazy.*

She reached the elevator, hit the button, and listened to the whirring noise as it ascended. With a *ding*, the doors opened. She stepped inside and hit the button for the bottom floor. It was like she was in a hotel, going to a fancy lobby, not in the *elevator of doom* taking her to cells holding killers. She chuckled at the name. Elevator of doom. She'd heard that her father's team had named it that. It stuck, all these years. She wondered how many times he'd stood right here where she stood now, riding the elevator to the bottom of homicide, preparing himself to face a human monster.

She'd had her share of staring down killers. The worst one had been Viviana, the younger sister in the Poison Sisters case. Viviana was simple to grill. Weak, easily influenced, she spilled everything that Stella suspected. It didn't hurt that they had a mound of evidence.

Lolita's olive-skinned face shimmered on the gleaming elevator doors.

The ball of sick festering in Stella's belly surged. She swallowed a generous mouthful of cold coffee, forcing down the uprising. *Not now.* She didn't have time for nerves. Or for doubt. She had to believe the words of her boss, her father, her partner. She had to trust herself.

The elevator stopped. The doors slid open.

A hallway, bright and sterile, opened up before her. She stepped out of the elevator and walked down the polished floor, her heels clicking loudly, echoing through the vacant space.

It was just her and the *Skin Peeler*, down here in the depths of homicide.

# Chapter 84
# Whiskey-Infused Skin

Footsteps approached outside the door. Lolita would give anything to get out of this room. It was luminous, sterile, and small. The four walls closed in on her, crushing her mind.

The door opened. *Strawberry-blonde whiskey treat.*

The slutty groupie who had slathered Orson with her attention the night of his big show at *Vinyl*. She walked into the room, dripping her fruit-infused bourbon scent all over it. Lolita licked her lips and leaned against the cold metal chair. She ran her eyes along the supple skin of the woman. The creamy flesh taunted Lolita. Saliva pooled at the corners of her mouth. She looked at blondie's right hand. The smooth, pale skin pulled at her loins. Her fingers trembled at the thought of crawling them over the sleek flesh and peeling it away.

Desire swelled from the pit of her stomach, creeping up her insides and clawing up her throat. She swallowed.

What she wouldn't give for a syringe brimming with her favourite oxytocin-laced cocktail. One for her, and one for strawberry whiskey.

# Chapter 85
# Skin Peeler Eyes

Stella stepped into the room. Lolita sat on the far side of a silver table, staring straight at her with those intense eyes.

The legs of the chair screeched across the concrete floor as Stella pulled it away from the table, rippling a chill down her spine. The chipped coffee mug clacked against the table as she set it down. The folder whispered a low sigh as she placed it next to the mug. As she sat, a whiff of citrus and spice wove up her nose. Tingles trickled through her insides, turning into waves of sick coursing through her gut.

Stella closed her eyes and cleared her mind.

This wasn't the time to relive her fucked-up intimate encounter with the *Skin Peeler.*

Her jaw clenched as she opened her eyes. Lolita jolted. Her mysterious eyes explored Stella. Stella relaxed her face. She needed to remain a blank slate until she could feel this out. She had no idea how Lolita would respond. She folded her hands together and rested them on the table.

Looking straight into Lolita's enticing eyes, she started her interrogation. "Lolita Salim. I'm Detective Mahoney. I'm here to take your statement of the events that led you here."

Cold darkness trickled from Lolita's eyes.

Stella opened the folder, shuffled through the files, and retrieved a series of photos. She set three pictures down on the table and slid them toward Lolita.

"Donovan Goldering. Melvin Bradley. Karol Kain. How did you know them?"

Lolita stared at each photo, her eyes widening. She pressed on the photo of Karol Kain, the singer, and slid it toward herself. "I..." Her voice shook. Tears spilled down her cheeks, trickling over her contorted skin. "The show...the singer..." She gasped, her hand flying to her mouth, and she went silent.

Stella sat down in the chair and waited. If she could get Lolita's version of what she did to these victims, she could validate her profile, perhaps even evolve it. It could help identify where her techniques were spot on, and where they needed improvement. Furthermore, if she could get Lolita talking freely about these three murders, she might get comfortable enough to talk about others. If there were more. That's what Sutton wanted.

She didn't want to be in here, at first. Now, sitting across from this killer, she felt centred. She wondered if this would help her to deal with her own demons.

"Lolita, what do you remember about Karol?" She relaxed her face again, making sure she appeared neutral.

Lolita remained fixated on the photo, grazing her finger over the woman's face. Dying to know what was going through Lolita's mind, Stella harnessed the urge to talk too soon. Patience. It had always worked in the past. Ask the right questions, allow ample time between each, give the killer the chance to ponder, to reflect, to reveal.

Stella flipped through pages stamped in her mind. Pages from a book, written by a criminal profile expert, describing techniques of how to get inside the mind of a certain breed of killer.

*Don't accuse. Ask complex questions that would be too tempting for him or her to resist. Provide plenty of space between questions, allowing the killer time to relive the response to your question in their mind. Remember, their main driving force is fantasy. Validate their responses. They perceive their killings as their life's work.*

The words had resonated the first time she'd read them. The title and author of the book were etched in her mind forever—*Evil Mind Dive, Dr. Quesnel.*

After several minutes of silence, Lolita remained fixated on the photo.

"What does this singer mean to you?" Stella attempted another tactic, rephrasing the question to link it closer to the fantasy of the *Skin Peeler.* The killer who recorded their own music, whose rhymes held a higher level of importance to them than anything else.

"The eyes. It's him. Orson." Her gaze and her face froze. The fear gripping her expression was undeniably real.

Orson. These were replacements for Orson. Her theory had been dead on. What had really happened to him? She needed to find out.

Stella opened the folder and slipped out a photo of Orson. She slid it right up to Lolita.

Lolita's face and shoulders twitched. Anxiety and fear flowed from her pores, filling the space between them. It was either one hell of a show, or Lolita had transformed into the affectionate version of herself. The one that had lured Stella in with her lust.

"Tell me about Orson." Stella softened her expression slightly.

Lolita glanced up from the photo, dropping her hand into her lap. Her mouth twitched. She scratched erratically at her drooping lip. "He's my boyfriend. Or...he *was*. Or...he *is*." Her hands grabbed at the dreadlocks, pulling them. She shook her head. "I don't know."

"You don't know what?" Stella asked.

"I don't know what year it is."

Was she for real? Stella hid any skepticism, washing her face with concern and belief. "It's 1999." She waited.

Clarity washed over Lolita's eyes. "1999," she whispered in a hoarse voice. "OK." Her face relaxed, her shoulders sagged. "Orson *was* my boyfriend. He was the lead singer of our band."

*Fantasy.* Unravel her fantasy.

Stella painted concern over her face. "What happened to him?"

Lolita seemed as though she bought it. She swallowed. Her lip trembled. She scratched at her contorted skin a couple of times, then lowered her hand. "He..." she paused, "he died. After a show. Drugs." She blinked as she inspected the photo.

"I'm sorry." Stella forced sympathy into her eyes and over her face. "That must have been tough for you."

The contorted corner of Lolita's lip twitched. "Yes. I...I guess I haven't been the same since."

*Fantasy. Unravel her fantasy.*

1993.

Stella pictured the plethora of music paraphernalia, the magazines, the VHS tapes, the cassettes, the LPs, all from 1993, cluttered in Lolita's living room.

Lolita had literally been living in a 1993 bubble.

"Orson died in 1993," Stella proceeded with caution.

"1993." Lolita stretched her legs out in front of her and rested her hands on the table, the cuffs clinking against the steel.

*Good.* She was relaxing. Feeling safe. Comfortable.

Stella needed to push herself further into a patient stride. This was *not* the time to go full blast. "I'm sorry that he died. I'm sorry that it's been difficult for you." Stella let her concern sink into Lolita's mind.

Lolita smiled meekly.

The citrus spice wafting from Lolita faded. The effect it had on Stella dimmed with every step of the interrogation. A sick rot tainted the minuscule tendrils of lust still pulsing inside of Stella. The rot thickened with every question she asked this woman. Her confidence tugged at her. She let it lead. She leaned over the table, stretched her hand out, and rested her fingers close to Lolita's.

The *Skin Peeler* took that bait. She brushed her fingers over Stella's. The tingles that followed dissipated in a flash as Stella focused on her line of questioning. She pictured Lolita, that night, standing beside her at Vinyl. She concentrated on Lolita's lips. *I knew he'd be big.*

"That night, it was painful for you." Stella paused. Lolita's fingertips remained on hers.

"It was." A tear trickled down Lolita's cheek, catching in the contorted skin in the corner of her lip. "It was supposed to be *me.* He stole *my* rhymes." The warmth in Lolita's eyes and voice drained away. A coldness spread through her gaze. Her voice deepened. "*You*...you were there." She yanked her arms away. The cuffs clanked against the metal table. "You tried to take *him.* He was all I had left."

Lolita thought she was someone else, some woman who was there the night Orson died.

*Play out the fantasy.*

"I *was* there." Stella remained steady, unemotional.

Lolita flushed red. The darkness in her eyes became rabid.

"I should have given it to *you*," Lolita spat.

"Perhaps you should have." Stella leaned over the table.

"He was too enthralled with *you* to notice what I slipped into his drink." Lolita's lip twitched.

"Oxytocin." Stella eased against the chair.

"My fucking mother poisoned me. I poisoned him."

There it was. The *Skin Peeler* had a deep wound stemming from a childhood that Stella could only imagine. The oxytocin had likely been used to attempt to fix whatever damage was festering in Lolita's brain. Ed Gein's speech had slurred, and his eye had wandered lazily due to the beatings administered by his loving father.

Lolita raised her cuffed hands and scratched at her drooping lip.

Stella pondered the contorted skin, wondering how injured Lolita's brain was, and if it was the cause of the deformation. Her shoulders relaxed as she waited to see what else the woman who peeled skin from hands would reveal.

# Chapter 86
# Open Up

A muted orange glow engulfed the room. Acoustic guitar music flowed through the space. Stella removed her leather coat and settled against the cushioned seat of the corner booth. She had an impeccable view of the entrance. She'd be able to see him come in.

It had been one hell of a day. After her intense interrogation of Lolita, the Skin Peeler, she had secluded herself in the war room late into the night with Parker and Sutton, putting the pieces together. Jake had dashed back and forth between his desk and the stuffy room, feeding them data. She would stop at nothing to put together an iron-clad case.

Lolita had grown up in the quaint town of Richdale. Her mother had continued to consume a toxic concoction of alcohol and drugs well into her pregnancy. Scans of Lolita's brain had resulted in the conclusion that she had an extremely rare abnormality in her exterior lobe. There was an irreparable crack in her amygdala connectivity. The lateral hemisphere of the brain controls, among other things, speech and emotion. In general, her ability to control her emotional behaviour could be directly impacted. More specifically, tying emotional meaning to memories and decision making could be compromised. A slew of doctors had been consulted and experimental treatments fed to her, including oxytocin. Several nearly empty bottles of the expired prescription had been found as the search of the askew little house near Electric Avenue continued. Blackwood had managed to unearth the toxicology report of Orson Cruz. Traces of oxytocin activity had been detected in his system. It had slipped through any suspicion at the time given how many dangerous substances he consumed regularly.

Several recordings had been found in Lolita's recording studio on ADAT tape. Her voice had been identified on all of them. The additional voices were suspected to be those of the victims. Traces inside an amplifier case, also discovered in the basement, had matched each of the victims. Half a dozen silver shirts had been located in Lolita's bedroom closet. The tags were removed. It appeared unlikely that they'd be able to determine the source of the shirts.

Stella shook her head, forcing the investigation from her mind. She'd done everything she had to. She atoned for her mistakes on this bizarre case. It was time to correct the remaining mistakes in her life.

Butterflies fluttered through her stomach. She closed her eyes, took a substantial breath, and released a long exhale.

"Your drinks, miss," a resonant voice gently grabbed her attention.

The waiter, dressed in a neatly ironed ivory shirt, the sleeves rolled above his elbows, nodded as he placed two crystal glasses on the table and nodded.

"Thank you." Stella smiled.

As he walked away, she focused on the glasses. Rich amber liquid filled them about halfway. A single sphere of ice chilled each. A sliver of burnt orange peel curled over the crystal lips. She'd consulted the seasoned waiter the moment she walked in, wanting to set things right before she could mess them up.

She slid one of the glasses across the table and placed the second in front of her. Caramel and cinnamon notes infused the warm air.

Movement from the entrance caught her attention.

*Tad.* His golden locks fell over his muscular shoulders. His amber eyes scanned the room, landing on her. Heat rushed through her. Tingles followed.

He walked over, set his coat down, then settled across from her. He noticed the drinks and smiled. He picked up the glass, took a leisurely pull on the bourbon, and let it linger in his mouth. After he swallowed, he settled his gaze on hers. "Nice. Not sure I recognize this one. It tastes *vintage.*"

"Old Weller Antique," she said.

"Must be a special occasion." He took another sip, his gaze never leaving her face.

She swallowed. "I..." She took a sip of the soothing alcohol, then gathered herself. "I'm sorry." She stared at the table. "I *do* feel something. For you. It *was* real. I don't know how...to...do *this.*" She met his eyes.

He slid around the booth, right up close to her. With his fingertips, he pulled her chin, making her face him. His gaze melted her.

He leaned in, pressed his lips against hers. She gave in, closed her eyes, and lost herself in the kiss of all kisses. Flames of desire licked her insides.

When he pulled away, she nearly lunged forward, not wanting it to end.

He picked up his glass and raised it. "To new beginnings."

Stella reciprocated, raising her glass.

# Chapter 87
# MTV 1993

Lolita pulled her legs into her chest and leaned against the wall. She rocked back and forth, resting her forehead on her knees. Her dreadlocks fell over her face, dimming the electrifying light. Why did it have to be so glaring in here? She couldn't function. The light seared her brain, exacerbating the fissure. She could *feel* it.

After a series of fresh brain scans, she'd been informed that the irreparable crack in her amygdala connectivity had deepened over the last few months. The sudden deterioration had compromised her mind, her ability to grasp reality and to function as a part of society.

She closed her eyes tight and pictured the living room in her off-center little house. A warmth rushed through her as she imagined herself sitting on the velour couch, cross-legged, her fuzzy blanket around her shoulders, orange flames licking the sides of the brick fireplace. Her shoulders relaxed.

She took a step further into the bubble as she created it in her mind.

Her favourite mug sat on the coffee table in front of the couch. Lemon citrus wafted from the warm tea filling it. The burning fire warmed the room.

It almost felt like she was there.

She took another step, following the path inward into the bubble as she blew images into it, blowing it open in her mind. Her shoulders relaxed further down her back. The strain on her mind eased. A slight warmth swelled in her feet as they touched the ground. A little more. She could feel the rootedness, so very close.

She saw the TV on the antique stand, images flickering over the hazy screen. The title on the bottom was sharp and in focus.

*Nirvana "Heart-Shaped Box" In Utero DGC Records*

A performance from another time.

Focusing on the images as the video played out, she narrowed in on the singer. His face. His tourmaline eyes. His white-blond hair. His voice. It was Kurt Cobain, according to the screen. She only saw Orson. She knew he'd be big. She'd been telling him that all along. His voice flowed through her ears, every word matched perfectly to the beat it belonged to, every line easing off his lips like velvet, reaching an edgy curve at the end. The lines wove together in the impeccable rhyme.

She could hear his voice in her ears, feel it inside of her, in her soul.

The rootedness reached up her legs, into her core, grounding her. The twitching stopped. The anxiety eased. Everything within her let go. She chose the 1993 MTV bubble.

She stared intensely into Orson's emerald eyes. All she knew at this moment in whatever time it was, is that he loved her. She was his. He was hers. That's all that mattered.

A screech violated her mind, slamming the brakes on her thoughts. The beautiful images she'd created disintegrated in a split second.

Her eyes flew open. Her shoulders clenched. The bright, sterilized walls glared at her. She searched for the source of the intrusion. The door creaked open and a woman dressed completely in white, down to her shoes, shuffled across the room.

"What are you doing over there, dear? You should come and sit in the chair. It would be more comfortable." The woman's songbird voice trickled through the room.

She set a tray down on a table next to the single chair. The only other furniture in the room was a bed, a nightstand, and a lamp. A room for one. A sterilized, polished, bright as hell, room for one. Lolita had no control over the lights. They were on during daytime hours, to prevent her from sleeping all day.

This woman didn't even have the decency to let her live in her 1993 MTV bubble.

The grotesque formation on her lip itched. Her face twitched.

"You should come and sit. Eat something." The woman smiled at her then walked to the door and left the room.

The door creaked closed. The latch screeched then clicked.

Lolita closed her eyes and tried to control the involuntary rocking that had taken hold of her body. She'd have to start all over again. It was exhausting trying to create the world she needed to find any sort of calm. To achieve even an ounce of rootedness.

This entire situation was impossible. No videos. No music. No spiced tea. She'd begged, but they wouldn't give her any of the things she needed to prevent herself from going insane.

At night, she woke in a sweat, several times, only sleeping a few hours at a stretch. Her mind would be wild with images. During the day, a rotation of attendants entered her room. She saw the skin peeling away from their hands. She saw their lips moving, their voices smooth, repeating the words that she had written for them, with their hands.

The images made her nauseated. They wouldn't leave her alone.

Something sick simmered within her. She couldn't put her finger on it. It nagged her, day and night.

The only solace she had were the few moments when she was able to move into an extensive 1993 MTV bubble.

SKIN PEELER

# Chapter 88
# Criminal Profile: Skin Peeler

C riminal Profile of the *Skin Peeler:*

*VICTIM TYPE*

- *Gender:* Primarily male

- Eye Colour: critical component, extreme green, emerald, tourmaline

- Hair Colour: primarily sandy blond

- Hair style: shoulder length, or short cropped, messy, tousled

- Height: 5'5" to 5'7"

- Build: thin, wiry

- Skin: Pale, Caucasian

- Age: Mid to late twenties

*TROPHY*

- Skin from the hand, taken in two clean sheets, one from the front, one from the back

- The ultimate form of the skin trophy is the skin glove created by stitching together the two peels of skin

- Represents the hand of the killer's lover/lead singer of band [Electric Skin]; The hand that wrote the ultimate lyrics;

- Power of ownership of the deceased and/or the muse that he offered [the ability to write the perfect rhyme], who the killer sees as the boyfriend, the ultimate possession

*FANTASY*
- The recreation of the night of October 31, 1993, on which the killer's boyfriend performed at *Vinyl* with *Electric Skin*

- Lolita had been the guitarist for *Electric Skin*. She was not included on the night of October 31, 1993; It is suspected that Lolita's condition [damage to the connectivity of the amygdala] caused the contortion of the skin at the left corner of her mouth and thus a droop which deteriorated her ability to rhyme and perform;

- Boyfriend fixates on a certain woman [groupie/fan, strawberry-blonde hair, petite yet curvaceous figure, pale skin] who had made multiple appearances at his shows

- The fantasy puts ownership of the woman to the killer; the killer 'takes her' for herself, taking the power from the boyfriend, and putting it into her own hands

- Killer drugs the boyfriend by slipping oxytocin [obtained

by prescriptions in her name that were provided to her as treatment for her brain condition] into his drink

- The death of Orson Cruz [lead singer of *Electric Skin*] is deemed to be an overdose due to the high levels of a variety of substances in his system, the circumstances, and verified regular behaviour

- Orson Cruz is found dead in the alley behind *Vinyl*

- The current victims [Donovan Goldering, Melvin Bradley, Karol Kain] were taken as replacements for Orson Cruz

- The motivation for the current series of murders was to recreate the events of the night of October 31, 1993, thus allowing Lolita [*Skin Peeler*] to recreate the events of the evening in the manner that she wanted them to occur, and thus giving her ownership of the ultimate possession [Orson Cruz] and her *muse* [his lyric-writing hand]

*MODUS OPERANDI*

- Pre-mortem: viewing the candidate at least once, perhaps multiple times

- Prepping the oxytocin-laced liquid in the syringe, thus allowing the killer to take him/her easily into a waiting car

- Prepare a book with a cover made of paper with a chemical composition matching that of a J-card [used for cassette inserts] and ample blank pages

- Tie the victim, secure wrists and ankles, seating them in a chair in the recording room studio [basement of killer's house]

- Extract blood and mix with ink, thus creating the *blood ink* required to write the message in the book

- Attempt to persuade the victim, once ungagged, to perform the rhymes as written in his/her blood ink in the book, while recording live

- Continue dosages of tranquilizer, GHB, LSD, and oxytocin as required to subdue the victim, and to attempt to make him/her co-operative

- Preparation of *Skin Glove:*

  ◦ Slice the victim's hand around the perimetre, creating a 'front' and 'back' sheet of skin

  ◦ Peel each sheet of skin

  ◦ Dry sheets of skin

  ◦ Stitch together the two sheets with clear thread

  ◦ Hang/display the 'skin glove' on a stand allowing air to enter within, thus further drying and allowing the glove to be wearable

*Use of Skin Glove:*

- Use the skin glove to write the lyrics in the prepared book with the prepared blood ink to be performed by the victim

- Repeat attempted recordings until satisfied with the quality of the performance, or the victim is unable to perform

- If every attempt has been made, and the perfect performance is deemed unattainable, medicate the victim until death, if not already dead

- Wash the victim with warm soap and water; This will require removal of clothes, cutting of clothes to remove as required;

- Re-dress the victim;

- Fold the victim's body and place into the amplifier case for removal and transport to final destination

- At final destination, remove victim from the case and position against the wall in seated position

- Position the hand such that it can hold the book

- Position the book to the open page displaying the lyrics in the hand of the victim

- Position the head such that the eyes are directed at the open page

# About Author

Julie Hiner spent endless hours during her childhood lost in the pages of books. The only thing that took precedence over a book was her Walkman. To this day, Julie is a hardcore 80s rocker at heart.

In a previous life, Julie worked as a computer scientist, specializing in network simulation. On a break between contracts, she published an inspirational work of non-fiction, her own story of facing fear and anxiety on a bicycle in the European mountains.

Julie now writes psychological horror/suspense heavily infused with hard rock and metal. She had published an *80s metal murder* detective series, a 90s nostalgic serial killer novella, co-curated a horror anthology, and had several horror short stories published in anthologies. You can find her at KillersAndDemons.com serving up toxic cocktails of metal and murder.

# Acknowledgments

I require support and love when I write a book. If you shared with me a warm hug, a glass of lunchtime wine, a cold beer, loving words, a wheel of cheese, a head bang, droplets of sweat on the dance floor, or any other form of love and support, then thank you from the bottom of my heart.

A special thank you to Taija Morgan for once again going above and beyond to provide meticulous, insightful, and entertaining feedback. Without her editing magic, this book, and every other book in the series, wouldn't be what it is.

A massive thank you to Cami Schulte for devouring *Thrash Track* and providing insightful feedback. Cami has been a critical part of my production process since the very first book. Her enthusiasm to thrust herself into a wild metal infused world is unmatched.

The biggest, sweatiest, neck wrenching head bang to Lÿnx. When I discovered this badass hard rock meets glam metal band, it was a dream come true. They took the 80s metal book launches to a whole new level. Their support and encouragement has been nothing less than a dip into paradise city. Their music has captured my 80s rocker heart. They have reminded me how it feels to love a piece of music so much that it hurts.

A head bang (or two) to Hazzerd for their earth shattering vocals and instrumentals on the *Thrash Track* soundtrack. They literally brought the characters and the story to life. Their incredible talent and creativity took the *Thrash Track* soundtrack to mind blowing extremes. A head bang (or two, or three) to Cody Anstey for coordinating the entire project to create the *Thrash Track* soundtrack and for his amazing mixing and recording skills. His vision and guidance have made a dream that has been bubbling inside of me come true!

A massive hug and a sweaty head bang out to Dan Bronson for helping me to find the perfect music fusion for two worlds to collide. When he directed me to Children of the Korn, the core of the characters and the outrageousness of the plot skyrocketed to new heights.

A huge thank you to the bold authors whose writing infused me with the confidence to stop holding back and write the story how I know it needs to be. Mark Towse. Bryan Bowyer. Kristopher Triana.

A loving thank you to James Hiner for inspiring me to express my creativity without fear, for providing me with insightful feedback, for guiding me to the best rap of the early 90s, and for supporting me during all my ups and downs. An extra thank you to James for tolerating all the thunderous thrash metal vibrating the walls of the house.

# Also By

Detective Mahoney Series:

Final Track – Book 1

Acid Track – Book 2

Back Track – Book 3

Devil's Track – Book 4

Dead End Track – M.E. Blackwood Story

Novellas:

Owen's Terrarium

Metal Demon

Anthologies:

The Omens Call – Edited by Hiner and Willcocks

Short Stories:

*Ice Metal Queen,* Solstice in Purgatory, The Seventh Terrace☐

*Attic Puppet,* Terrors From The Toy Box, Phobica Books☐

*Candy Lady,* October Blood, Hawke Haus Books☐

*Hallowed Killer,* Pulp Harvest, Blood Rites Horror☐

*Corpse Forest,* The Other Side, Devil's Rock Publishing☐

*Tuny,* Terrace VI: Forbidden Fruit, The Seventh Terrace

If you enjoyed *Thrash Track* please consider leaving a review Goodreads, Book-

bub, or your retailer of choice. A review is worth a lot to an author.

Come visit @ KillersAndDemons.com